HEY YOU, PRETTY FACE

LINDA COLES

Blue Banana

All rights reserved. This book or any portion thereof may not be reproduced or used in any manner whatsoever without the express written permission of the publisher except for the use of brief quotations in a book review. This is a work of fiction. Names, characters, places, brands, media, and incidents are either the product of the author's imagination or are used fictitiously. Any resemblance to actual events or persons, living or dead, is entirely coincidental.

Copyright © 2018 Blue Banana

To Carole. For your support, and love of Jack.

Chapter One

Sunday 19th December, 1999. Almost Christmas.

It was going to hurt. She knew it would hurt far more than the act of giving birth itself had done, not an hour ago. But life for the little one would be so much better without her, with someone else who could take care of her, give her everything she would ever want for, a life the young woman hadn't a chance to offer her.

"Goodbye, little one. I'm doing this because I love you, not because I don't want you. It'll be better for you this way."

She kissed her baby's forehead before wrapping her tightly in the swaddle she had. The infant whimpered a little. Perhaps she was trying to communicate, asking her not to go. Perhaps they could find a way to be together; it wouldn't be that bad. But the woman knew it could never be anything else, and as tough as it was, she knew she had to stick to her decision. Inside her, two voices screamed loudly at each other, straining her chest: one urging her to leave her child, the other sobbing, pleading with her not to go through with it.

Deep down, she knew there was no choice and, mumbling words of comfort to herself, she tried to quiet the voice begging her to stop. With the whimpering child wrapped in a towel and tucked inside her only coat, she placed the tiny bundle inside the porch of the church doorway, tucked away from the relentless biting wind and sleet that was beginning to fall. With the baby safe for now and out of harm's way, she was sure she would be secure for the night. Someone would surely open the church door in the morning and take her in. The child's life from that moment on would be so much better than the alternative. She shivered and hugged her arms. She knew she would be cold without her coat, but the little one needed it more. It was the least she could do, her last solo act of kindness for her daughter before she walked away.

Forever.

The young woman barely felt the wetness falling on her shoulders as she disappeared back into the street and the darkness, the hot tears streaming down her face cooling quickly as they fell away. She rubbed her arms, more out of needy emotion and comfort than anything else. The sleet melted on contact with her thin sweatshirt, soaking the fabric. Even though she was shivering, she didn't notice the vibrations shaking her body. Her only focus was the sheer desperation of the situation, the intense hopelessness that was her short life so far. At least her baby wouldn't have to be part of it now, would have a fighting chance with someone else, someone more able, someone less useless, someone less scarred.

Someone a million times better than she was.

Inside the church, an older woman sat praying quietly, grieving for how her life had turned out so far but without tears. It was a comfort to her to simply sit here in the dim light, praying in silence, though she'd never bothered with the church before she'd gone away. No time for it, she'd always said. Not relevant to her. No interest in hocus-pocus. How the tables had turned and times had changed since she'd returned to Croydon only four weeks ago.

Prison changed you, for one thing, and it did so particularly if you were the victim of continual abuse as she had been. Day after day, night after night they'd come for her both mentally and physically. The prison guards had turned blind eyes to her suffering, monitoring her from a distance until things went as far as the guards dared them to and then stepping in at the last minute. Even the infirmary hadn't been a safe haven.

But then, paedophiles deserved what they got, apparently. More so the female ones. The other prisoners couldn't comprehend what went on in her head to have committed such an abhorrent crime. It was far worse than murder, in their opinions, and her punishment should be that much harsher. She'd cried like her victims had, willing her death to come.

Oh, how she'd prayed, but those prayers had gone unanswered. But she was free again now.

Gathering her few belongings and wrapping her flimsy scarf around her head, ready for the icy wind outside, she made her way to the front door and steeled herself for the walk back to the halfway house she'd been placed in. It wasn't far, but in mid-winter, and in this weather, it would be far enough on foot. The valuable little money in her pocket was better spent on food than bus fare. Opening the heavy wooden door, she shuffled out into the porch and pulled her scarf a little tighter before descending the few steps, holding tightly to the handrail as she went. But halfway down, the woman stopped. Had she heard something over the howl of the wind? She stood still, straining to listen in the quiet street. On a night like this and so close to Christmas, sensible people were huddled away in their houses, more likely their beds at this late hour; there was not a soul outside but her.

Yes, there it was again – a sort of gurgle. The longer she stood listening, the more it gained strength. Was it coming from above her, where she'd come from? As she made her way carefully back up the steps, the sound became louder, more insistent, then developed into something she recognized, something acutely familiar. There was no doubt what it was.

The cry of a baby.

Chapter Two

The Jolly Carter, shortened to The Jolly by the locals, was much the same as any backstreet public house around Croydon, or in fact in any other part of the country. A foggy haze of cigarette smoke hovered overhead with nowhere to go, as more and more rose from the mouths and noses of drinking customers. Whether you smoked or not, you ended up smoking by default. There was no choice, unless you wore an oxygen mask – although that would have given you added protection from the smell of urine as you passed the gents toilets. The gaudy décor of the establishment had, over the years, been covered with a thick veil of caramel nicotine that ran in streaks down the walls.

Workingmen – and they were mainly men – propped the bar up, some with a newspaper, others holding court and regaling the others with tales, each one better than the last. Some stood alone, searching for answers at the bottom of their pint pots. Tom Jones was "Burnin' Down the House" on a jukebox. It was Sunday lunchtime.

"Another when you're ready, please, Jim," Jack ordered, waving his empty glass in the barman's direction and catching his eye. The red-faced landlord nodded and made his way over to grab the glass.

"You're not going to be late for your lunch, are you, Jack? Your missus will be mad as hell..." He let the words dangle knowingly but Jack shook his head.

"I've time for one more, then I'll be off. A nice bit of roast beef, all the trimmings, a glass of wine maybe, and my old chair to sleep it off. What more could a man ever want for?" Jack grinned his contentment at his day ahead, but Jim was already retreating to the bitter pump to refill his glass. Jack watched the creamy head of ale come back his way a moment later and handed over a fistful of change.

"I wish I had someone upstairs to make my dinner and let me have a nice sleep after it."

"Then you need to get yourself a good woman, like my Janine," Jack said, taking a long mouthful and wiping the froth from his upper lip. "She's a good woman, that's for sure, though she'd give me hell if she could hear me telling you to find yourself a good woman. She'd tell you to get organized and do it yourself, stop being a lazy arse. And she'd be right."

"I ain't got time to peel spuds and shop for beef. I'm here all the time. Another reason I haven't got a woman – not many come in here, and those that do only come in to drag their husbands back home."

There wasn't much more Jack could add to that. He nodded his understanding and resignation to the landlord's retreating back as he made his way further down the bar to serve someone else. Jack studied his own pint for a moment, then was interrupted by the ringing of his mobile in his jacket pocket.

"That'll be Janine now, I'll bet. Right on time," he mumbled affectionately to himself. He flipped the top of the phone and answered it. It wasn't Janine. She wasn't calling him home for his Sunday lunch and an afternoon nap.

"DC Jack Rutherford. Hello."

"Jack, I need you to get yourself over to the hospital." It was the desk sergeant back at the station.

"What's up, Doug?"

"A newborn baby was handed in at the hospital not long ago. Seems the little one had been found abandoned in a church doorway. Someone dropped it off and must have left almost immediately after. As did the woman who handed the baby in. We need to track her down and find out who the baby belongs to. It's lucky to be alive if it spent the night out in the cold. Last night could have been the coldest one this winter. Could have frozen the balls off a brass monkey."

Jack looked at the remaining half of his glass of bitter as the sergeant went on, all visions of his Sunday roast fading away, not to mention his nap. And Janine wouldn't be too pleased, either.

"Any idea who the woman was and why she left so soon?"

"Nope and nope." Useful.

"Right. Best I get on my way, then."

The sergeant gave him the details of who to contact at the hospital and hung up. Jack took a last gulp of the remaining half and left the rest on the side, signalling to the barman he was off with a quick wave of his hand.

"Save me some, eh?" Jim called across in hope.

"I'll be lucky if I get any now. Been called into work."

Jim gave him a look that said "tough luck," and carried on wiping the bar with a damp cloth the colour of slate rooftop tiles. Jack hoped he didn't wash glasses with the same dirty cloth.

Heading towards the door and the cold midday air outside, he paused for a moment. He'd better give Janine a call and tell her he wouldn't make lunch. He pulled out his phone and pressed dial.

"Sorry, love. I've been called in. A baby has been found so I've got to go. Will you keep mine warm?"

"Oh, Jack! I was looking forward to a movie with you after lunch, too." She sounded disappointed. He hated doing that to her, but it couldn't be helped. As a detective's wife, she was used to it.

"I know, love. I'll be as quick as I can. You go ahead and eat. I'll have mine later. Then we'll watch the movie."

They said their goodbyes, Jack knowing full well that whatever happened between now and bedtime, he'd never see the movie past the opening credits.

Still, he'd be back home on the sofa with his Janine, and that was enough for him.

Chapter Three

It was a good job he'd only had a pint and three quarters. A DUI for a detective never sat well with the public – or his boss, for that matter. Still, it wasn't a problem now, though Jack could have done with a sandwich to soak up the beer that was sloshing around his empty stomach. Janine had got him watching his weight, and so the Sunday breakfast routine they'd shared for as many years as he could remember had gone south. With her hands on her hips like an old ward matron she'd told him if Sunday lunch was to stay in place, he couldn't have both that and his afternoon pint. The thought amused him as he locked his car door and headed to the hospital's main entrance in search of Monica Johnson, the matron who had called the police.

The front entrance doors slid open automatically as he neared the sensor and he stepped inside; the bland pale greenish-blue décor and the smell of cleaning fluid were the same as most hospitals he'd ever been inside. Even on a Sunday, doctors, nurses and orderlies moved briskly about, some headed home, some on their break and some headed to the next part of their working day. They all minded their own business as they went, with no conversation between them, so Jack fell in behind a man wearing surgical scrubs, joined the human train and followed the signs to the special care baby unit where the infant was being cared for.

The baby. Who would abandon their child, and on such a cold night? Who would be so desperate or stupid to hope someone came for it before it was too late? Why not take it directly to the hospital straight off, or the police? But Jack already knew the answers: because she was scared. And this case would be no different.

Of what, though?

And ditto for the woman that had found the child – why not call an ambulance and the police straight away when she'd found it?

The sign for the SCBU was up ahead and he pushed the buzzer for admittance, his warrant card ready and visible through the glass partition. He waited, then he saw her. He instinctively knew it was her: Monica, authority written across her ample chest as she walked towards him. She reminded him of Hattie Jacques from a *Carry On* movie.

He chanced a smile. As she opened the door, she returned a flicker of one, though it vanished in an instant. Her name badge did indeed confirm she was Monica Johnson. And in charge.

"Good afternoon," Jack said politely, keeping his voice low. The ambience of the ward told him loud noise was not acceptable, and he was aware that his shoes sounded like the quick slaps of an elastic band on the lino as he followed her back towards her desk. He tried, and failed, to walk on the tips of his toes.

"Take a seat," Monica instructed, waving her hand to a spare chair. Glad to stop the sound of his own shoes, he sat, fiddling to get his notebook from his inside pocket. She sat opposite him, waiting.

"Why don't you start from the top and tell me everything you know? Then I'll ask a few questions." He beamed a reassuring smile and received another flicker in return.

"I'd only been on duty a few minutes, so it was not long after seven this morning. There was a phone call from the main entrance reception. The security guard called up saying a woman with a bundle needed help. She'd found a baby abandoned. Naturally, I went down to meet her and took a nurse with me, but when we'd got there, she was nowhere to be seen. The guard was holding the baby. I asked him what had happened, and he said the woman had found the baby last night about 11 pm at St George's church. She'd kept it warm until this morning, but it was hungry. Then she left without giving any more details. Another staff member went after her, but she wouldn't say another word apparently, so they gave up. All we can tell you is that she was about retirement age, grey-haired, and dressed a bit oddly, like from a charity shop perhaps. We've no idea where she comes from or her name." She sighed and ran a hand through her hair. "I wish I could tell you more."

"Has security checked the camera footage? I assume you have footage of the main desk and the outside of the building?"

"Yes. I have a copy for you, not that it shows much. She was alone and on foot, and had a scarf around her head and neck, to keep the cold out, I expect." She handed Jack a CD copy of the front desk and immediate outdoor camera footage.

"I may need to see more footage from further out. Who do I need to contact to get it?"

Monica wrote down the name and telephone number of the head of security and handed him the piece of paper.

"And how is the little one now? I hear it's a little girl."

"Doing well, considering her rough start. She was hungry, but no hypothermia or else I don't think she'd be still with us. Last night was a particularly cold one, so she was lucky the lady found her. I wish she'd brought her straight here, though."

"Any sign of the mother? I'm guessing she gave birth elsewhere and you haven't seen her?"

"Correct. Everyone is accounted for on the maternity ward and in here, so I'd guess you are right, though she may need help herself. I suspect she gave birth in secret and on her own. She must be scared, confused maybe, and in need of medical attention."

"We'll keep an eye out, and we'll also check other hospitals and clinics nearby in case anyone has shown up needing help. Can you remember anything else, no matter how trivial you may think it is?"

Jack was hoping for something he could use, big or small. He'd take small over nothing.

"The guard said the woman who dropped the baby off was extremely nervous herself, as though she couldn't stand to be in the hospital – frightened, maybe, though I don't know why she would be. Then she was gone without another word. It doesn't make any sense. Perhaps she had a bad experience in the past."

Jack wasn't convinced. "Maybe it wasn't the hospital that she was scared of. Maybe it was the camera she didn't like."

Chapter Four

By the time Jack had been to the hospital, completed the necessary paperwork and notified the relevant authority. It was way past lunchtime and his roast beef would surely be past its best by now. He arrived home to find he was correct in his assumption.

"Ah, damn," he said to himself as he lifted the plate from the warm oven and removed the tinfoil that had been protecting his meal for the last five hours. A voice from behind startled him.

"Well, you have been gone a long while. I thought about turning it off." Janine stood in the doorway, arms folded in front of her, though she wore a smile on her face. She wasn't one to be annoyed in situations such as this. It wasn't her style.

"No matter, love. I'm glad it's still here and hot, even if the gravy has dried up a bit. I'll put some butter on it." Butter was Jack's answer to everything that looked a bit dry.

"Oh, no you don't, Jack Rutherford, or the doctor will be on at you for your cholesterol again. It's not good for you, not with the amount you put on things." He let it go. The battle was not one he'd win. He'd try and swipe a bit when she wasn't looking. Taking the plate to the table, he sat down and opened the jar of mustard. He smeared a bit next to the beef, then did the same with the horseradish. When he was satisfied, he picked up a Yorkshire pudding and bit into it, the crunch from the upper shell reverberating in his ears until it softened in his mouth. He dipped the rest into the horseradish as Janine watched, leaning back against the sink.

"You always make the best Yorkshires, Janine. Did you have a glass of wine with yours? I could do with one if there is some."

"I'll get you one. I only had the one with my dinner. A bit of a headache again."

"Again? You've had a lot recently, love. Why don't you go to the doctor?" He started on the second Yorkshire and repeated the process, dipping it in horseradish. He watched as she poured him a glass of wine and set it down in front of him. She pulled out a chair and joined him at the kitchen table while he ate.

"Women get headaches all the time. Anyway, what's the story with the baby? Where was the little one found and is it alright?"

"Mercifully, yes. It will be fine. It's a little girl. A woman handed it in at the hospital this morning then fled, even though it wasn't hers. She found it in the church doorway last night and took it home, we assume. Until we can trace her, and preferably the mother too, we haven't a lot to go on. In the meantime, the baby will stay at the hospital for observation, then it will go to a foster home, I expect. Poor mite. What a start in life, eh? They reckon it's only a day or two old." He slipped a roast potato into his mouth and chewed thoughtfully. "I wonder what possesses someone to abandon their baby like that, and on such a cold night too. Why not take it to the hospital?" Jack was thinking out loud.

"She must be in a desperate situation, is all I can think, and probably young, too. If she's underage, she'll not want anyone to know, not even the hospital, for fear of getting in trouble. Or maybe get her boyfriend in trouble? If he's still around? Maybe he's as young as she is."

"Hmm, maybe. We've all made mistakes at that age. Though this is a big one."

"I agree, but until you find the mother, how will you know

anything about the situation, and possibly return her child to her? Can you do DNA testing?"

"It's a bit trickier than that, I'm afraid. DNA is only of use if there is someone in the system with a match, though I know for a fact that with nearly all offences now, DNA is taken and stored in the system. That means that even begging, being drunk and disorderly, or taking part in a demonstration could put you on the DNA register whether you like it or not. It used to be taken only for more serious crimes. But like I say, there has to be someone to match it to. The added fly in the ointment is that a baby's DNA is never likely to be in the system because they've not had chance to commit a crime. And with paternity testing, you usually have at least one parent present, usually both."

Janine sat thoughtfully for a minute.

"What's up, Janine?" Jack asked her. "What are you thinking?"

"There was an article of the news, a couple of months back, I think, about DNA testing. There's a good deal of data in the database that they say shouldn't still be being kept, from folks not convicted and whatnot. Anyway, the reporter said something about a new test, from somewhere up north Leicester way, where they are trying to match family members' DNA to other family members. Apparently, there are a few bits of our DNA that show who's related, and they were trying to make the test more accurate. It was rather interesting, actually; can't you use that?"

"I've never heard of it. It must be new and not fully available yet." He finished his meal, licked his knife and fork clean, and then sat back holding the remainder of his glass of wine. "But I like your thought. If we had access to the technology, maybe we *could* find out who is a likely parent of the child because there's the baby's mother to think about too, her own need for medical attention perhaps. And the father." He drained the glass and stood up quickly, making Janine jump.

"Janine, you might be on to something there. I'll make some calls and look into it first thing tomorrow. But right now, I think it's time to let that exquisite roast beef dinner go down and start that movie in front of the fire, don't you?" He smiled.

But as Janine knew, Jack would be fast asleep not long after the opening credits and would pretend it had been a great film when he awoke at the end. It amused her that he thought she didn't know, and she'd never let on to him otherwise.

Chapter Five

Jack had just boiled the kettle in the small tea room at the station, unofficially known as 'the coffee cupboard' because in fact it wasn't much more than a closet with a tap and sink. But it was closer to the squad room than the main one. It had become the place to hide out with a mug of Nescafe for many of the team, particularly after a late night on the town. And that's why Eddie was headed inside – coffee and quiet. With two people in there, the cupboard was full.

"Morning, Eddie. You look like shit. Another late one, eh?"

"Do us a favour and put some hot water on a teaspoonful? Two sugars."

Jack watched Eddie nurse his right temple, a pained expression on his face.

"You don't want His Highness to see you like this again. What's going on? Woman trouble, or is it their man trouble again?"

Eddie had been caught with more than his fair share of married women over the couple of years they'd worked together, and had only recently found himself getting a hiding from a surprised husband who had come home early. The bruises were only fading now.

"Leave it out, won't you?"

Jack watched as he rubbed his temple again. "So, what happened?"

"Sue dumped me last night and I went on a bender, if you must know. Shame, really. I thought she might have been the one, but apparently, I wasn't to her."

Jack passed him a mug of instant coffee and watched Eddie take a couple of mouthfuls, looking like a camel at a desert watering hole.

"Thanks," Eddie said. "I needed that. My bloody head is splitting. Got any paracetamol on you?"

"Sorry, I don't carry them. I don't get headaches. Maybe you should, though. You seem to have a few of late. You and my Janine are a right pair."

"I doubt your lovely wife was out getting bladdered last night, or any night come to that. What's she doing with headaches anyway? Are you stressing her out, Jack?" His eyes danced mischievously. Eddie could get away with almost anything with anyone, and he knew it. And played to it.

"Watch it, you," Jack warned jokingly. "I dare say it's women's issues."

"Well, I know all about them, let me tell you."

"I'm sure you do. You've had so many of them. Enough women to launch your own study, I'd say."

"You're only jealous."

They sipped their coffee in the quiet of the cupboard, then Eddie spoke again.

"So, what did you do over the weekend, then? A couple of pints and fall asleep in front of the TV again?"

"Ha-ha. Actually, I was called to the hospital yesterday afternoon. A newborn had been found and handed in. Evidentially, it had been abandoned Saturday night in the church doorway and an older lady dropped it off Sunday. Problem is, we know nothing about either woman – no details, no nothing except the one who handed her in was older and rather nervous. I can't help but wonder what her issue is."

"And you're guessing the other one, the mother, is perhaps in distress for some reason? Maybe young?"

"I am, yes. It's hard not to. Abandoned babies are not as common as they once were, but still, it's not often a woman in a stable home environment abandons a child. It's usually those in a bit of a pickle that can't deal with a baby."

"So, what's the plan, then, Jack?" Eddie emptied his mug and set it on the drainer.

"Well, we have to find them both, so let's start with what camera footage we can get between the hospital and the church, see if we can pick anything up. The older woman wore a headscarf, apparently, and that would fit because it was as cold as a snowman's big toe on Saturday night. You make a start on footage from around the church. I have a phone call to make, then I'll join you." Jack rinsed both their coffee mugs out and put them back on the shelf.

"Right, will do. So, we have no idea what the mother looks like. I'm looking for someone possibly carrying a bundle, I'm guessing. That could take a while."

"Indeed. The monotonous part of police work, I know, but there's no other way. At least we have a time frame of around eleven pm, so that's a start, I suppose. I doubt she'd have a pram or buggy, though she may have had the child in a hold-all, maybe? Anyway, you know the drill. See what's what."

An observer would never guess that Eddie Edwards was, in fact, Jack's immediate boss and not the other way around, Eddie a DS to Jack's DC.

"I'll just make another coffee before I start, I think; the sugar will do me good. Are there any biscuits in that tin, do you know? Otherwise, I'll have to go to the vending machine."

"No idea."

Jack left Eddie sat in the coffee cupboard and went back to his desk. When he put his mind to it, Eddie was one of the best detectives there was in Croydon, possibly even the whole of the Metropolitan police, but when he had woman troubles, he was continually distracted and that meant Jack would end up covering for him yet again. Why women couldn't resist Eddie Jack would never know – he looked fairly average and wasn't exactly a David Hasselhoff lookalike. There were no ripped abs or sun-bleached hair for young Eddie Edwards, though he had a permanent glint in his eye that women found irresistible. Jack smiled. Maybe the man wore red silk shorts under his trousers – perhaps that was his secret charm.

Still smiling to himself, Jack made his way to his desk to make a few calls. If Janine had heard the news story right, perhaps they could use the new DNA know-how to find the abandoned baby's parents. Or at least one of them.

Chapter Six

Leanne Meadows was like any other fifteen-year-old living with their parents – for the most part, they got on but when she didn't get her own way, tensions ran high and dummies were spat. The Monday before Christmas was one of those days. Leanne's parents tried their best to give their daughter everything they could, sometimes at great personal expense to themselves, forfeiting holidays and weekends away so the funds could be put towards her cycle training and equipment. As a young national cycling champ for her age group, Leanne Meadows was on her way to stardom, and a cycling career that would take her on tours around the globe – as long as she carried on the path of hard work and commitment laid out before her. The cost of coaching and her never-ending equipment requirement, not to mention the constant toing and froing from events, was often the cause of rows between Leanne and her parents. But Leanne wasn't selfish, and she knew her parents did their utmost for her in time and money, which she appreciated with all her heart. Leanne contributed to the cost by earning what she could through babysitting and working part-time at the garden centre. But then the latest row had kicked off about Leanne wanting to ride with her buddies on Christmas Day morning instead of being at home with her parents opening presents. Tempers were getting frayed.

"Every day is important, Christmas Day or not!" Leanne yelled at her mother, who was having none of it.

"I'm asking for one full day without having to worry about you while you're out on your road bike. Just one day! I don't think that is too much to ask under the circumstances, young lady."

"But don't you see how important it is for me to train? I'll bet other totally serious riders will train that morning. I'll bet Froome or Deignan will be out – that's what makes them champions. And I want to be a champion!"

Their voices were getting louder and louder when Dave Meadows walked into the hallway.

"What are you two yelling at now? They can probably hear you at the end of the street! And from what I could hear from the bathroom, you need to show a bit more respect to your mother, Lea, and not shout the odds."

"But Dad, you know I have to train every day."

"No you don't, Lea. You need to train six days a week, so Christmas Day is your rest day this week."

"But Dad ..."

"That's the end of it, Lea. Your mother is right. It's one day together with no cycling. Rearrange your schedule for your rest day because it *will be* Christmas Day. And that's the end of it."

"But—"

"Lea, no. Now I suggest you carry on with whatever you were doing because this conversation is over and I've got to get to work. I've got an expensive daughter to pay for."

Leanne stood at the bottom of the stairs along with her mother, neither daring to say another word, because when Dave said it was final, it really was final, and that was how it was. Dave Meadows wore the trousers and got the last word. Leanne, though, was not happy, and as the tears threatened to break loose, she hurried back up the stairs to her room and slammed the door dramatically to let both parents know exactly how she felt.

"She'll get over it, Penny," Dave said to his wife. "She needs to know it's not always about her at every waking moment. She'll be down when she's hungry."

"I know." Penny looked at her watch. "She'd better not be too long. I think she's at the garden centre later this morning. I said I'd drop her off."

"I rest my case. You're dropping her off – again. She could cycle if it was that important to her, couldn't she? Anyway, I'm off." He bent to give her a peck on the cheek before heading out to the car. Penny stood in the doorway and watched him leave, gave him a quick wave as he pulled away then closed the door. There was no sound coming from upstairs. She decided to leave her daughter to cool off a bit.

Every family rowed from time to time, but that didn't mean she enjoyed it. Teenage sulks were the worst. They had a habit of making the parents feel it was they who had done wrong and never the other way around. But Penny would never swap Leanne from their lives, not for the world. She'd lost one child, many years ago, and on occasions like birthdays and Christmas, she always wondered what she'd have grown up to be like all these years later. Would she have been like Leanne, or would they have been chalk and cheese? Still, Leanne was her baby, and that was why she couldn't help but climb the stairs to her daughter's room. She knocked gently on the door.

"Come in," said a tiny voice.

Leanne was sprawled on the bed face down, head buried in her pillow. After a moment, she finally lifted her head up and looked at her mother, tears staining her red blotchy face. A bit of black mascara had leaked on to the pink pillowcase. Penny sat on the edge of her bed and gently stroked her daughter's long blonde hair.

"What time are you working today?"

"I'm on at ten."

"Do you want a lift over?"

"No, I'll cycle. It'll do me good."

"Okay, though it's another cold day outside and it could sleet again later, so keep safe if you're going to be a champ, eh?" She carried on stroking her daughter's hair, a loving smile on her face. Leanne sat up on her bed and hugged her tightly.

"I'm sorry, Mum. I didn't mean to upset you."

"I know you didn't, darling, and we understand your ambition, but we'll have a great Christmas Day together, won't we?"

Leanne blew her nose on a tissue she'd had up her sleeve, and dabbed her eyes dry.

"Of course we will, Mum."

"Come on, you'd better sort your makeup out before you go. Shall I make you a hot chocolate?"

Leanne nodded, a small smile brightening her face a little as she edged off the bed and ran her fingers through her hair, gathering herself together.

"Love you, Mum."

"Love you too, Leanne."

Chapter Seven

Her shift at the garden centre finished, Leanne changed from her jeans into her cycle clothes and, with her other belongings in her backpack slung over her shoulder, set off towards the back entranceway where her road bike was securely parked and padlocked.

It didn't take long to cycle the route home. The Wickham Road was a busy one, running back into Croydon from the west. The garden centre was only about ten miles from home and if the traffic was forgiving, it didn't take her long to get to and from work. Coming up to Christmas, she was glad of the money the extra shifts gave her, despite the cold.

Leanne checked that her cycle lights were turned on as the first spots of sleet began to fall. The late afternoon air was cold and damp and getting wetter by the minute, and the light was fading fast. She waited for a gap in the traffic, wishing she had her warm winter leggings on, then joined the mayhem of headlights headed back towards Cedar Road and home. In the near darkness, considerate cars gave her a wide berth, but a truck buzzed her hardly an inch from her elbow. Leanne yelled a curse after the driver, holding tight to her handlebars to steady the bike.

Leanne hated heavy traffic, though she was used to it. Being a cyclist meant many hours on the road with all kinds of hazards; luckily it was only a short journey home.

She had gone only a couple of miles when she discovered a problem. Knowing precisely how her bike handled, Leanne instinctively knew she had a puncture.

"Damn it," she exclaimed, and slowed to a stop around the corner of a side road away from the traffic as the last of the air leaked out of the tyre. She slipped off her cycling gloves and laid them in the grass as she crouched over the offending wheel. In the fading light, she got to work quickly, taking the tyre off and removing the inner tube, swapping it for the spare she carried in her puncture pack. Her fingers were bitterly cold, and getting the new tube to sit properly inside the tyre was taking far longer than it would have normally. Leanne was getting more and more frustrated and cold the longer it took.

"Oh, come on!" she growled under her breath. It had been one of those days from the start. Blowing on her fingers to try and warm them a little, she looked up from what she was doing and spotted something moving on the road ahead. Crouched down still and low, she strained to see what it was, but her eyes couldn't penetrate the near darkness enough for her to make anything out. Should she call out? Was it an animal heading for the busy road, maybe? Instinct told her to keep her mouth shut. Suddenly her ears picked up the sound of muffled deep, male voices, then the start of an engine.

Funny, she thought. Why no lights? Did the driver know they weren't on?

A door slammed, but it sounded more substantial than a car door; a van door, maybe? She was about to resume the task at hand when she realized the vehicle was headed her way, towards the junction, still without lights on. Should she try and warn the driver? Would they even see her in the near darkness? The vehicle was approaching too quickly for her to make a firm decision so she stayed put where she was, more out of missed opportunity than good judgment. But as the van pulled alongside her, she inadvertently locked eyes with the driver. The glow of light from the dashboard gave his face a ghostly glow. He was looking right at her. She froze. Then, the man turned towards the passenger seat for a moment, then looked back, right at her. His face was unsmiling. Everything around her seemed to still and quieten for a moment. Something deep inside her told her she was in trouble, but what should she do? Run, or hope he hadn't actually seen her huddled in the grass at all? Was she imagining it all? Could she be sure? After all, there was no light shining on her from their headlamps because they were still off. The lane was in darkness, wasn't it?

Her cycle lights were on!

He must have seen them glowing out from under her bike as it lay on its side beside her. Damn! Leanne knew for sure now that she was in trouble. She sprang from the grass and began to run towards the main road, hoping to stop a passing car and get to safety.

But the night had other ideas. Her plastic cycling cleats slipped and slid on the smooth tarmac as she careered around the side of the van.

And into the bulky arms of the van's passenger.

Chapter Eight

Penny looked at her watch for the umpteenth time. It read a minute later than the last time she'd looked. It was nearly six o'clock, totally dark outside, and Leanne wasn't answering her phone. But then if she was still cycling home, she knew Leanne wouldn't hear it; her phone would be tucked safely in her backpack against the elements as usual. Still, she should have been back more than an hour ago and Penny couldn't help wonder if she was staying out on purpose after the morning's heated discussion. So, when the front door opened, Penny all but flew across the lounge to the hallway, expecting to see her daughter coming through the door. But it wasn't her.

"Hello, love," said Dave. "Something smells good." He beamed. When Penny didn't return the smile, his smile vanished. "What's she done now?"

"Nothing like that. She's not come home yet and I'm worried. Her shift finished at four-thirty, so she should have been home an hour ago. I can't get her on her phone."

"Have you called the garden centre?" He took his overcoat off and hung it on the hook by the door. "They probably asked her to stay on and she's punishing us for this morning by not ringing. That'll be all."

"I haven't yet, but I will now. I didn't want her to think we were checking up on her."

"Let me know what they say. I'm going to take a quick shower before dinner."

As Dave climbed the stairs, Penny called the garden centre from her spot still in the hallway. After several rings, a harassed-sounding woman's voice answered at the other end.

"Hi, it's Penny, Leanne's mum, here. Can you tell me if she's left for home as yet, please?"

"Yes, Penny, she left at four-thirty on her bike. I could have done with her staying, actually. We've been busy since she left. Is everything alright?"

"Oh, you know teenagers. She's probably stopped off somewhere and I can't get hold of her. I'm a bit worried, though, so if you hear from her, do me a favour and let me know?"

"Sure will. Hope she's back soon. Got to go."

"Thanks. Bye." Penny stood with the phone in her hand and stared blankly at the hall wall. Where the hell could she have gone in this foul weather at night?

The bathroom door upstairs opened and Dave called down. "What did they say?"

"They said she left at four-thirty on her bike. I'm worried now, Dave. What do you reckon?"

"Well, first off, we'll give her another hour, in light of this morning's conversation, then we'll start calling her friends. If that doesn't do any good, I guess we call the police, eh?"

"Okay. One hour, though. No more."

"Agreed. Now, why don't we eat if it's ready? No point in us all waiting for Madam to show her face." He made his way back down the stairs, pulling on a sweatshirt on as he came, then took Penny in his arms at the bottom. He kissed her cheek lovingly.

"She'll be home soon, Penny. I know she will. She's not one to be a toe rag. She's a sensible girl who's still upset that we put our foot down – you'll see. She'll be moaning to one of her friends as we speak – I bet you a fiver."

"Well, I hope you're right, and I lose a fiver." Penny looked at her watch again. Six-fifteen pm. Leanne had until 7.15, then she'd be on the phone in a flash.

By 8 pm they'd called everyone they could think of and nobody had seen her – Leanne was still not home.

"I'm ringing the police now. This has gone on long enough, Dave, and I'm really worried. Then we'll drive out to the garden centre and see if we can see anything. Maybe she's had an accident and is lying in a ditch in the dark. I don't know, but I can't sit here and do nothing."

"Agreed. I'll give them a call, see what they say. She's still a minor and this is out of character." He was dialling as he spoke. When he'd finished speaking with the police, Dave said, "The duty sergeant will organize someone to come round and take a statement He asked us to get a recent photo out ready. They'll be over shortly."

Penny was already taking a picture out of a frame that sat on the mantlepiece, one of the few pictures of recent in which Leanne wasn't wearing her cycling helmet. It had been taken before she headed out to a school dance back in the summer and her sun-kissed face smiled back at Penny. She started to cry.

"Hey, hey, don't cry, Penny," said Dave, rushing to put his arms around her. "She'll be back soon enough. And now the police are involved, it will all be okay. We'll find her."

Penny wasn't convinced by his positivity, but she knew one of them had to be. No sooner had he said the words than there was a knock at the door.

Dave left her to wipe her tears and unlatched the door.

A detective stood on the step.

"Mr Meadows? I'm DC Jack Rutherford. May I come in?" The detective held up his warrant card.

Dave opened the door further and motioned for him to enter. "Thanks for coming," he said. He closed the door and the two men walked down the hallway to where Penny was now stood. She introduced herself and the three of them sat in the lounge.

"Would you like some tea, Detective?"

"That would be lovely, thanks. No sugar, thanks. Just milk."

Dave handed over the picture of Leanne.

"It's from the summer, so not long ago. Is that good enough?"

"Perfect," said Jack. "When Mrs Meadows comes back, we'll start from the beginning and I can assess where to take it from here. A family liaison officer will be joining us shortly and will stay with you for a while, okay?"

Penny walked back into the room carrying a tray and caught the tail end of the conversation as she handed Jack a mug of tea.

"Thanks," he said to her. "Now let's start from the beginning. Tell me everything you know and then I'll fill in the gaps with some questions." Jack had interviewed many parents of missing children in his time and it never got any easier to watch their pain and anguish. The good news, which he immediately shared with them, was that about a third of missing girls Leanne's age were simply staying out with a mate, inside, safe and warm. Another third made their own way home without the intervention of the police, and another chunk were simply out walking the streets cooling off. It was common for kids in this age group to go missing, in other words, and extremely rare for it to end in tragedy.

There was a comfort for the Meadows in the statistics. But which category did their daughter fall into?

Chapter Nine

Leanne Meadows wasn't the only child who went missing that cold Monday evening. When Jack returned to the station after talking to Mr and Mrs Meadows, he was surprised to see Eddie at his desk entering a report on his computer.

"No date tonight, Eddie?"

"Nah, got called to a missing person instead."

"Eh? I've just been to one myself. Nobody said anything to me about another misper. Who is it?"

Eddie carried on typing as he spoke. "A twelve-year-old girl, Kate Bryers, didn't make it back from walking her dog tonight. What's yours?"

"Similar, actually. A fifteen-year-old girl didn't make it home from her casual job at the garden centre on Wickham Road. Had a falling out earlier this morning with her parents, so I'm hoping she's cooling off somewhere. She's a cyclist, so she was riding home on her bike. Uniforms are retracing her steps as we speak, and I'm off to join in the search. You?"

"Uniforms are door knocking, then same. I've called the hospitals. Nothing there, so that's sort of good news." Eddie stood and pulled his jacket on. "Right, I'm off. I hope these two aren't connected. Will you check they don't know one another and let me know? Of course, if they did and they are hiding out together someplace, that would be ideal. Bring them both home together in time for hot chocolate, eh?"

"Will do," said Jack as he watched his colleague go. "Not sure why a fifteen-year-old would hang out with a twelve-year-old, though," he mumbled, half to himself. Still, he pulled up the report for Kate Bryers anyway and scanned it.

"Hmm, she lives not far off the Wickham Road, though. That could be a coincidence – or not." He picked up the phone to call the FLO who was with the Meadowses.

"Can you see if Mr or Mrs Meadows knows Kate Bryers, age 12?" he asked her. "It seems she's been reported missing this evening, too, so gently as you go. Let me know when you've broached it. She's a bit young to be hanging out with a fifteen-year-old but maybe Leanne was helping her with something. Or it could be nothing."

"Will do. Nothing to report here," the officer replied. They rang off, then Jack grabbed his own coat and went out to his car to join the other officers. He had just about fastened his seatbelt when his phone buzzed again. He flipped it open.

"DC Rutherford," he said.

"Jack, it's PC Clarke, about the Leanne Meadows case? We've located her bike, we think. Looks like it's got a flat tyre. On the corner of Wickham Road with Sparrows Lane."

"I'm on my way over. I'm guessing no sign of her?"

"Correct. There's a set of gloves here as well as her bike, a backpack with a change of clothes and her phone. Nothing else. Looks like she was attempting to mend the tyre. There's a new tube as well as the old. We're securing the area now."

"Did you say Sparrows Lane?"

"I did. Any reason you ask?"

"Another missing child tonight lives on Sparrows Lane. You'll see the squad car parked outside, I expect, if you drive down."

"Now that is weird. You think they're missing someplace together?"

"I don't think anything at the moment, apart from what you've already stated, but it's weird. DS Edwards is coordinating that one and will probably coordinate this one too now, same area same night and all. Anyway, I'll be there shortly."

He disconnected the call and concentrated on getting out of the car park onto the wet road. Sleet was starting up again, making tiny splodge patterns on the windscreen in front of him. Sleet was usually a good indicator snow was on its way. The bookies would love that, so close to Christmas. It was too cold a night to be outside, that was for sure, and Jack hoped that both Kate and Leanne were keeping warm somewhere safe. His phone rang again, and he struggled it out of his coat pocket.

"DS Rutherford."

"It's PC Clarke, Jack. They're not aware of a connection. Leanne had a small circle of close friends. The rest were all cycling buddies, all around her own age. Sorry."

"Right-o. Thanks." He tossed the phone onto the passenger seat and cussed. "Shit. That leaves us with no obvious connection. It could be a long, cold night."

Up ahead, he saw the lights of the squad car on the corner of Wickham and Sparrows Lane and he pulled to a stop a little way before the scene. A crime scene tent had been erected and mobile lights set up, and he spotted two figures in white paper coveralls. All was in hand. The sleet was still falling, and he wished he'd got better footwear on for a grassy ditch inspection. He pulled his coat collar up as far as it would go and stepped out into the cold night, hands stuffed deep into his pockets. If he slipped, he'd have no chance to save himself and end up on his arse for sure.

Better not slip, then.

"What have you got, Clarke?" he asked the PC who was walking towards him. "Anything new?"

"SOCO have photographed and are about done. A couple of officers have questioned the neighbours in Sparrows Lane and talked to the FLO at Kate Bryers' home. We've lifted the bike and the other belongings, so we'll see if it's definitely hers. There's no evidence of a struggle, though there are some strange marks on the loose gravel at the edge of the junction. They look like maybe slip marks, but they're thin. We're thinking maybe she had cycling shoes on and slipped for some reason. There are only a couple of them. Other than that, nothing obvious or new to add right now."

Jack didn't like what he was hearing – or thinking. "So, Leanne isn't here. I'm betting those few houses down there haven't seen her, and there's two slip marks near her bike. By a busy road. What are the chances she's accepted a lift with a stranger?"

"Don't know, but it's not looking good, is it, Jack?"

"No, Clarke. It's most definitely not looking good."

Chapter Ten

Mr and Mrs Bryers were understandably worried sick. Their twelve-year-old daughter was missing, and now another girl was missing, disappeared from the end of the lane. Their heads were filling with all kinds of scenarios. Neither parent had ventured out to work the following morning. Both were too tired, too anxious to concentrate and wanted to stay at home for when Kate returned.

Because she *would* return. They had to cling to a positive outcome.

They knew the stats, but being so young, Kate was extremely vulnerable. The statistics for her age group were not as positive as for the older girl's. The only comfort they had was that maybe Kate wasn't alone. Maybe she was with the older girl, someone they could count on to help bring Kate safely home. At fifteen, she would be a bit more street-smart. But who knew where they might be, or what condition they were in?

If they were, in fact, together.

The FLO was still with them, had stayed with them through the night – not that either of them had slept much. This morning they were all going to meet with Leanne's parents and try and piece together a connection, some common ground.

The meeting was set for ten that morning, and both Jack and Eddie would be in attendance.

Right now, both detectives were finishing off the morning briefing in the squad room back at the station.

"Before we go to the Bryers' house, let's both go to the Meadows' and relook at Leanne's room," Eddie said. "We can also pick up her hairbrush so we've got her DNA. At least when it's lodged in the misper's system, if anything turns up elsewhere, we'll know. We'll do the same at Kate's home, too. I know it's early days, but let's get it done."

Eddie was in full swing for a change. His sometimes-questionable methods, mixed with hard graft, were what would bring them home, if anything would.

"After this meeting," Jack added, "I've organized to talk to their closest friends, see what shakes loose, see what Kate's plans were. I have a short list to work from but since school is closed for the holidays, it could be tough to find her wider circle. I'm speaking with her head teacher, though, and she'll help out. We know what Leanne was doing – on her way home from work – but Kate? I don't suppose she had her own phone?"

Jack was hopeful, though he suspected she wouldn't have, given her age. Not many youngsters had a phone in 1999. Not that many adults did.

"That would have been useful, but no, she didn't," Eddie said. "Leanne only had one because of her cycling and going off so far and so often. Her parents wanted her to be contactable or to be able to call if she ever got stranded. Shame she hadn't called last night, eh? We can still follow up with the phone company, though. There could be texts."

"And I suspect, given those skid marks, there wasn't time," Jack said. "I also suspect someone took their chance while she was distracted changing her flat, so Leanne could be anywhere by now if that's the case. In fact, they both could be. Although, of course, we could still be dealing with two quite separate incidents. Has PR organized a press conference yet?" Jack wanted the word out, the sooner the better.

"I believe so. We need these girls' pictures on the evening front pages and on the news. I'll double-check what time. Posters are in hand, too. The rest is legwork. And CCTV won't be much use until we know what we're looking for. Both girls were well out of the town centre. Nothing out there filming."

"Let's see what the press cough up for us. Somebody must have seen something of either girl. And the fact that we now know Kate was dropped off by her regular lift at the end of her road as usual narrows things down. Two girls from roughly the same spot? I'm wondering if one was premeditated and one an opportunity for whoever – if Leanne was not meant to be a victim. And the more I think about it, I'm wondering if, from her spot in the ditch, she saw something and that's what made her a part of all this."

Jack pulled at his upper lip, something he did when deep in thought. Janine had chided him that he should grow a moustache, something else to play with other than his lip. "So, Kate could be the main target, and Leanne was the fly in the ointment they weren't counting on. That could put her in even more danger then: they won't want a witness to whatever they have planned. Hell, this gets worse by the minute."

Eddie didn't like it either. "Then we first need to figure out why Kate. If we can do that, we should find Leanne."

"Agreed."

Eddie addressed the rest of the room as a whole, his voice elevated for all to hear. "Right, everybody, that's the plan. Let's figure out why Kate. Talk to your snitches, get the word on the street, find out about locals with a fondness for children like Kate, the fruit loops in the area. I want anyone and everyone with a possible connection to Kate interviewed and drivers on that main Wickham Road spoken to." Clapping his hands together loudly, he shouted, "Let's get busy, then!"

Turning to Jack he said, "Right, we've got a meeting to attend. No word of this in front of the parents, right?"

"Right-o."

Chapter Eleven

Leanne was frozen to the marrow. Her cycle clothing wasn't meant to be warm; it was meant for riding in, not sitting all day in. She rubbed her legs to try and get some warmth into them. Thank goodness she'd been wearing her long-legged pants and not her shorts. She'd have dressed in warmer gear had she known she was going to be abducted, she thought wryly.

Abducted.

Her parents would be going out of their minds with worry and she'd no way of letting them know she was alright. All right but imprisoned. As the man had unceremoniously bundled her into the back of the van, she'd kicked and fought her way to no avail – and gotten a punch to her stomach for her troubles. That punch had bent her over double, disabling her long enough for the men to get her inside the van without any further commotion. When she'd finally raised her head after the winding, she'd noticed she wasn't alone in the back. A young girl sat crouched in the near darkness, making tiny whimpering sounds. By Leanne's reckoning, she looked to be about eleven or twelve. But before she could speak to her, one of the men had tied Leanne's hands together, stuck tape across her mouth and fastened her to the back of one of their seats by some sort of leather restraint. The young girl had already been restrained in the same way. Then the van had driven off. Not a word had been said by anyone.

Leanne was a smart girl for her age, and a strong one from racing regularly with both male and female riders. But it wasn't her physical strength she pulled on inside that van – the leather restraints were more than her match. Rather, she instead turned her attention to the situation at hand, drawing on the focus she'd learned over her years of competition. There was no way to turn her head and see through the windscreen – she'd tried her hardest, straining her peripheral vision – so she began to listen carefully to figure out where they might be going. By her estimation, they'd travelled on a motorway; the traffic noises and continual speed of the van told her that much. But whether they had travelled north or south, she'd no way of knowing. She had heard aeroplanes flying low overhead, meaning an airport was nearby, but it could be Heathrow, Gatwick, or Stanstead, all of which were in different directions.

After a time, the traffic had eased, the van slowed, and the outside sounds had died away. She'd wondered if they were in the countryside. They'd driven for about an hour, and neither of the men had uttered a word. When they'd eventually stopped, a bag had been placed over her head as she was led outside, the cold biting through the thin fabric of her clothes, her cycling shoes making walking difficult as they made their way up some stairs to the room where she was now.

The first thing that had hit her was the smell. It was stale, as if the windows hadn't been opened in years and whoever lived there hadn't washed during that time either. The room was dimly lit and there was a faint smell of urine. She knew the other girl she'd arrived with had been a few steps behind her – she had heard her tiny whimpers – and had been taken past her doorway, presumably to another room. When the man had taken the bag off her head, she saw that he and his partner both wore black balaclavas. Leanne figured that was a good sign: if they weren't showing her their faces, they weren't intent on killing her.

She hoped.

They left her as quickly as they'd deposited her. As she lay on the sagging single bed with no more than a thin blanket for warmth, she concentrated on locking the details and events so far into her head, ready for when she was safe again and asked to give a description. *When* she was safe, she told herself. Not *if*. She was skilled at staying positive, even during the worst parts of a race when the pain reached critical and she still had a way to go. Her racing mantra played in her head now: "I give myself permission to win. I give myself permission to win . . ."

She pulled on that inner strength now, because she knew if she didn't she wouldn't survive it. How she wished with all her heart she was with her parents now and she could take back the row they'd had that morning about Christmas Day. It all seemed so trivial now.

I'll be back for Christmas Day.

Nothing had happened since her arrival; that now seemed like an age ago. and since she was not wearing a watch, she'd already begun to lose track of time. Without a window to the outside world, she had no way of seeing whether it was day or night. The place was silent; there were no sounds of trains passing nearby or aeroplanes above. There'd been nothing whatsoever since she entered the small, dim space. Either she was in the middle of nowhere, deep in the countryside, maybe, or she was deep inside something else, a room in a much larger building possibly. The only way out of the room was through the door she'd entered by – and that was kept locked.

I'll be back for Christmas Day, she told herself.

Christmas Day was her goal. If she was going to get out of the room alive and well, that alone would keep her going – she had to have something.

The sound of the door being unlocked brought her back to the present, all senses on high alert. Leanne sat up quickly against the wall, holding her breath, and waited for whoever it was to enter.

It was a young woman.

Her long, lank hair spilled over her face, which was equally grubby; her eyes barely lifted from the floor. She was carrying a tray of food – Leanne's first meal. She watched as the woman locked the door behind her again, taking no chances Leanne might bolt. Taking the woman in, Leanne relaxed a little and let the wind back out of her lungs as the woman placed the tray on the end of the bed. She was not much more than skin and bone, Leanne noted, no match for a strong fifteen-year-old girl, Leanne thought.

"Your food. Eat." It wasn't much more than a whisper, but with an accent, though Leanne wasn't sure from where. Eastern European perhaps?

"Where am I?" she tried, but the woman did not reply. "Please, I need to know."

"Eat. No more food."

"Please! Tell me where I am!" But the woman was already hurrying back to the door. Leanne leapt off the bed and started after her but someone must have been listening in and was ready with a key to unlock the door on the other side. It opened rapidly and the woman disappeared back through it, the key turning before Leanne reached it. She threw herself against it and began banging with her fists, screaming to be let out, her racing mantra forgotten as she sobbed for her mum and dad.

Her sobs died in her throat as a woman's scream sounded on the other side of the door.

Chapter Twelve

Leanne froze. Was it the woman who had just been in her room, or someone else? Maybe there were other girls and women being held here. Maybe it had been the little girl from the van.

She turned to the tray of food. The bowl of once-hot orange soup tasted like it had come from a packet. A stale bread roll accompanied it. Leanne hadn't eaten since late lunch at the garden centre, so ripped the stale bread into pieces, soaked them in the soup, and grimly began to eat. If she was going to keep her strength up, she had to eat something. She hoped and prayed the food was safe and not full of sedative – or worse. Shame they'd given her only a plastic spoon and not a metal one, a possible weapon.

There was nothing else on the tray save for a glass of water, which she drank down; she was not really thirsty, but it would fill her stomach. At least they might let her out to use the toilet and she could gain some valuable insight into what was on the other side of her door.

Several hours after she'd eaten her soup and bread, she heard a key in the door again. She sat bolt upright, back to the wall, both eyes focused on the door as it opened into the room.

This time the visitor was a man.

And he wasn't wearing a balaclava. That wasn't a good sign.

Her stomach rolled. Did that now mean she wasn't going to get out alive, or that they had no plans to ever release her? Was he one of the ones from earlier, or another? Her bottom lip began to quiver in panic as the man approached the bed, his eyes never leaving hers. Leanne held his stare, fighting to keep herself calm. He sat down on the edge of the bed, the mattress dipping under his ample weight, and smiled slowly, a smile that rolled her stomach again, threatening to bring the orange soup back up into the room like a hosepipe. He wore a dated comb-over that tried its best to cover a balding scalp; his stomach hung over his shell suit bottoms where his stained T-shirt couldn't reach, like raw sausage meat spilling over a mixing bowl. It was the same pinkish colour. Leanne swallowed hard as the man reached a fat, fleshy hand out towards her thigh, watching her all the time. then pulled back at the last minute as Leanne screwed her eyes tight shut in anticipation of contact. Then the man did something she hadn't expected – he laughed at her. She opened her eyes but didn't say a word.

"Relax, you're not my type. Too big, too old," he said mockingly.

Leanne understood exactly what he meant but forced herself to speak, willing her voice to sound strong and even.

"What am I doing here? Where am I?"

"You are a fly in the ointment. But I dare say you could be a useful one, though I'm not sure how or where yet. You don't need to know anything more."

"What about the other girl that was in the van, where is she?"

"Ah, now she was part of the plan, a young chrysalis waiting to become a glorious butterfly one day." His smile played with the orange soup inside of her and she swallowed hard to control it.

"Is she here too?"

"Oh, yes. But you won't be seeing her again." He rose up as if he was done, had said what he came to say, though really there had been nothing.

"I need to use the toilet." She was grasping at straws.

"I'm sure you do, but you'll have to wait – or do it in the corner."

"In what, my soup bowl?" she said sarcastically, unable to help herself.

The man's hand whipped out and landed a stinging slap across her face. "Yes, I guess you will," he said calmly. He smiled as she rubbed her face. "You'll soon learn how to behave so we all get along."

Leanne watched in silence as he walked back to the door and left the room. She heard sound of the lock reengaging on the other side.

All alone again, she let the floodgates open into the stale pillow so they wouldn't hear her. Leanne at fifteen wasn't as strong as she thought she was.

Chapter Thirteen

Chloe had always been sporty, had always enjoyed the limelight when she romped home across the finishing line first or second. School sports day had always been her favourite part of the term. She must have been in the front of the queue when long lean legs and power had been handed out. Chloe loved her athletics and even though the sports centre was nowhere near her home, she made do with the running track she'd created for herself on the quieter back streets of Manchester. It gave her the outlet she needed as a teenager. Like many girls her age, she carried the world's troubles on her shoulders – albeit her own small world.

Then one day her world had erupted like a volcano. At first, she'd put the heavy morning sickness down to anything but the suspicion she was pregnant. But soon reality had set in, and as her pregnancy progressed, her clothing style changed to a much looser look. But still, neither of her parents had noticed that their daughter was knocked up. And that suited Chloe, because if nobody noticed and spoke of it, she wasn't pregnant – was she?

Except she was.

And not through any misdeed of her own. While her friends from the estate often sported bruises on their faces and arms, the abuse Chloe was dealt at her mother's hands was far worse: night after night, for as long as she could remember, her mother would give her a glass of sedative-laced milk at bedtime and let grubby strangers into her young daughter's room to have their way with her.

And that was how the pregnancy had come about – and how Chloe's mother had found out about it: a punter had expressed his displeasure at her growing belly and had told Chloe's parents he wouldn't be back. No longer a money-making machine, Chloe arrived home one day after school to find her bag packed and a note on the kitchen table telling her they had moved to Scotland to take up a new job and she wasn't going with them.

There was £200 in an envelope to help her get settled somewhere. "Stay with one of your mates in the meantime," the note said. It had been in her mother's handwriting, and not even a kiss or good luck at the end of it.

She'd stayed the first couple of nights at a friend's place until the girl's parents had asked her to leave; they didn't want someone cluttering up their sofa, they said. So, she'd decided to thumb it and catch a ride south to the bright lights of London. Her lift had taken her almost to the City centre, where she'd got the tube the rest of the way in, figuring the centre would be where it was at. Whatever 'it' was.

Kings Cross had been her home on that first night, and she swore it wouldn't be on the second. She'd moved on to Croydon the following day, where she had wandered the streets aimlessly until she'd all but collapsed outside a small café. The owner had made her some tea and toast. If it hadn't been for Roy taking pity on her, who knows where she would have ended up, and with whom.

She's been allowed to sleep on Roy's sofa for a whole week, no strings, and he had helped her find a place at a women's refuge where she could stay until the baby was born. After that, the worker told her, the council would find her and her baby a more permanent place to live. Naturally, they had thought she was older than she was, and when they talked about foster homes, Chloe had scarpered quick smart. With less than £200 to her name now and no way of earning anything, she knew it was going to be tough and had braced herself to be ready. Roy had told her she could pop in occasionally for tea and toast, but that was all he could offer. Now, she had to make it her own way – on her own, broke and her baby due to make its entrance at any moment. Until it arrived, she'd manage.

And so, on a freezing cold night a few days before Christmas, she gave birth outside Selhurst train station in a dingy, draughty doorway. No one had bothered to stop and see what all the noise was about; everyone was in too much of a hurry to get home and out of the cold.

Folks were only ever concerned about themselves.

Chapter Fourteen

Chloe was at Roy's, a habit she couldn't shake, though she didn't really want to. There were only a couple of people in her world now, and Roy was one of them. The other was an older lad called Billy whom she'd met at a soup kitchen one evening a couple of weeks or so; they'd kept each other company for a couple of hours. His 'place,' which was where he stored his few belongings, was in an unused garage on Pitt Street that belonged to an old lady who allowed him to squat there as long as he was quiet. It wasn't far from the train station and was one of the few houses that had a garage, though most people parked on the street these days. Chloe had stayed with him a few nights, as mates, and they were careful not to let the old lady notice, nor the neighbours, for fear she'd throw them both out. The old side door entrance was useful in that respect, and they were careful to come and go when the street was quiet. But it was relatively safe and dry, and Billy had turned out to be a good friend as Chloe adjusted to life living rough. He also knew about the baby, though Chloe had threatened him with death should he tell anyone about her leaving it in the church porch.

Nobody else knew.

"So, when do I get to meet Billy, then?" Roy asked as he placed another mug of tea in front of Chloe.

She wrapped her hands around it for comfort. "You want to meet him? Why?"

"I don't know, really. Make sure he's suitable?" Roy was smiling as he said it and Chloe giggled a little, like the child she really was.

"He's suitable to be a friend, and he's nice. You'll like him for sure."

"Well, next time you call in, bring him for tea and toast too. I'm sure he'd appreciate it. It's been bitter these last few days."

"Thanks, Roy. He would appreciate it. I didn't want to take advantage of your generosity; otherwise, you'd have a shop full of homeless people queuing up."

"I can't feed everyone, but I can look out for you, I'm sure. Which reminds me – I've some extra blankets for you. I had a clear-out so they're yours if you want them."

"Thanks. They'll come in handy."

Roy sat down for a moment, and it was plain to see he had something on his mind. He spoke in a low voice, though there was no one else in the café to overhear anyway.

"Listen, Chloe. I couldn't help but notice you've lost weight – quite a lot, actually. Only there was a story on the news a couple of nights ago saying a baby had been found abandoned on the steps of a church. I wondered if perhaps you've been pregnant and it was yours?"

Chloe dropped her head, unable to meet Roy's eyes. Should she tell him the truth? Could she trust him with such a secret, a man she'd only known for a handful of weeks?

He tried again. "It's okay if it was. The baby is safe and well, by the way. I saw it on the news. Only I thought *you* might need some medical attention too."

"I'm fine!" It came out too fast and too loud. *Shit.* She'd given the game away. "Now look what you've made me do!" She stood in a hurry, slopping tea over the tabletop. "You can't tell anyone – promise me, Roy!"

"Your secret is safe with me, Chloe, but let me take you to a health clinic. They don't have to know who you are, but they can check you out. You don't want an infection, now, do you? There are places you can get help. Just to be sure."

She sat back down, a sulk on her young face, a face that was trying to be more grown-up than she felt at that moment.

Barely audible, she said, "I'm fine, Roy, really I am. But thanks. I can't risk this coming out, that it was me. I didn't do it lightly, you know." Tears started to fall; Chloe was powerless to stop them.

"I can't imagine how hard it must have been," Roy said gently, "but it was probably for the best until you get on your feet. Are you still in touch with the father? Does he know?"

"No, I'm not, and I don't want to talk about it!" Chloe snapped. She wasn't about to answer questions about who the father was; it was too painful to think about. And she didn't know anyway.

Roy backed off and was quiet. After a moment, he took her hand in his. She snatched it away and wrung both hands together in her lap, the tears still streaming down her face.

"Sorry, Chloe," said Roy, abashed. "I'm sorry for bringing it all up and upsetting you." He changed the subject. "Look, why don't I grab the blankets and drop them at the end of your road by the bus stop. Perhaps you and Billy could pick them up from there in, say, two hours? Then you don't have to carry them all the way. And while I grab them, take a hot pie for each of you. I'll be closing soon anyway, and they'll only go in the bin."

Chloe knew they wouldn't have; Roy would have them for his evening meal later. But since he was offering. . . She nodded.

It was warming to know that someone cared about her, even if they were almost a stranger. She'd take that.

Chapter Fifteen

"Your friend Roy must be a good sort. These extra blankets are magic while it's this cold," said Billy, as he and Chloe sat huddled in their makeshift home together under the new blankets. The two of them had made their hot pies last, relishing the warm tasty gravy as they chatted, a torch between them for lighting. It was far from ideal, but compared to what some others had who slept rough, it was deluxe accommodation.

"He is, isn't he? I expect he gets a bit lonely all on his own, has time to help others that drift by, like me. He reminds me a bit of Roy Cropper off *Corry*. My mum used to watch it. He's a gentle soul, too." Chloe licked the last of the gravy off her fingers, wishing she had another pie to follow, but there was only a sliced loaf on offer. It would have to do. "Want a piece of bread?"

"No, I'll save mine for breakfast, thanks. Which reminds me, how much money have you got left? Enough for food tomorrow?"

Chloe wrestled her purse out from under the blankets and Billy opened his wallet. They pooled all the money they had between them on the candlewick spread that, in its day, had probably been a pretty shade of pink. Chloe wondered why Roy might have had a pink bedspread at one stage; it wasn't exactly a single man's colour.

Maybe he'd married at one time, or had had a woman friend. She busied herself counting the coins and the couple of notes.

"We have a grand total of thirty-six pounds and forty-two pence, so we can eat for a few more days if we keep it frugal, but that bit will soon run out. I think I should start begging again tomorrow – what do you think? I hate nicking stuff. It's not right."

"Nicking is quicker, though. It's too cold for you to sit out begging, and the shoppers that are out have their minds on present lists, not people like you and me. Meagre offerings at this time of year." The thought of Christmas made him smile. "What wouldn't you do for a place at a Christmas feast? All those hot roast potatoes, chicken legs and lashings of gravy. What heaven, eh?"

Chloe had to admit it sounded good. "There will be a dinner somewhere though, won't there? I mean at the soup kitchen? Or one of the shelters?"

"Yeah, there will be, and we'll queue up like the rest and enjoy it, but it won't be a patch on what my old gran used to make. She made the best roast spuds this side of Watford."

"Well, I'm going to find myself a dry doorway tomorrow and make myself comfy and see what we can get," Chloe went on. "If we can get twenty pounds, that will give us a buffer; then we can buy some toothpaste and a brush. My mouth tastes disgusting most of the time, plus a shower wouldn't go amiss either. I'm going to the shelter tomorrow, see if they'll let me in and get clean."

"I'd go in the morning rather than when it's dark again – far safer. Be good to have a mobile shower unit, eh? One that parks at the end of our street?" Billy was back to dreaming. He'd been on the street way too long.

"Billy, you really live in a land of hope, don't you?" she chided him. She finished the last of her slice of bread then gathered their bit of money back into their purses. They never stored all the money in the same place. Personal robberies were too common and they couldn't risk someone else getting their hands on it all. It was their bit of lifeline and all they had.

"You seemed a bit upset when you came back from Roy's," said

Billy. "Did something happen?" Billy had wanted to broach the subject earlier but decided it was best to give her the space he'd quickly learned she needed. Now seemed like a better time: she had food in her stomach and they were both relaxing in relative warmth. In the low light of the torch, he noticed her drop her head at the mention of meeting Roy. Gently he prodded her again. "A problem shared and all...?"

Taking a deep breath, she said, "Roy knows about my baby. He put my sudden weight loss and the abandoned baby in the news together and asked me, and I gave the game away like a fool. Now someone else knows," she said despondently, but what was done was done. "He said he won't tell anyone, but he wanted me to get checked out somewhere. Well, it'll be obvious the baby was mine. I bet they don't have too many getting checked after giving birth that don't go through the regular channels. Someone's bound to be suspicious."

"Surely they won't tell if you ask them not to? Privacy and all – doesn't that count?"

"Maybe abandoning your baby is an offence. I don't know. I never looked it up. Remember, Billy, I stupidly ignored what was going on, hoping it would go away, and it didn't. I had to give birth that day, ready or not, and I knew I couldn't keep her, so I did what I had to. Whoever takes her home from the hospital will do a whole lot better than I could in this mess, and I'm not going to prison for wanting better for my girl. It's not like her dad could have taken over."

Billy's ears pricked up at the mention of the baby's dad. It was the first time she'd mentioned him. When she didn't elaborate, he left it be.

Chloe was quiet for a moment, then said, "I wonder how she's doing, what they've called her."

Placing a comforting arm around her shoulder, Billy leaned in and said, "This close to Christmas, I expect they've called her Mary."

"Mary." She tried the name out. It was appropriate, and she

hoped someone was looking over her, keeping her safe, giving a better life than her own had been. "I like that. Mary. At least I can refer to her with a name now."

Billy squeezed her shoulder gently. If Mary gave Chloe comfort, then that was a good thing.

Chapter Sixteen

It was every officer's nightmare when children went missing, mainly because they knew the statistics on a child ending up safe and well. If they hadn't wandered home of their own accord within the first few hours, it meant something more sinister was at play. In the case of Leanne Meadows, it seemed to Jack and Eddie that they were looking at possible abduction. The skid marks at the side of the road strongly suggested that something had gone wrong while she'd been changing her flat. The fact that Kate Bryers had also gone missing at around the same time and from the same location pointed to a connection between the two cases.

Eddie and Jack were on their way back from interviewing some of Kate's friends in their homes; all the children were home for Christmas holidays now, meaning they couldn't simply interview them as a group in the school gymnasium as was usually done. Unfortunately, nothing helpful had come out of any of the conversations, only tears and distress for their missing friend.

"Why was someone so young even out in the lane at night in the dark?" asked Jack. "There are no street lamps along there. Couldn't her parents have taken the damn dog for a pee themselves?"

"It was all part of her responsibility, one of her chores. No different to other kids, I suppose, but with hindsight, it seems a bit risky. But then no one ever expects their child to be abducted, and that's what we're saying has happened," Eddie said.

"Do you think they're together?"

"Probably, though I'm still thinking Leanne was in the wrong place at the wrong time, what with the puncture and all. I only hope that if they are being kept together, they are able to comfort one another until we can find them. Wherever they are. I must admit, we have zip to work with; no one has seen a thing." Eddie looked as despondent as he sounded as they turned into the station yard.

"Do you think it's sex-related, that paedophiles have taken them?" Jack asked.

"Had it only been Kate missing, I'd say it could be, though there is no direct evidence to that effect. But Leanne would be too old, wouldn't she?"

"Depends on the customer's taste, I suppose. It's a dark world behind some folks' closed doors. Human trafficking doesn't discriminate, and includes all age groups, not only children. But I agree: on the surface, we've said she was in the wrong place, not the target. When will forensics have something? There must be at least a tyre track to work with, or a cigarette butt."

"I'm hoping for something later today. I've tried to push a favour through." Eddie turned and smiled at Jack. Jack grinned back. He knew how Eddie worked, particularly with one of the women who worked in the labs.

"Oh? What have you promised her this time?"

"A curry out at that new place on the high street."

"Don't suppose you want me to come along for a threesome?" Jack was only teasing. His ideal night was a curry in front of the TV with Janine.

"Bugger off. No way!"

Eddie shut off the engine and he and Jack jumped out and hurried towards the back entrance where a uniformed officer was braving the cold and finishing his cigarette on his break. Ice-cold rain had been pelting down all morning and showed little sign of stopping. The sky was heavy and leaden grey. It was no weather to be outside in, thought Jack as he brushed rain droplets of his coat.

"Coffee to warm up, then I'll give the lab a buzz, see if I can't work my charm," said Eddie. As they walked through to the squad room and the coffee cupboard, Jack heard his name being called from behind. He turned to see Clarke about to catch him up.

"What's up, Clarke?"

"You had a call from the DNA lab. Apparently, you were asking them about a new DNA test? Here's the number to call to speak to someone directly. You need to ask for Barbara Winstanley. She's the scientist working with it, fam something or other. No doubt she'll explain it." Jack took the yellow Post-It Note and looked at it before grunting his thanks and following Eddie into the cupboard. The kettle was coming to the boil.

"What's all that about?" Eddie asked.

"Ah, it may be nothing, but I thought I'd give it a go. It's for the abandoned baby case. I'll let you know if it comes to anything."

"Not a lot to do there, is there? The baby will go to a foster home and be adopted, right?"

"Yeah, but it would be nice to find a parent for the little mite, don't you think?"

"And how are we going to do that?"

"Well, nothing came up from the report on the evening news, but there is a DNA test that I'm looking into. Hence this message." Jack flashed the yellow note. "I'll let you know what comes of it."

"Don't go wasting your time, Jack. We've two missing children out there. Baby is safe for now, probably better off where she is than with the woman that dumped her. Now, am I pouring you a coffee or not?"

Jack knew when he was being silenced on a subject and nodded for coffee. But there was no way he was going to forget the little one. If he could find a way to figure it out, he'd do it in his own time if need be. He knew from experience that when an officer discovered a baby abandoned, it stayed with them most of their lives; they were always wondering. And while he wasn't the one who had handed her in, he had been the one on duty that day and had gone to the hospital and seen the tiny bundle with his own eyes. That made him her tenuous guardian in his mind, and he'd do what he could. Taking the steaming mug back to his desk, he picked up the phone and dialled the number, hoping Barbara Winstanley was available to talk.

He was glad he'd called her.

Chapter Seventeen

What Dr Winstanley had told him had given Jack hope, though that hope was balancing precariously on a seesaw of protocol and data. Still, there was a chance. Thanks to science so new it wasn't even officially available yet, it seemed there was a possibility of finding out who the baby's parents were. While Jack knew the baby's mother would have her own reasons for abandoning her infant, he also knew she might want to make contact with the child in the months or years ahead. He also knew that the child herself might want to find out who her natural parents were when she was old enough.

There was a small gift shop in the lobby of the hospital, offering helium balloons, small bouquets of cheap carnations and chrysanthemums in plastic funnels filled with water, and an array of greeting cards spinning on a swivel stand. Jack considered taking the baby a balloon, but "Congratulations!" seemed inappropriate for a small being that had been wrapped in an old coat and left to fend for itself alone. He picked up a small pink stuffed rabbit and went to pay the cashier.

"Congratulations. Your first?" she enquired.

Her assumption flummoxed him for a moment, and then he replied simply, "She's not mine, actually."

"Shivers, I'm so sorry. I just assumed..."

"I know. Don't worry." He smiled briefly to show there were no hard feelings and took his change along with the rabbit, heading to the maternity floor and the special care baby unit.

He was heartened to see the ward sister, Monica, was on duty as he buzzed for entry. She waved as she walked towards him. With a click of the door, he slipped inside.

"Hello again, Detective. Have you some news for us? I'm assuming your visit is about the baby that was found?"

Jack fiddled with the rabbit in his hands then remembered he needed to hand it over. "I thought I'd drop by and see how's she doing, bring her this." He proffered the pink toy and Monica took it from him, petting its head lightly as she did so. "But as for news, we have nothing yet, I'm afraid. You probably saw the news?"

"Yes, we all did. Sad, isn't it? Though she's quite well enough to go on to a foster home now, no damage done. She's only in here because of the circumstances and the need for extra security. Social services will be taking her later today, in fact."

"May I see her, please?" Jack wasn't entirely sure why he wanted to, but something was pulling at his conscience. "Does she have a name?"

"Of course you may, and yes, we figured since it's almost Christmas, the staff chose something appropriate – we've called her Mary. It seemed apt."

"Mary. That's nice. And yes, festive too." He followed Monica over to a cot at the end, where a little bundle wrapped in pink lay alone. She gurgled in her sleep, looking warm and healthy like any other newborn baby with a full tummy in a warm, safe place. A bubble broke from her tiny mouth and another formed behind it. Her left leg kicked up and down on the small mattress. Jack's heart ached for a moment as he watched.

"Hello, Mary. I'm Jack," he said gently, waving a couple of his fingers at her. *Welcome to the human race ....* "I've brought you a bunny." Monica handed it back to him and he tucked it at the corner of Mary's cot so she'd see it when she woke up. More bubbles came and went as he watched over her, but he said nothing more, content to be in her company for a while.

"I'll leave you for a moment. I must get on. Come and see me before you leave if you would," said Monica. Then she was gone.

Jack pulled up a chair and sat by Mary's cot, just watching her. Janine and he couldn't have children, though they had wanted them. Janine had been devastated when the news had come that the problem had been with her, but they'd got through the rough days and the tears, had both pulled through in the end.

Like Mary was now, being strong.

Still, it didn't stop the longing that they both still felt on occasion, occasions such as these when new babies came into their lives via friends and family. No, it still hurt like hell.

"I've come to tell you something, Mary. I am going to try my absolute hardest to find your mum, I promise. There's a new test, you see, and if your mummy or daddy is in our system for some reason, we might be able to figure something out with some new science." More bubbles, and then another gurgle followed by a half cry.

"Hey, shhh, shhh," he soothed, not wanting to disturb her. He kept his voice gentle and low, as people do for the very young who are asleep. "I'll see if we can get permission, eh? See what we can find out, who your mummy is. Will that be alright?" Another half cry, followed by a full one that caught the attention of Monica. He felt her behind him.

"She's due her lunch. Probably hungry," Monica said, and Jack took it as his cue to leave her.

"She's a delight, isn't she? I wish I could take her home myself. Anyway, there's a new test I'll need to get the relevant permission for, to see if we can trace her parents. It's a long shot, but worth a try. What time are social services coming for her?"

"Not until about four o'clock, I think. Why?"

"I'll need to take a swab from her mouth, gather a sample of her

DNA. Hopefully, I can get the paperwork out of the way before she leaves. But if you wouldn't mind, not a word to anyone; not yet, anyway."

"If you say so. Not my business, and as long as everything is in order with Mary and her welfare, that's all I care about. Might see you later, then." Jack thanked her and headed to the door as Mary picked up volume behind him.

There was plenty to be done. Now all he had to do was find her mum.

Chapter Eighteen

After his conversation with Dr Winstanley, Jack needed some luck on his side. From what she'd told him, it was possible though barely out of trial mode. Jack was filled with optimism and had a spring in his step as he approached the office of his DI, Will Morton.

As usual, Morton's head was firmly fixed in the racing pages as he ate his sandwiches, ham and cheese with mustard pickle. There was a yellow blob in the corner of his mouth. It was the same filling every day. On Fridays, he had a packet of ready salted alongside. DI Morton was a creature of habit.

It was probably about time he retired, many thought. His heart was already somewhere else, namely the Scottish Glens with a bottle of malt and his Red Setter close by. Still, he needed to give another two years to get his full pension entitlement and that meant a half-baked focus on many of the cases he oversaw. The brass would have been better off putting him on traffic duty and freeing up his spot for someone with a bit more go in them. But Morton was well liked, just ineffectual. Eddie, desperate to rise in the ranks and up his pay grade himself, had often vented his frustration but discovered it was a pointless exercise, as the DI's boss preferred to leave the status quo in place. Rumours had developed behind Morton's back that he had something on the chief inspector, something that enabled him to sit comfortably until it was time to retire, though nothing had ever been proven. Still, it rankled Eddie. Jack, for his part, couldn't care less as long as he was left to get his own work done. He preferred to be a detective rather than climb the ladder and be a pencil pusher.

Jack rapped his knuckles on the open door and, without looking up, Morton said, "Come in, Jack."

"How did you know it was me?"

"I'm a detective, not a fool. Plus, I saw you approach, so seeing you kind of gave the game away." He spoke in a monotone, as he always did. There was never any energy in the man, and Jack often wondered if anything ever got Morton excited, anything at all. He pitied Mrs Morton.

"Right, yes. I can see how seeing me might help," he said drily. "Anyway, I need your signature on something, if I may. It's for the abandoned baby case. I'm hoping to find the mother, make sure she's okay too."

"You are aware abandoning your baby is a custodial offence, aren't you, Jack?" Morton still hadn't lifted his head from the racing post.

"That I am, sir, but in extenuating circumstances, like other crimes, we have some discretion, and that's why I want to take it further. If she's a young lass, she may be scared. She may have come from a broken home or worse, so until we see, my concern is merely to find out what happened. So I need your signature for a new kind of test."

Finally, Morton looked up. "What is this test?"

"Glad you asked. It's called familial DNA testing, and rather than checking for an exact match, it checks for close family member matches. It's based on the assumption that people who share a large number of genetic markers are likely to be closely related, so if we have either parent already in the system, it could throw out some possibilities. Or even *their* parents could give us something, another generation of DNA. It's brand new, sir. Janine heard about it on a news story on the radio, and I spoke to one of the researchers earlier."

"Well, if it's so new, does it stand up in court?"

"Doubt it at this stage, but at least it could help with the first aspect of finding Mum, eh? Do I have your permission?"

Morton wiped the yellow pickle stain away with his handkerchief. He sat up properly, looking at Jack.

"Why the interest in this case, Jack? Haven't you got enough to be doing with two missing children out there only days before Christmas? Don't you want them home opening their presents on Christmas morning, all nice and safe and snug? Because I know I do." Morton's face resembled that of a maths teacher quizzing a student who didn't know the answer to a basic problem. He was going a bit pink around the edges. Undeterred, Jack stood his ground.

"I do, of course, but this child also deserves to be safe and snug on Christmas Day with someone who loves her. I'll do it in my own time, if that's what you want. I'm intent on helping her any way I can, so please, will you sign this form to allow the test to go through or not?" Jack could hear his tone change and he corrected himself quickly, not wanting Morton to get uptight about it. He needed his signature, after all.

"Let me look, then," Morton conceded, and Jack passed the document over, waiting nervously for Morton to take his pen and sign. After a heavy sigh, Morton scrawled his name across the signature section, handed it back, and stuck his nose back in the racing post.

"Keep me updated."

Jack was dismissed, it seemed. Containing his desire to smile until he'd left the room, Jack went straight to the fax machine and dug in his pocket for the yellow note that he'd written the number on. The familiar dialing tone sounded as he waited for the machine to connect, then he watched as the page was slowly sucked through the machine. In a matter of moments, his message would be on Dr Winstanley's desk. Now all he had to do was get the child's DNA on a swab and get it off to the lab, and that meant getting back to baby Mary before 4 pm when she would be taken into care. He checked his watch: plenty of time, but still, he'd go now and get it done. No sense leaving it until the eleventh hour.

Grabbing his coat, he headed out, shouting over his shoulder to Eddie that he'd be back in an hour.

Chapter Nineteen

Sister Monica Johnson was waiting for him when he arrived on the ward.

"What's going on? Have you found something?"

"Not quite, but I'm hopeful of a bit more to go on soon. In the meantime, I need a swab from baby Mary, from inside her mouth. Are you able to do it for me, please?"

Jack was almost breathless with excitement, and Monica picked up on his vibe. "Er, yes. Do you have the kit with you?"

Jack removed it from his coat pocket. It was nothing more than a long cotton bud enclosed in a plastic tube with a lid and label on it. He'd already filled the details out, though without a surname.

"I'll only be a minute. Please wait here." Jack watched as Monica made her way to back to Mary's cot at the end of the ward. A moment later he had the sample in his hands.

"Still no news since you were last here? Nothing from the security cameras, I'm guessing?" she asked him.

"Unfortunately, that's correct, but now I have this." He raised the thin tube in his hand. "I'm hoping the gods are smiling on us and we start to get somewhere." He gave her his brightest, most encouraging smile, thanked her again and turned to leave the hospital once more.

By the end of the day baby Mary would be taken by yet another stranger and placed with a foster parent until her future could be decided up. It was probably a good thing the poor little mite knew little of how much her life was being directed from behind closed doors by yet more complete strangers. It wasn't the best start to life, but as a foundling, she had little choice. Someone had to make the decisions.

Jack hurried to his car, pulling up his collar against the sleet. He needed to get the tube over to the lab so they could start work on it, and with Christmas holidays about to start, he didn't want to waste another precious moment. He was hoping someone might take pity on the case and bump the job up the queue. Unlike Eddie, Jack relied on good manners and conscience to get what he wanted. He was hoping Dr Barbara Winstanley would appreciate his way of doing things.

He pulled his scarf tighter around his neck. He'd felt on the edge of a cold for a couple of days and was anxious to keep it at bay and enjoy Christmas without being ill. Perhaps a hot toddy and a soak in a hot bath later would help. At the lab, he braced himself against the icy air as he dashed across the wet tarmac towards the front entrance. The glass doors opened automatically and he gathered himself in the lobby. The receptionist at the solitary desk looked bored.

"Soon be Christmas," he said, smiling at her, but she didn't look convinced that it would change anything.

"Who are you here to see?"

"Dr Winstanley, but I'm happy to go up to her. She doesn't need to be bothered coming down," he said, giving her another winning smile.

"Sorry. Can't do that, since we're a lab and all."

Jack was tempted to exclaim 'No shit,' but refrained, again. Manners.

"Who shall I tell her is here?"

"DC Jack Rutherford."

He waited while she made the call.

"I have a DC Jack Rutherford here to see you." Try as he might, he couldn't tell what was being said at the other end. After a moment, she rang off and glanced back up at him. "She'll be right down. Please take a seat."

Jack smiled at her again, but declined the seat offer and instead leaned against the wall by the lift, supposing Dr Winstanley would make her entrance from there. He wasn't disappointed. The lift pinged its arrival; she must have come straight down after she'd gotten off the phone.

As the doors opened, Jack did a double take. The woman in front of him nothing like what he'd been expecting, but he instinctively knew it was her. She held her outstretched hand in front of her as she stepped into the foyer.

"We meet at last, Detective Rutherford. Nice to make your acquaintance."

Nice, and articulate too, thought Jack.

"Indeed, and yours too. Thanks for seeing me on such short notice."

Her bright-blue eyes twinkled as he spoke, and Jack idly wondered if she was wearing coloured contact lenses, but since the rest of her was equally as beautiful, he figured not. Her hair was styled in a short blonde bob that accentuated her fine features, and her pale pink lips were almost as mesmerizing as her eyes. In short, she was a natural beauty, which confirmed in his mind that those blue eyes were for real. Jack dragged his mind back to more important thoughts and stuttered for a moment, words jostling for order before he spoke again.

"I'm sure you've heard about baby Mary on the news?"

"I have."

"Well, this is her DNA," he said, holding the tube out, "and about all we have to go on. I'm hoping this will work." Jack flashed his best smile yet again, and Dr Winstanley returned one of her own.

Then, tilting her head to one side she asked, "She's special to you somehow, isn't she?"

Taken aback, he replied, "Um, yes, I suppose she is. It's obvious, then, is it? I must try harder."

"Yes, and no. I mean yes, I can see it, but no, don't try harder. You shouldn't have to hide it. The little one has you on her side trying to help her, and while she doesn't know it yet, I'm sure she'll appreciate your effort and involvement when she's older."

Jack nodded and looked at the floor. He felt a blush rise and hoped it didn't show.

"I can see I've embarrassed you." She put her hand on his arm and added, "I'll get this going right away, Jack. Let's see if we can get a result before Santa comes down the chimney, give her a special Christmas present."

Recovering, he said, "That would be perfect if you can. I really can't thank you enough. Here's my mobile number, day or night. As soon as you have a result I'll call in and get it." He handed his card over and she slipped it into her lab coat pocket.

Smiling in his direction for the last time, she said, "I'd better get to work then," and pressed the button to call the lift, leaving Jack to exit with a grateful wave and venture back outside into the freezing cold.

Again.

Good manners and humanity generally worked in his favour. He must tell Eddie.

Chapter Twenty

Eddie looked pleased about something when Jack returned to the office. He walked back to his desk, wringing his hands animatedly to get some warmth back into them after the short trip in from his car.

"What's up, Eddie? You look pleased about something."

"Finally, we have something to work with. The tyre tracks at the end of Sparrows Lane near the drag marks or skid marks or whatever they were – the tyres are Continentals, which are used mainly on Transit vans, and given the depth of tread, they're probably new ones. They got some good casts of them with the wet weather – the mud was good and soft. I have a uniform checking if any of the residents down there have a van like that, which I'm suspecting not, then I've organized with traffic to filter out van drivers travelling that road for the next twenty-four hours to pull them over and see whether they were on it when the girls disappeared. If we get lucky, we can look inside a few of them at the same time. Long shot, I know, but it's something."

"Have the press been told yet?"

"No. I don't want to spook the actual culprits until we've done some checks, then we'll go to the press. Those vans are ten a penny, predominantly white, and sold all over the UK and beyond. But we'll need the public's help. Someone may remember seeing a van as they drove by but didn't realize its relevance at the time to come forward with it. No doubt we'll get the usual red herrings when we've put the press release out – everyone knows a man with a van these days, and some folks are happy to dob someone in, particularly an ex."

Jack nodded unhappily in agreement. The press was a help to get the word out, but the majority of the responses would end in wild goose chases, he knew.

"Let's hope it throws us a bone to worry, then," he said.

A call across the squad room interrupted their conversation, Clarke stood at her desk, telephone in her hand.

"Boss, you'll want to hear this," she said, and both men walked over to her. "Uniform reckon one of the residents saw a dark-coloured van; the mention of one must have jogged his memory. He was nearly back at his place after taking his dog out and saw it at the end of the lane, though from quite a distance. He said he knew it wasn't a car – the headlights were all wrong and it was virtually dark – but he's sure it wasn't a white one. Nothing else to report other than it was only there a moment or two."

"Well, that's something at least. We can narrow it down. Thanks, Clarke. Let traffic know what we're looking for, will you? No point in stopping the white ones at this point."

"Right. Will do, Sarge."

Jack checked his watch. It would be dark again in another hour, making van sightings even more difficult; a set of headlights approaching made it hard to see the vehicle they were attached to. But time was marching on and they needed to do something.

Eddie must have read his mind. "I know, Jack," he said, "but it's the same time of day and if it's a local driver, we could be in luck. Best we go out there, too, and give them a hand. Grab your scarf. It's bitter cold."

Jack wondered if it was a day for stating the obvious, and once again he refrained from adding 'No shit.' "I'll be right there," he said. Manners and all.

After two hours of sitting in their tin can half a mile north of the checkpoint, they had spotted precisely two dark-coloured Transit vans and radioed ahead. Neither had resulted in anything. Neither was from around these parts, and neither of them had passed by on the day of the abductions. And more importantly, neither of them had Continental tyres with the same tread pattern.

It was almost 6 pm, and Jack was ready for his dinner. He called ahead to Janine to let her know he'd be home later and tell her not to wait for him. After ten years of marriage, she was used to his last-minute plan changes and told him to keep warm. It was freezing out there.

Was there no escaping it?

"Here's another," Eddie said, and did the necessary, radioing to the boys ahead. They both watched as the van's red tail-lights went on and the driver pulled over.

"Please let us catch a break. Please," Jack muttered under his breath.

But after a few moments, they watched in dismay as the van drove off again. The radio crackled and, sighing, Jack picked it up.

"Better luck that time," said the constable. "Same tyres."

Jack and Eddie looked at one another and grinned.

"Great!" said Jack. "We can follow that one up at least. Were they locals, by chance?"

"Negative. From out Tilbury way. So still not that far."

"Worth looking at in more detail, though. Tilbury Docks springs to mind straight away when you mention Tilbury. And the things that go on in containers. But let's not jump to conclusions yet. It's the first of many more we'll come across, I expect."

"I agree. We'll keep on, and you do what you need to do to follow up," the PC said. They rang off and Jack hung the mic back on its hook. He looked across at Eddie.

"At least it had the same tyres. It's a start," he said.

Chapter Twenty-One

She'd shivered most of the night under her thin blanket and had barely slept at all. The man's visit had scared her, sending her emotions spiralling, the tears streaming until she had no more left to give. Her face had stopped stinging from his slap some time back, but her face was red and swollen anyway from crying so hard. Leanne wasn't stupid, and while the sting from his hand had gone, she could still feel the sting of his words.

"*Relax, you're not my type. Too big, too old.*"

Was the other girl in the van more his desire? Was she here in the same building, or had they moved her? Disposed of her, even? But a more urgent question was what had she found herself mixed up in if she wasn't what he wanted? And furthermore, did that make her surplus, put her in even more danger? She'd seen his face and knew from movies and crime shows that that was never a good thing – she'd be able to identify him.

The sound of a key in the lock again startled her. What could they want this time?

Leanne hoped it was only someone else bringing food.

The overhead light bulb went on and she struggled to focus after the darkness even though it wasn't particularly bright. But it wasn't the man; it was the woman from yesterday, the same dank hair half covering her petite face, grubby clothes, and she was carrying a tray. She thanked her lucky stars it wasn't the fat repulsive man from yesterday – was it yesterday? As the woman made towards her, Leanne heard the lock being fastened again. Someone was guarding outside her door, though guarding who against what she'd no idea. Was the woman a prisoner too?

"Food. Eat. No more," the woman said to her now, her eyes staying low. In the crook of her elbow hung a plastic shopping bag and as she put the tray down, she handed Leanne the bag. "Warmer clothes. Put on. Cold."

"Thank you. Toilet, please?"

"No toilet. Bucket."

"Please, I need the toilet," Leanne said, her voice rising in frustration. She shuddered at the thought of her own waste building up inside the small room. It smelt bad enough as it was; the tatty carpet in the corner already soaked with her urine, and hers wasn't the first to have been deposited there, she was sure.

"No toilet. Bag," the woman said, her voice rising a notch in reply, eyes darting rapidly to anywhere but Leanne's own.

Leanne spoke to the woman again, deciding on a softer approach. If she was a prisoner too, maybe Leanne could befriend her for her own needs, as a way of escape. "Do you live here too?" she asked with a small smile. The woman shook her head slowly, choosing to answer without actual words. Leanne watched her as she picked up the tray from yesterday and made her way back to the door. Hurriedly she said, "Thank you," hoping her gentler demeanour would encourage the woman to talk on her next visit. Being locked in a room all day and not knowing where or why she was there was distressing enough; she had to figure a way out. There was a click of the lock turning and the door opened briefly, allowing the skinny woman to slip through the door. Then it was relocked. Was there someone stationed outside the door all the time, she wondered? She doubted it. Probably the guard was there only for when the woman entered in case Leanne tried anything on.

She could overpower the frail creature. But to what end?

There was no doubt Leanne was big for her age, and strong too from cycling, but she needed a chance to use them to do any good now. She turned her attention back to the tray of food and the plastic bag. The food looked as appetizing as a bowl of wet cat biscuits, but she needed to keep her strength up. Dutifully, she spooned the sloppy mess – probably cold cereal – into her mouth. A mug of pale and tepid tea followed it down, and that was breakfast. It filled a small corner inside her otherwise empty stomach, and for that she was grateful.

Leanne then turned her attention to the plastic bag and tipped the contents out onto the narrow bed. Track pants, a long-sleeved top and some socks, all of which looked like they'd once belonged to someone else – another prisoner, perhaps? She touched the grey sweatshirt and idly wondered whose it had been and what had happened to them. Had they gotten out of the building alive? She pulled the socks on over her own thin ones, and then pulled on the track pants and shirt, hoping for comfort in the layers. It was better than nothing; there was no heater in the room.

With nothing else to do, she flopped back on the bed and took comfort under the thin blanket. What she wouldn't do to see her mum and dad right now. How she'd cry on their shoulders and tell them how sorry she was for being an ungrateful cow, how much she appreciated what they both did for her. If only she'd accepted her mum's offer of a lift, she'd be tucked up snug in her own bed instead of here in this hell hole. The tears flowed again as she stuffed her hands into the track bottom pockets to keep them warm. But there was something there, something long and smooth, right at the bottom of one of them. From her touch, Leanne instinctively knew what it was but pulled it out for confirmation.

It was her weapon, ready for when she chose to use it.

Chapter Twenty-Two

She turned the teaspoon over in her hands; its handle had been filed to a point. She assumed the frail woman who had brought her food had put it there. While a key to the door would have been the ideal gift, the spoon would have to do for now. When the time came to use it, there'd only be one chance to get it right. She'd have to choose her moment carefully. It seemed someone was on her side at least, and she felt sure it wasn't the man with the sausage-meat stomach. Leanne sat up on her mattress, the thin blanket around her shoulders, twiddling the spoon between her fingers. Her fingers were the coldest things about her now; she'd have killed for a pair of mittens. She estimated it had been several hours since the woman had brought breakfast, assuming the meal had been breakfast, and Leanne idly wondered what her next meal might consist of. Would there be another gift, perhaps? One thing she knew was that if her secret benefactor was the woman, she'd work on getting her on side even more, and hopefully find out what had happened to the young girl she'd arrived with. Was she close by? As she lay on her bed earlier, she thought she'd heard faint crying noises, but wasn't sure if she'd imagined it or not. Try as she might, she hadn't been able to ascertain where the noise had come from – up or down, one side or the other. Was it the girl? Were there other girls besides herself?

Standing up, she walked over to the door and crouched down again to look through the keyhole, but as with the previous times she'd done so, the result was the same – nothing. The key was most likely still in the lock, blocking her view. There was a slim gap under the door itself, the perfect depth to drag a key back through, her way out to freedom if only she could dislodge it out of the lock. She'd tried to push it out from her own side with her spoon, but it had been fruitless. But there had been a draft blowing through, directly into her eye, and that meant she wasn't inside a building with many rooms like a hotel or boarding house. It meant the outside world was not that far away.

Still crouching at the door, she listened for voices, for movement, for cries even. Hearing nothing, she decided to give the key another go. There was no point sitting freezing, waiting for something appalling to happen to her, because it would do if she stayed put; otherwise, why hold her prisoner? It wasn't for ransom; her parents weren't well off. If the man had said she was too old for him, she wouldn't be too old for someone else's perversion, and she didn't want to take the chance of finding out. Grabbing a piece of newspaper that had been left in the room, she tentatively pushed it under the door, ready to catch the key when it fell, hoping it wouldn't make too much of a clatter as it did so.

She pushed the length of the teaspoon into the lock and prodded the end of the key gently, increasing the pressure gradually so as not to send it shooting out and missing the newspaper altogether. Then it would be obvious what she'd been up to, and she would be in even more danger. After a minute or two of patient and gentle manipulating, she felt the key start to give, but as warm optimism filled her cold soul, it was washed away in an instant.

Someone was coming.

But what to do with the newspaper? It was too obvious sitting out on the other side of the door like a flag. If she pulled it back in they'd be bound to see it moving and know she was up to something, but if she left it there, they'd surely ask why. Her mind scrambled to come up with a story as she bounded back to her bed and blanket. She jammed the spoon under her pillow. The footsteps weren't small like the woman's; they were heavy and sounded tense, the tread of someone on a mission. Leanne held her breath and forced herself to look defiant as the door banged open.

It was the man with meaty hands, his face deep pink like bubble gum.

"What are you doing?" he demanded, waving the newspaper at her.

Leanne's heart sank to the soggy cereal in the bottom of her stomach. "I wondered if you had anything else to read. I've read that paper."

"What, so you thought you'd put it out like an empty milk bottle, to be replenished? You're not in a hotel, you know. We don't work like that around here. Don't you get that? Otherwise, a chef would be cooking you a full English in a morning, not a bowl of cereal." Raising his voice to a full shout, he added, "Are you a stupid bitch or what?"

Leanne watched as his face became a deeper pink with the effort of exerting himself. The veins bulged in his neck.

"I'm sorry," she stammered. All thoughts of staying strong vanished as the burly figure approached her bed and she prepared herself for his hand to make contact. She scrunched her eyes up tight and raised her hands to protect her head, waiting for the inevitable.

She smelt him as he spoke, felt his putrid breath warm on her ear as he whispered to her.

"That's more like it. Less cocky and more submissive. It will be better for you in the long run. Who knows – you might even get to enjoy it."

Leanne didn't move a muscle until she'd heard the door open and close again, the turn of the key. The hammering of her own heart was the only sound in the stillness.

Chapter Twenty-Three

After three full hours sat in a freezing cold doorway on a piece of cardboard, all she had to show for her efforts was £3.60, barely enough for a mug of tea and a biscuit. Billy had chosen a different spot. Their plan was always to cover two places at once; that way they doubled their chances of attracting sympathetic passers-by. She stretched her legs and groaned. She needed the toilet. And she was hungry. She hoped Billy was faring better than she was.

"Any spare change, sir?" she'd asked almost every male that had walked by. Most of them had hardly glanced at her, and most had not bothered to answer. Only one male had stopped, had taken some pity on her in the cold and tossed her a £2 coin. Her only other donation was from a young woman not much older than herself, who had supplied the other £1.60, all she had in change. Chloe had thanked them both heartily, but no one else had volunteered to share. Chloe found it easier to coax money from the men who passed; they were less critical of her somehow. The women, however, took the time to glare, show their contempt for the unwashed who made the streets their home. They didn't seem to see them as humans at all.

Chloe knew she looked a sight; she was hoping to grab a shower after the lunchtime crowd had scurried back to their warm shops and offices. Even though this was better by far than living with her vile parents, what she would have given for a warm office to sit in and munch on a Penguin biscuit with her mug of afternoon tea. Inwardly she smiled at herself; she was getting more like Billy each day.

By 1.30 pm, she couldn't hold her bladder any longer and decided to call it quits and move on – to the toilet at least. She gathered her piece of cardboard and the makeshift sign asking for change and headed towards McDonald's, where she knew it would be warm. Inside, she could use the loo and wash her hands, if she was quick and the manager didn't sling her out as soon as he spotted her. She hung back near the front entrance until a group of five teenagers approached together, then added herself to the back of them, hidden relatively well by their big coat hoods and scarves. Once inside, she filtered off towards the back of the building and waited out of sight for the toilet door to open, which she'd catch and slip through. So many cafés and fast-food chains had codes on their toilet doors to stop the likes of her going in, as well as tourists who merely wanted to relieve themselves without making a purchase.

The warmth of the restaurant was comforting. Her pink, chapped face and fingers smarted as they thawed, but there was no time to linger – the toilet door was opening. Now was her chance. She held it back for a Japanese lady who was coming out and won herself a quick nod and smile. The gesture reminded Chloe how much she missed positive human contact. No one wanted to hug her, touch her arm, dish out a warm smile or say something welcoming; it was all negative, crappy, soul-destroying negative. At least she had a friend in Billy, and vice versa, but still, a hug went a long way to not feeling like a sewer rat all the time.

There was no one in the toilet room. The three cubicles were empty, so she took advantage of the space and gave her hands and face a good wash with the available hand soap. Running a basin of warm water, she soaked her chapped hands, relishing the warmth, until another woman entered and stared at her in disgust before going into one of the cubicles. When she'd finished and come out again, she tutted as she washed and dried her hands at the opposite end of the room, no doubt not wanting to get too close. Chloe was tempted to say something, but kept her mouth shut. The older woman's camel coat looked expensive, and Chloe wondered why she was in McDonald's and not supping tea from a china cup out Knightsbridge way.

"What are you staring at?" the woman questioned.

"I was admiring your lovely coat. Nice and thick, I expect," Chloe said with a small smile.

"If you got a job, perhaps you could buy one," the woman replied curtly, and then hurried back out into the restaurant. Probably with the grandkids, Chloe thought. She washed her face, and briefly wondered if she should try and wash her hair in the basin and dry it under the hand dryer. She decided not to bother; someone would probably report her. No, she'd have to hope for that shower. Finished in the bathroom, she made her way back into the restaurant and the smell of warm burgers and chips, her stomach growling in hopeful anticipation that would not be fulfilled. Chloe was nearly at the exit when she spied an unattended tray with two burger boxes and two packs of fries; the customer had probably gone to get extra salt or something. She quickly glanced round to see if there was anyone making an obvious beeline for the food, and when nobody appeared to be moving towards it, grabbed both boxes and both packs of fries and joined the stream of people leaving, her stash pressed close to her stomach to conceal it as best she could.

Once out the door, Chloe turned left with the throng and kept moving until she came to a side street and slipped down it. Nicking wasn't something she enjoyed, but it was a darn sight easier and more productive than begging in a doorway on a day like today. Opening one of the boxes, she smiled at the Big Mac inside it. She reached for the first packet of fries and emptied that in beside it.

She'd save the second burger and fries for Billy, she decided, and laid them both carefully inside her shoulder bag. He'd enjoy them later back in the garage, she was sure. But right now, it was time to eat, and she made herself comfortable on the cold floor and prepared to dig in.

The stench of urine around her went unnoticed as she devoured her first hot meal in a while.

Chapter Twenty-Four

Chloe licked the last bit of salty grease off her fingers, glad she'd washed them before she'd stolen the food. She felt bad about stealing, but she assumed the person she'd stolen from could afford a replacement meal, unlike herself. The small amount of money she'd earned so far wasn't going to keep them in much more than a cheap white loaf for dinner, some cheese or plastic meat filling if they were incredibly lucky. But her stomach felt good for now, and as tempted as she was to tuck into Billy's burger and fries, she restrained herself, knowing how much he'd appreciate it later, and that he wouldn't dream of depriving her had it been the other way around.

It was quiet in the side street. The hustle and bustle on the main thoroughfare had also died away, but Chloe knew it would start up again a few hours later when workers began the mad dash to train stations and bus stops for the journey home.

Home.

It was only natural to miss the creature comforts of what she'd had in her life, and even though her parents couldn't have cared less about her, she'd had a warm bed and there was always food on the table. Even if it hadn't been much, it was more than she was getting currently. Her mind wandered to her own brief parenthood and the baby girl she'd left in the church porch. Her heart ached again, but she knew it was all for the best. Had the hospital named her Mary as Billy had suggested? Whatever name they'd chosen for her, Chloe would always think of her as Mary. One day she hoped to meet her, explain her actions to the girl and hope to make amends, but that would be light years away. But for now, she had to earn some money and she hoped the afternoon shoppers would be a touch more charitable as she gathered her meagre belongings and set off back up towards the high street to find a different and more productive spot than the morning. The smell of burgers and fries inside her bag gave her comfort. It would be a nice surprise for Billy later, albeit a cold one. Still, he'd not grumble.

Billy had fared a little better in Croydon town centre. Having jumped a train ride, he'd made his way from East Croydon station into town, the walk keeping him warm after the steamed-up carriage of hot bodies. He'd been tempted to sit a while, but without a ticket, he knew he'd be kicked off. He had waited on the platform for the right moment to dodge out the turnstiles. He'd spent the morning in an empty doorway like Chloe had, but Billy had his cheeky personality on his side, which he used to his advantage. If he could have sung and busked, he would have, but he could do neither, so he fell back on his sense of humour.

"Spare a shekel for an old ex-leper?" There weren't many people that hadn't heard of Monty Python and *The Life of Brian*. And even if they didn't toss him a coin or two, it made many of them smile, something Billy fed off because at least it was a smile, a warming human emotion.

"Spare a shekel for an old ex-leper?" he said again, trying to catch the eye of a gentleman approaching, feeling sure he'd appreciate the humour. He was wrapped up warm in his coat, his scarf almost covering his face to keep the chill out, thick gloves on his hands. Billy saw the man take a glove off and feel inside his coat pocket, then pull out a note and some change. Billy took his spiel up a notch in volume. As the man arrived in front of him, Billy repeated it, looking the man straight in the eye, hopeful. The man spoke first.

"If I give you this five-pound note, what will you buy with it?" No smile as yet; Billy was going to have to work for it.

"My girl wants a new toothbrush and some toothpaste, so I'll start with that. With the change, something other than bread. Man can't live by bread alone, you know." Billy painted on his best smile and willed the man to part with his cash.

"I guess you are a Monty Python fan, then?"

"'That I am, sir. Bloody do-gooders." Billy gave another cheeky smile as he quoted from one of the most famous scenes. Finally, the man showed the start of a smile, and Billy knew he had him.

"Then go and buy her a new brush and paste to go with it. She's not Roman by any chance, is she?"

"Oh no, sir. What have the Romans ever done for us?" Billy laughed as the man finally handed the note over.

"What the hell. Take it all," he said, adding the loose change too, making a total of nearly £7. "Buy yourselves something to eat to go with that bread."

"Thank you, sir, thank you!" Billy called after the man as he slowly walked off. "Very kind of you, sir!" he called, and the man raised a backwards hand over his shoulder in acknowledgment. Some folks could be generous with both time and change, and Billy was grateful for both from the stranger. He wondered who he was and where he was headed. Perhaps he'd see him again on his return trip. Maybe he'd stop and chat a little more. Billy pocketed the money and smiled to himself. He needed to stop and buy Chloe a toothbrush and paste on the way home later. There was a budget grocery store not too far away.

But first he needed to get back to work.

"Spare a shekel for an old ex-leper?" he called to anyone who would listen.

Chapter Twenty-Five

Jack parked the car in the driveway of their semi-detached home. They lived on a quiet street, not far from the town centre. It was only the second home they'd owned together. The first had been a small flat not far from their current spot, and they'd saved hard to make it up another rung of the property ladder. With Janine and himself both working full time, they had done well for themselves though it had been a struggle at first to meet the mortgage repayments. While their friends were going out on a Saturday night to the cinema or for a meal, Jack and Janine would rent a DVD and stay in with a budget bottle of wine, and Janine would make a nice supper. They'd never been flash with their cash, and since they enjoyed each other's company, staying in with a movie instead of going out didn't much matter to either of them. One thing all their scrimping and saving had taught them, though, was the value of money. Their home had become their savings bank for the future, a place to start their family in. Unfortunately, Mother Nature had had her own agenda, and so the spare room had never been turned into a much-yearned-for nursery. Instead, it now contained boxes of stuff they no longer used – board games, old books that stood no chance of being read again by either of them, clothes for the charity shop, an old iron. All in all, the room looked messy, drab and sad.

Jack was stood in there now, looking through the window out into the darkness dappled in orange sodium at the other houses in the street, the odd car making its way back home for the night. They knew a few of their neighbours, and their street over the years had become like a bowl of stew with various ethnicities continually coming and going, the pot's contents changing constantly. There were a couple of houses where more senior owners still lived, most now on their own, their partners long gone, Jack and Janine were the decent neighbours who looked in on them occasionally. And that reminded him that he hadn't done so in a few days. With the current cold spell, he'd call in on them all tomorrow. He looked around the small room again and tutted at its lack of purpose; they could do better with it. Maybe a room for him to relax in, though why would he sit upstairs when he could be down with Janine? Perhaps a sewing room for her; she'd used to enjoy making clothes for herself but couldn't recall her doing so for some years. He'd have to ask her.

"Jack," Janine called up the stairs, "dinner is ready."

"On my way," he called back. He headed down, thoughts of the spare room fresh in his mind. He took his seat at the table, where a plate of hot meat pie and gravy awaited him.

"This looks good, love," he said, grabbing the salt pot, something he always did before he'd even tasted the food, and something Janine could never understand.

"How do you know if it needs it before you've tasted it?" she'd asked him on so many occasions that now she didn't bother. She gave him a questioning look anyway.

"What?" he said, smiling, though he knew anyway. He tucked in, gathering mashed potato onto the side of his fork.

"What were you doing up there"? she enquired, and waited for him to finish his mouthful before he answered.

"I was in the spare room. We should do something with it rather than leave it gathering stuff that should be at the charity shop. It's a real waste." He cut a forkful from the meat pie and savoured it, gravy gathering in the corner of his mouth as he chewed. "Do you still have your sewing machine? You used to make clothes. Why don't we make it a sewing room for you?"

"Well, that's a thoughtful gesture Jack, but I've not made anything for maybe ten years, and I don't even have the machine anymore. Clothes aren't that expensive these days and working full time, I've not that much spare time anyway." She returned her attention to her own meal but added, "I get your point, though. It could do with a clear-out. Maybe we could decorate it, smarten it up a bit. It wouldn't take long when it's empty."

"Then we should do something with it. What about a lodger?"

"Yes, I agree, but not a lodger. I like my space and privacy. And with you coming and going all hours, I'd rather know who was in the house with me at any one time. No, we'll think of another use for it. Though if we can get the stuff down to the charity shop, I bet someone would appreciate the old board games and books at Christmas. It's only a couple of days away."

Jack piled peas onto his fork and hastily bent to eat them before they rolled off. Only a handful made the journey and he mixed the remainder into his mash instead. They couldn't escape from him so easily.

"Let's do it when we've finished dinner. I could drop them all in tomorrow when I go past as long as I can get a parking spot close by. I don't fancy dashing in the rain getting soaked but I'll be past again later so I've a couple of shots at it."

"Talking of shops, have you done all your Christmas shopping?" She smiled at him coyly and he knew exactly what she was referring to – had he bought her gift yet or not? There wasn't much time left. Luckily, he had and could reply honestly.

"I have bought your present, as it happens, my love. I've just got to collect it from the store. It's all ordered and paid for," he said in his best-satisfied tone. "You'll not catch me missing Christmas present-giving. I've had all year to get it organized."

He looked smug, and Janine smiled at his cocky attitude as he pushed mashed potato and peas into his half-smiling mouth.

Chapter Twenty-Six

It looked to Jack like Eddie had been burning his candle at both ends again. He was rubbing his already swollen eyes as he entered the squad room. Jack and a few of the others including Clarke had already been in for a couple of hours, albeit to sip coffee and mull over the case so far while awaiting their official briefing from Eddie. And from the way Eddie looked, they wouldn't be getting one until he'd had at least another two strong mugs full. Clarke glanced at Jack as she too noted the condition he had arrived in. Had he slept in his suit? Jack crossed the room and ushered Eddie to the coffee cupboard, where he closed the door behind them.

"What the hell, Eddie?" he hissed. "You're the boss, for goodness' sake. What's happened to you? We've all been here a couple of hours already. Where have you been?"

"Long story, but I thought Sue wanted me back so I went round."

"And?"

"And I was wrong. In fact, she was there with her new bloke and that got me pissed off so I banged a few times on the door with my fist."

Jack knew where the story was going. Eddie had a temper.

"And the new bloke didn't take too kindly to your knocking, and you ended up scuffling, that it?"

"Pretty much. I went back to the pub for a couple, got hammered and slept in my car. And before you say anything, I know. I screwed up and I look like shit."

"On that, I have to agree. And you smell like it too, I'm afraid," Jack said, wrinkling his nose up. "You'll have to get off home and have a shower, take the smell of stale booze off at least. I'll cover for you with Morton. He's probably down the bookies, anyway. I've not seen him yet either. So turn around and get off, then you'll be back in a better frame of mind to do some bloody detective work."

Jack couldn't help raising his voice over the last sentence, because he meant it, whether Eddie Edwards was his boss or not. With more vans identified by the traffic cops, they had work to follow up with; there was no time to bother about whether Sue had a new bloke or not and deal with the fallout from Eddie getting inebriated.

"Right. Back soon," Eddie said, and made a dash for the door before anyone else stopped and smelt him.

Jack shook his head. With more junior officers already in and working, between him and DI Morton, who the hell was supposed to be showing a bit of leadership? He took a couple of deep breaths in and out and felt a little calmer. If the team needed leadership, that left Jack to do the job. Clapping his hands loudly, he made his way to the front of the squad room. The crime boards displayed both Leanne's and Kate's pictures and precious little else save for an image of a dark Transit van that someone had probably lifted from a web page. The whole board looked far too sparse for his liking.

"Listen up, everyone." He waited until all heads were turned his way before starting the briefing. It wasn't something he'd done much of before. "DS Edwards will be back shortly, so in the interest of time marching on, I'd said we'd go over the case together in his absence and fill him in later. So let's get cracking." He looked directly at Clarke. "Clarke, where are we at with the van list to follow up on?"

Clearing her throat, she stood and addressed the other half dozen people in the room, a mixture of detectives and civilian researchers. "Thanks to traffic, we've a list of six to follow up with, and preliminary vehicle checks have been done with all of them through the system. I believe Mo has been looking further into owners and drivers. Mo?"

As Mo stood, Jack couldn't help watch as her midriff settled itself at the sudden movement of standing. As a researcher on the team, she spent large chunks of her day sitting in front of a computer terminal looking things up, usually with a packet of digestives close by her never-ending mug of tea. Her low-cut shirt showed off her ample chest, which was rapidly turning beet red from standing and addressing the team. It never got any easier for her.

"Interestingly," Mo began, "one of the vehicle owners is a name we've come across before, though not where minors have been involved. Remember that case a few years back when a woman was kidnapped and taken to Manchester? GMP found her in a derelict house on the outskirts of town, safe but severely traumatised, several weeks after her abduction. We never did find the real reason she was taken, but she did manage to identify one of the men in the ring. He was successfully prosecuted and served five years in Strangeways. Despite being offered a deal, he didn't cough up the names of his accomplices, so that's why he did time. He was released last year. His name is Martin Coffey, and obviously not the rather dead Martin Coffey."

"Dead Martin Coffey?" Jack asked, for the benefit of the rest of the room.

"Yes, hanged in Strangeways in 1946 for murder. He was one of the last to be executed there, but no relation."

"So, Martin Coffey has a dark Transit van that was down here recently for us to spot it. That warrants a deeper look. Right – Mo, you get on to Martin Coffey and get digging. Let's see his whereabouts. Find as much camera footage as you can from the nearby trunk roads close to Wickham and Sparrows Lane. See if we can place his van anywhere near there on the day of the abductions. If it was in or around the Croydon area, let's know about it. Now, that's going to take some time, but it's all we have so let's get to it. Good work, Mo. We have a name at least."

Mo's ample cheeks reddened at the compliment, and he half felt bad about delivering the compliment publicly, though praise for a job well done went a long way. Heads swivelled back to computer screens and Jack walked briskly to the coffee cupboard for a quick one before DI Morton made it in.

Chapter Twenty-Seven

❦

By lunchtime, Jack's stomach was growling like an angry lioness protecting her cub. He craved something hot and tasty and not the cheese sandwich that was sat on his desk. Through the opaque Tupperware lid, the outline of the roll looked meagre and unappetizing, and Jack wished there were a couple of hot fat sausages and a smearing of ketchup in it instead, but since he'd put it together himself before breakfast, he knew there was no chance of that.

Not unless the fairies had been while he'd been away from his desk.

Still, if the lion were roaring, the sandwich would tide him over until he braved the outside cold and a mobile food van down the side street not far away. Some men had a secret woman on the side or a quiet gambling habit, but not Jack. While he loved Janine, she did keep a tight watch on his diet, so secret hot sausage sandwiches were his side vice, although he tried to limit his intake. He set the cheese roll on the plastic lid as a plate and took two enormous bites, filling both cheeks with food so he looked like a giant hamster. The roll was gone in three more mouthfuls.

The squad room was relatively quiet. Most desks were empty now, as his colleagues had also gone off in search of sustenance after a busy morning. The discovery of Martin Coffey's name and the presence of his vehicle in the area had to account for something, and none of the team believed in coincidence. Jack wiped his mouth with the back of his sleeve as he swallowed the last bite and looked at his watch. The charity shop would be open now, and the boxes were in his car, so he figured he might as well head over while things were quiet.

"What the hell," he said to himself, knowing he was using the trip to the charity shop as an excuse to arrive back via the mobile food van. He was only kidding himself. Jack grabbed his coat, wrapped his scarf around his neck and headed out to his car. For a change, the sky was pale blue like a faded deckchair left out in the sun too long, the sun barely warming the tarmac under his cold feet, but at least it wasn't raining. Thank goodness for small mercies.

Ten minutes later, he was looking for a parking space not far from the charity shop. He spotted a small green shopping trolley-type car about to pull out so he put his indicator on to show the driver he wanted the spot – he hoped his car would fit. Cars were building up behind him as he waited for the old lady to finally pull out; he saw her small dog balancing its front paws on the dashboard. He was tempted to use his horn to hurry her up, but a car two back honked so now he didn't have to. Finally, she pulled out and Jack squeezed his in at an awkward angle, leaving the rear end hanging out into the road. The car that had honked swerved past him now, its driver showing his displeasure with a one-finger salute and a rev of the engine.

"Yeah, yeah, yeah," muttered Jack. He stepped out of the car, opened the boot, and lifted out the two boxes of games and books, balancing one on top of the other. As he turned to close the boot lid, he could feel the lower box wobble and he fought to control the both of them before one or both fell to the pavement. He was about to scream an obscenity when a voice broke into his thoughts.

"Steady on! Here, I've got it." A pair of hands took the box from the top and nimbly prevented things from crashing down. Jack looked up and was surprised to see a face he'd seen before, and only recently.

It was the young boy he'd seen begging, the Monty Python fan. Billy.

"Hello again," Billy said, his smile as bright as mirror glinting in the sunshine. When it registered who was back, Jack returned the smile. "Thanks for saving that lot. I was in a bit of strife there for a moment. I'm taking them to the charity shop. Had a bit of a clear-out last night and thought someone could make use of them over Christmas."

Billy took a look in the top box and noticed the game of Scrabble in its dented box.

"You're giving your Scrabble away? How come? It's a classic."

"Ah, it's not much fun when you know which of the two of you always wins. Seems pointless in some respects. Plus, she cheats, makes words up."

Billy laughed out loud and added, "That's all part of playing it. My gran always cheated. Said it kept her imagination alive. I'll give you a hand inside with the boxes. Lead the way." Billy held on to the box with the Scrabble on top and followed Jack the few doors down to the shop. They both put a box each on the counter and waited for one of the volunteers that staffed the shop to come over.

While they waited, Jack enquired, "Did you get the toothpaste and brush?" It seemed the thing to ask, though he wasn't sure why. Did it matter if the lad had spent the money on cigarettes?

"Of course I did. I said I would. She was delighted. A girl needs her little creature comforts, even in this life, on the street. Thanks again, by the way."

"Glad I could help." There was a pause while they waited. The volunteer was busy helping someone choose a coat close by. "Look, I know it's none of my business, but you seem a decent kind. Why do you live on the streets?"

Billy's face dropped and Jack immediately regretted asking such a personal question.

"Oh, listen to me. I'm sorry. It's not my or anyone else's business. Sorry, lad."

"Most people don't understand, think we're vermin and should go and get a job. But it's a long story and not one for today." Billy gave a tight smile before adding, "I'll leave you to it, then. Nice to see you again." He headed towards the door.

At the last minute, Jack grabbed the Scrabble and went after him, leaving the rest of the two boxes on the counter. The volunteer would get to them eventually.

"Hang on a minute," he said as he arrived alongside. "This might give you both some amusement – if you want it, that is. And once again, I'm sorry."

"It's no problem, and thanks. It will be fun on Christmas Day."

Jack's heart pulled a little, wondering where the young man and his girl would be sat when they played it; certainly not in a warm living room with leftovers for tea, he was sure. He reached inside his coat pocket for his wallet and pulled out a £20 note and a business card.

"Look, buy yourselves something nice to eat when you play, and here's my card." He could see that the lad was desperate to take the money but resisting the urge. "Take it. I know it will come in handy. And if you get stuck, in any way, here's my number. Just in case you ever need help, okay?" Their eyes met and Jack nodded, urging Billy to reach out to take it. They were both stood outside the shop on the pavement now. Shoppers bustled by in a continual stream, stuffed bags in their hands. The boy put the money in his trouser pocket, along with the card, then lifted his hand to shake Jack's.

"It's super kind of you. Thank you. I'm Billy, by the way."

Jack took his hand and they shook. "And I'm Jack, nice to meet you, Billy."

"Well, you have a good Christmas if I don't see you again," Billy said, and waved as he moved of into the throng of pedestrians, leaving Jack to add a simple wave of his hand and set off in the opposite direction.

Now all he had to do was collect Janine's present, which seemed overly lavish now after meeting Billy again.

Chapter Twenty-Eight

Jack couldn't get Billy out of his mind. After driving back to the station, he'd forgotten all about his sausage sandwich, which meant something was seriously taking up his headspace. The kid seemed so cheery, as well as well-mannered, and he wondered idly as he parked up what his circumstances were, why he was living on the streets of south London and begging. He couldn't have been more than about seventeen, Jack deduced; the kid had a youthful face behind the wispy hairs that would one day go on to be a beard. He was lucky he didn't have to bother shaving every day yet, Jack thought ruefully, never mind the expense for someone with so little income. And he had a girl too, a friend, some company to go 'home' to, wherever home was. Maybe under a flyover, in a derelict building, a hostel even? What did he have in the way of comfort, of possessions, apart from a second-hand box of Scrabble?

Jack had given him his number in case he needed anything, but he doubted the kid would ever call. More than likely he was too proud to ask for help – and certainly not from a copper – and he hoped the £20 note would buy Billy and his girl a bit of festive cheer, wherever they holed up. They'd both be freezing, surely; the weather hadn't been on bright side of the homeless for some weeks, and worse was yet to come.

Jack's mind turned now to thoughts of another homeless soul, baby Mary. She'd have been picked up by her foster parents by now, and safe in a warm crib with a bottle of milk. Jack was glad of that, but what of her future? Would she be adopted anytime soon? He doubted there would be much of a wait for a newborn; the list of hopeful parents far exceeded demand. He thought about his and Janine's anguish about adoption some years back. They would both have made wonderful parents, given the chance. Strange how anyone in any circumstance – rich, poor or destitute – could bring a child into the world and nobody batted an eyelid, yet *apply* to give a child a good home, and the hoops to jump through were endless, usually ending in being told by some bitter social worker that you weren't quite suitable because they said so.

After more than twelve months of interviews, scrutiny of their financial records and being vetted in every area imaginable, the process had come to a screeching halt. Their social worker had been suddenly taken off their case without explanation and they were asked to start to the whole process all over again. But neither of them had the emotional currency left to spend. The whole process had left them emotionally raw, totally despondent and almost broken. So, they'd decided to take a break from the process and retry a little later on, in the hope that the adoption process would have relaxed a little during that time. It never did, though, and they'd ended up withdrawing completely, feeling that's exactly what the social worker and selection panel had wanted to hear. It had made no sense.

Jack was aware of his name being called and he tuned back in to his surroundings. He was back in the squad room.

"Something the matter, Jack? You look like you've seen a ghost." It was Eddie, back in and looking like he'd scrubbed up and had a shot of something energetic – like intravenous caffeine. Maybe he had; Jack wouldn't put it past him.

"Sorry, miles away." Jack shook his head a little to rearrange his thoughts, like bringing the nuts to the surface in a packet of muesli.

"Where've you been? I've been looking all over for you?"

That's rich. I've been the one covering for you.

"I had an errand to run. Couldn't wait. But I'm here now. What's up?" Jack smiled to diffuse any tension from Eddie with his sudden change back into boss mode. The man was either all in or all out. It seemed he was back to all in.

"We've got a name to work with. Martin Coffey. He's been inside for—"

Jack interrupted him. "I know. Mo informed us at the team briefing earlier, after you'd left. They are following up, looking for that reg plate with the private cameras along the main trunk road to see if we can trace the van's journey, see where it came from, where it went on to. Have they found anything?"

Eddie looked deflated. "Not yet, but it'll take time. There's a lot to find and search through. Still, it's a lead."

Jack hung his coat on the back of his chair and sat down. Eddie remained standing by his desk. Jack sighed. "Best tell me which cameras I need to sift through then and I'll get onto it." It was Jack's way of saying 'yes boss, now leave me alone' without actually saying it; he knew which battles not to bother fighting, even if Eddie owed him big time. Jack needed to be left alone. He had some thinking to do.

It was nearly five o'clock before he came back up for air; there had not been a single sighting of the van in question. Sitting back and rubbing his tired eyes, he noticed the Tupperware box that had contained his cheese roll from earlier, the roll he'd moaned at, had wished was sausage and ketchup. Immediately he wondered what Billy would be tucking into this evening. Had he been serious about living on bread alone?

Then an idea came to him. But would Janine go along with it?

He'd ask her over dinner later.

Chapter Twenty-Nine

Janine was a good sort and had readily agreed to Jack's idea of having a guest or two at their Christmas table. Jack had explained that Billy seemed a sensible lad, and that he thought it fit to help where he could – if the young couple wanted his help, of course. Not everyone on the streets wanted off; some enjoyed the lifestyle, the freedom they got, though Jack couldn't see why. Freedom could be found living in a proper warm home, surely? But each to their own. It was not Jack's or anyone else's place to dictate otherwise.

"Now all I've got to do is find him and ask him," said Jack, finishing his porridge and pushing the bowl away. "You make the best porridge, Mrs Rutherford," he said, rubbing his satisfied stomach and reaching for his coffee.

"You need a warm start from the inside on cold mornings like this. See you through till lunchtime, hopefully," she said, gathering their bowls up and rinsing them in the sink. "And how do you think you'll find him again? Billy, I mean."

"I'm a detective, remember? I find people. It's what I do, and I dare say I'll find him again. He'll more likely be begging where I first saw him, so it's as good a place to start as any. The hard part might be persuading them both to join us. But if they refuse, why don't we send a couple of plates to their digs if I can wheedle the address out of him? That way, they can enjoy dinner, but without the stress of being at a stranger's table and feeling they have to be on their best behaviour or whatever."

"Good idea. They win either way."

"Precisely. Well, I'd better get off," he said, draining his coffee mug. "I'll see you later, love." He bent to peck her on the cheek before grabbing his coat and scarf and setting out.

He was sat in his car waiting for his windscreen to defrost, the heaters inside on full blow and sounding like an aircraft engine warming up, when his phone rang.

"DC Rutherford."

"Jack? It's Dr Barbara Winstanley. From the lab."

"Morning Doc. I hope you've got your thermals on today. It's a frosty one." He smiled as he said it but wondered if he'd overstepped the mark as his quip went unanswered and nothing filled the air. He was about to apologise when she filled the space anyway.

"Can you call in by chance? I have something to share with you and I'd rather explain it in person." Jack detected the seriousness in her voice and doubted it was at his earlier comment. She sounded all business and it sounded important.

"Right. Why don't I come over now, then? I can be there in twenty minutes, if that suits?"

"Perfect. See you then," she said quickly and hung up, leaving Jack wondering what on earth she needed to talk to him about in person. Still, he'd find out soon enough.

She was waiting in reception as he entered the building and Jack tilted his head in a questioning look. He tried not to notice how lovely she looked again, though her eyes were not dancing with the same energy as they had at their last meeting. Something was up.

"Let's go to my office," she said quietly and pushed the buzzer. The lift doors opened and they both stepped inside. Lifts were never meant for small talk, even when the occupants knew one another even a little, and they stood in silence until they reached her floor. Jack followed to her lab. The sterile environment was cool but not cold as they passed through and headed to a small room off to one side. She closed the door behind them and offered him coffee from a small machine behind her desk. He assumed she must drink quite a bit of it to have her own fresh jug. He added milk and sugar to his mug and settled back, waiting for her to fill him in.

"As you know, you gave me a DNA sample from baby Mary. I've run the test, giving it priority, and well, we have a result." She didn't sound too happy.

"I sense something is wrong."

"You could say that. As you also know, the familial testing aspect is so new it's only just officially possible. Well, we got a hit after I submitted the result into the database. And not quite the result I was expecting, if we got a match at all. Only about ten per cent of the population is in there, maybe less, and most if not all have been involved in a crime in some way."

Jack was starting to get frustrated. How long would she take to give him the answer before he had to physically drag it out of her? He knew all this so far. He nodded, urging her on.

"The test we ran looks for family members through bloodline and gives us several results – again, only if they are all in the system. Well, in Mary's case we got two results."

Jack felt like he was about to burst. "And what did the results tell you?"

"They gave us a female and a male. The male was in the system from a while back, to do with a bar fight up north. Things had got ugly and a man got a bottle in his face. This male was involved somehow. You'll have to dig out the details."

"And the female?"

"Well, here's the interesting thing. There's an extremely strong match to your missing girl, Leanne Meadows. We have her DNA in the system from her hairbrush. So strong is the link, in fact, that she's very likely the mother." Dr Winstanley let that sink in.

"So, you're saying our missing fifteen-year-old cyclist is a perfect match to baby Mary's mother, a girl that has since gone missing?"

"Yes, I'm afraid so."

"I'm struggling to get my head around this, Doc. Her parents would have told us if she'd been pregnant, and since she was last seen out on her road bike on her way home from working at the garden centre, she can't have just given birth the day before, surely? With nobody knowing?"

"I can only tell you what the results say, and the profile matches in so many ways." She paused. "Though there is one anomaly."

"And what's that?"

"It's where the male comes in. It seems he's the father."

"Great! We've found one of them at least."

"Not so fast, Jack."

"Oh?"

"The male is now forty years old. If your missing girl Leanne is the mother at fifteen . . ."

"Oh, shit. I need to find him, then."

"You'll not need to go too far to do that."

"Oh? And why's that?"

"Because the owner of that particular DNA is Leanne's dad, one Dave Meadows, the man in the bar fight."

"Holy shit."

"Indeed."

Chapter Thirty

It didn't make any sense to Jack. A cyclist training hard for the champs, a girl missing since the day after baby Mary had been found, a girl showing no sign of being pregnant – there must be some mistake. There had to be something seriously adrift with the test; that was the only explanation. How could Jack go and question Leanne's father about him being the father of an abandoned baby and his own daughter the mother, when she clearly *wasn't* the mother? Meadows would think he'd gone mad, and would definitely not appreciate the accusation at a time like this. This type of DNA testing was so new; perhaps it had been read wrong, or had been contaminated somehow. But Dr Winstanley had been adamant – data don't lie. There had to be another explanation. In the meantime, he had to be doubly sure about Leanne's pregnancy and then take it from there. He was now on his way over to the Meadows' house and hoped he found his tactful side before he opened his mouth with questions for them both. That was the reason he'd decided not to take Eddie along with him. The man had as much tact as a mosquito so had said he'd fill him in later. Mercifully, Eddie had agreed.

With windscreen wipers working double time clearing the sleet away, he pulled up outside the Meadows' home on Cedar Road and sat for a moment, engine running, hoping the weather would ease enough for him to get out. A twitch of a curtain in the front window told him he'd been seen, so he had no choice but to make a dash for it. He pulled his coat collar up and legged it, careful not to slip. The front door opened as if by magic.

"Thank you," he said to Mrs Meadows as she closed the door behind him and the warmth from the house touched his face.

"Come through, Detective," she said, and he followed her back into the familiar lounge where Mr Meadows was stood ready to greet him. He was holding one side of his face a little and Jack enquired if he was okay.

"It's nothing that a new filling won't sort out," he said brightly. "I can't get in until after Christmas. I keep catching cold air in it."

"A toothache can be nasty. I find whiskey helps," Jack replied, smiling, keeping the conversation light before he killed it with his questions to come.

"Take a seat. Can I get you some tea?" Mrs Meadows asked.

"No, thank you," he said, sitting on the edge of the sofa and making the cushion sag awkwardly. "I have a couple of questions for you that I didn't want to ask over the telephone, if I may. A little sensitive, actually."

"Go on." It was Dave Meadows. "What do you need to ask?"

Jack paused for a moment before coming straight out with it. "Could Leanne have been pregnant by chance?"

"I beg your pardon?" Penny Meadows leapt out of her seat as if she'd sat on a firecracker. "I think I'd have noticed if she was, not that Leanne is like that. She's fifteen, for god's sake! I can't believe you're even asking!"

Dave Meadows went to his wife, who stood wild-eyed, staring down at Jack on the sofa. If it had been a cartoon sketch there'd have been smoke coming from her ears, but it was no laughing matter.

Mr Meadows finally spoke. "You obviously have your reasons, Detective, so why are you asking?"

Jack cleared his throat gently. "I had to check the fact. I'm sorry to have asked. It's all part of a line of enquiry, but you have confirmed what I thought the answer would be."

"You said you had a couple of questions. What is the next one?" Dave Meadows had taken over from his wife.

Jack thought about how he might phrase the next firework. "Is Leanne your only child, Mr Meadows. Does she have any sisters or brothers, half-sisters perhaps?"

Dave Meadows' eyebrows shot up into his hairline. "What is this?" he roared. "Are you trying to make this as painful for us as possible?"

Jack doubted he'd ever seen a man go so red in the face so quickly, and slowly stood to try and calm the tension in the room, his hands spread like two fans, gently pumping up and down.

"I'm so sorry to have asked, but again, it needed confirmation. I don't want to upset you both any further. It's a painful time, I know. I'll see myself out." He had turned to leave when Penny Meadows spoke in a voice so low, he almost missed it.

"She died at birth." Jack wasn't sure if he'd heard her right.

"Penny, no. Don't upset yourself. It was such a long time ago," Dave said soothingly. "He's asking about children still living, I'm guessing?" He turned to Jack, who simply nodded, not daring to say anything else that might upset either of them. But Penny wanted to talk.

"Leanne had a sister. She died at birth." Her words came slowly, deliberately and full of sorrow. "Only a little older, but older nonetheless. She's in the cemetery at Adventist Church, the same one where that baby was found a few days ago. We named her Charlotte. You can check if you like." She looked worn out from the effort and Jack guessed correctly that this wasn't something that was ever mentioned.

"Thank you. It won't be necessary. I'm sorry to have asked." Making his way to the front door with a polite nod, he could hear her faint sobs as Mr Meadows tried to comfort his wife.

Back outside, he felt desolate at the destruction he'd left back in the lounge. Their answer had only confirmed what he had suspected, though he couldn't have guessed about the death of an earlier child. He could only imagine the pain they were now going through, raking it up back up, not to mention the prospect of losing another if Leanne wasn't found soon.

At least it had stopped raining. The cold damp air somehow felt cathartic on his skin, a penance for the upset he'd put them through. He hadn't asked how old the child had been, or how she had been taken from them, but the coincidence of Mary being abandoned at the same church jostled with the unanswered questions. He could find out back at the station, though, how Dave Meadows' DNA had come to be in the mix. He wasn't looking forward to asking that particular question.

What a holy mess. Pulling away from the curb, Jack felt sadder than he'd been in a long, long time.

Chapter Thirty-One

"Don't be long," her mum called out as Lesley closed the back door, her new Christmas puppy close at her heels on a lead. The small Golden Labrador looked everything like the toilet tissue advert with a personality to match, bounding along without having yet learned manners, chewing on her lead at the same time as doing everything else, her attention darting from one thing to another in double-quick time. Lesley's parents had given her the puppy a couple of days before Christmas Day itself because it made more sense than keeping it cooped up and quiet somewhere. Lesley would have found or heard it, and since she'd been a little unwell after a nasty cold, they'd both figured it would cheer their daughter up.

They had been right. Two mornings ago, they had both gone into her room, where she was reading a book, and presented the bustling box to her, its contents almost impossible to hide. Lesley had cried with delight. She'd wanted a puppy for so long but her parents had stalled and stalled until now. She'd named the little dog Dora after Dora the Explorer, and she now sported a pink collar with a nametag to match. The name fitted her personality a treat, and now she and her young mistress were virtually inseparable,

Dora sleeping in a basket by Lesley's bed at night. Lesley was responsible for toileting the puppy first thing when she got up in the morning and the last thing before sleep, though her father took her again before he himself retired to bed.

They walked to the end of the road and back, as was their routine while Lesley was on her own. She was under strict instructions not to go any further. Dora and Lesley could go out again later for a longer walk when her father got home and could tag along with them both.

"Come on, Dora." Lesley chatted encouragingly to the dog, who was straining on her lead by her side. Dora was desperate to run and explore but, it was too soon for the little pup to be out and off her lead, so Lesley picked up her own pace and began to jog lightly to keep up with her new four-legged friend, whose tongue was now hanging out the side of her mouth. The end of daylight wasn't far away; some streetlamps had already lit up, casting their amber hue on the damp pavement.

The two were nearly at the end of their street. Lesley was telling Dora what she hoped Santa might bring them both and how she knew how much her grandma and granddad would love to meet her new friend. It was going to be the best Christmas ever. So engrossed was she in describing how Christmas worked and what it meant that Lesley didn't hear the vehicle approach them from behind, nor the door open before it had stopped. Nor did she cry out when a giant hand covered her tiny mouth and strong arms pulled her back into a dark space, all alone save for the person that had dragged her in. The vehicle had then taken off with her muffled cries going neither heard nor answered, leaving her puppy behind to find her own way home.

An hour later, her worried mother had gone out into the street calling for her daughter. She'd seen nothing of either of them and had immediately called the police. It wasn't like Lesley to wander off or disobey her mother in such a way. Another hour later, when Dora had made her own way back, cold and tired after her adventure, Lesley's parents feared the worst, knowing she would never have left the puppy on its own.

Something had happened to their Lesley.

It was Eddie who called Jack at home to inform him another young girl had gone missing, and that, like Kate a few days earlier, she'd been out at dusk all alone. A search party had been put together immediately. Uniformed officers were making door-to-door enquiries along the route the youngster had taken, but it seemed nobody had seen or heard a thing in the twilight. Many hadn't been home from work themselves when it had happened.

Abduction was the most obvious conclusion, considering what they were already dealing with. The parents had been questioned, a family liaison officer appointed, and uniform and volunteers had searched through the night resulting in a big fat nothing. Lesley Raby had disappeared. The cold was a worry if she was still out on her own, but there was nothing left to do but carry on the search and pray she'd simply got lost and had taken shelter somewhere to be found the following day.

Then, when a shift worker who had arrived home unwell at around the time of Lesley's disappearance told an officer he'd seen a dark Transit van but nothing else, nothing to cause suspicion, he didn't realize how helpful he'd been. The team, and certainly Jack, didn't believe in coincidences. They'd spent the night examining camera footage leading out from the area and finally, at nearly five in the morning, they had found what they were looking for: a dark-coloured Transit van with the same registration as the one they'd been checking into, the one belonging to Martin Coffey.

"Coincidence my ass," Jack had told DI Morton. It was time to bring Martin Coffey in for a chat.

Chapter Thirty-Two

"Any luck locating Coffey?" Eddie shouted into the squad room as he entered, his body oozing authority and focus for once. Maybe Sue was back on again, Jack thought, or there was a new someone to fill her shoes, more likely. He watched as heads lifted up from what they'd been doing before the arrival of their boss, who was now at the front of the room awaiting a reply.

"Anyone?" Eddie pressed again. Mo stood up, almost toppling over in the effort but managing to steady herself at the last moment, sending the flesh on her bare arm trembling. She was the only person in the room dressed for late summer and Jack assumed she had her own personal central heating or, at the very least, a faulty inbuilt thermostat.

"It seems he's not been home for a while," Mo began. "He has a house in Thornton Heath – nothing special, as you'd expect for an ex-con – but nobody has seen him for a week or so. Neighbour thought he might have gone away for Christmas. Seems unlikely, though, don't you think? Where to exactly in this weather?" Nobody said anything. She referred to her notes. "No family around the south; all up north. He came down south when he left Strangeways, stayed in approved premises for a few months, then moved on to Thornton Heath. Either way, he's not been home and not been seen." She sat down again. The pink tinge that had risen up from her cleavage now covered her face and she took a deep breath to refill her lungs.

"Thanks, Mo. What about sightings of the van registered to him. Anyone?" It was Clarke's turn. She took the stage and added her findings. "It's been like sorting cooked spaghetti into straight lines, but we've got two separate sightings, one on the M25 heading east towards Tilbury again and one on the high street here in Croydon yesterday. No visibility on who was at the wheel, but the reg matches, so the same van. Add that to our third victim going missing, a young girl of twelve called Lesley Raby, who didn't return after walking her new puppy last night. We're assuming the van had something to do with her disappearance. A dark Transit was seen in the area, as you know."

"Right. Good work," said Eddie. "But I want Coffey in for questioning quick smart, so do what you have to do and bring him in. Anyone got anything else to add? Jack?"

Since his news was nothing to do with the missing girls, he shook his head no. The DNA mixture from Mary was still puzzling him, but as it wasn't relevant to Leanne's case and since, according to her parents, Leanne definitely hadn't been pregnant, it would only confuse things. He did, however, still want to ask Dave Meadows for an explanation, but after yesterday's upset, he'd have to find the right moment to talk with him alone – preferably in an interview room. He made a mental note to call the doc again, see if she had any ideas as to the strange bowl of DNA stew and how the hell it contained what it did. There had to be another answer.

"Right. Keep me up to date. I want to know the moment you find him and I want eyes and ears at his home address in case he shows. We'll pick him up soon enough."

Since there was nothing further to say or report, Eddie headed for the coffee cupboard. Jack marvelled at the man's lack of effort and idly wondered how his neglected team managed to cope so well and so cohesively.

Tomorrow would be Christmas Eve. It was now extremely unlikely that either of the three missing girls would be home in time to unwrap their presents. All they could hope for now was that they were alive and unharmed somewhere, and preferably together for comfort. He thought of Billy and his girl. Janine had agreed for them to join their festive meal, but he hadn't done a damn thing about trying to find the boy. Now with Lesley added to their list, the case was going to take all his time and energy, and had become infinitely more urgent. Depending on how the day went, he'd slip out later and do his best with the time he had left.

Back at his desk, he picked the phone up and dialled Dr Winstanley. Perhaps she could throw some light on his DNA stew.

"Hello again, Jack. How's the case going?" Her voice was like honey on his inner ear.

"Totally confusing, if I'm honest. At least the DNA case is. The other case, the missing girls – that's simply frustrating, rather than confusing. But it's baby Mary's case I'm calling about. Have you a moment?"

"Of course. How can I help?" He imagined her eyes dancing as she spoke and felt immediately guilty for thinking of it at all.

"The missing girl, Leanne, was most definitely not pregnant, according to her parents, not even in secret. She worked at the garden centre and was training hard for the cycling champs, so out and out not possible. Leanne did, however, have a sister, but she died at birth so there are no more sisters, nor brothers, nor half siblings. Again, this is all according to her parents, but I'd still like to get Mr Meadows in for a chat. As you'd expect, they were both extremely upset when I left them both yesterday."

"Understandably. What can I do?"

"Give me another scenario. How else could the test results have come to be? Somebody has to be the mother and, likewise, somebody has to be the father." He tossed the problem back at the doc, his mental energy almost depleted, and rubbed his eyes wearily.

What she said next didn't help him any further.

Chapter Thirty-Three

The three men sat around the makeshift table in the kitchen, cradling mugs filled with cheap instant coffee. In the blue haze of three smouldering cigarettes resting between nicotine-stained fingers, tensions were high.

"It's your fault for bringing her back," Martin shouted, spittle landing on the table in front of him. He didn't attempt to wipe it away but left it gleaming like a glow-worm on a darkened cave wall. Nobody was going to say anything. There was no point riling him up any more. When Martin got angry, it was best to let him vent and keep your head down to avoid a stray backhander. Finally, Rob broke the silence, his brawn far outweighing his brains.

"We couldn't leave her there. She'd seen us! We couldn't take the risk. If we had, we wouldn't be sitting here now. More likely we'd be in a remand cell. Would you have preferred that?" The big man took a long drag on his cigarette to calm his nerves and stop himself from adding something else he might later regret. It wasn't ideal, and certainly had not been part of their plan to have acquired a fifteen-year-old girl. It wasn't their market. Her existence was causing them a problem.

"Rob, don't be a stupid idiot," Martin said menacingly. Leaning into the other man's big face he asked, "But why did you have to bring her back here? Why didn't you deal with the problem somewhere quiet on the way back before she'd seen too much? She's a loose end now. You've caused us a bigger problem we didn't need to have."

"Come on, Martin," the third man, Bernard, said. "Give us a break." It came out almost whiny and he scrambled to rectify his tone, adding, "Rob and I had to make the decision quickly so we grabbed her. Yeah, it's not what we planned, so we'll get it sorted, won't we, Rob?" He turned to the youngest of the three, the pock-marked muscle who did the grunt work for the trio. He'd only been working with the group a couple of years. Martin and Bernard had made their acquaintance inside, having shared the same wing. Bernard had been in for aggravated robbery, and Martin was in for his part in a kidnapping. When they'd both been released, they'd hooked back up and somehow Rob had tagged along. He was a friend of an acquaintance and pretty handy with his hands, though not in a DIY homemaking kind of way. Unlike his collaborator, Rob was fit and strong. Bernard was the pasty and overweight one.

"Well, as far as we know, she's only seen my face, not either of yours, so we needn't panic yet. She's still got a value if we offload her rather than get rid of her permanently. Why don't I put some feelers out and see if we can't get her moved on? With that blonde hair and her size, she could pass for eighteen easy enough with a bit of slap-on and some heels. Make someone a bit of money, like, not to mention we get a payday too."

Smoke puffed from their three mouths as they thought through what Bernard was suggesting. The air was clogged and almost devoid of clean oxygen. While it was risky that Leanne could identify one of them, she'd probably never see the light of day again anyway, and her new owners could dispose of her when the time came. Martin hated dealing with corpses. They meant too much evidence left lurking that could be linked back to them in a whole manner of ways, so he avoided them at all costs. Being linked to a murder, or murders, meant a good deal longer time in prison, a place he'd rather not go back to. What Bernard was suggesting took that aspect away and made good business sense.

While Martin sat thinking, the others waited for his decision. The strip light overhead flickered a little, as though it too was giving its opinion on what to do. Finally, he spoke.

"We'll sell her on," he said quietly. "Set it up, Bernard. Let's get her gone. We haven't got the room to keep her here any longer." He stubbed his cigarette out on the old Formica tabletop. The ashtray was too full and overflowing for one more butt. He stood up to leave, stretching his arms above his head, then rubbed his stubbly face and gave a slight smile only big enough for him to notice.

"Key still in the lock?" he asked almost innocently.

"Fancy a bit yourself, do you?" Bernard asked. "Before she goes, give her a taste, eh? Dirty bugger." He laughed.

"With your tastes, I think dirty bugger is your domain, paedo. You're the sicko. I like mine to have tits," Martin joked as he made his way towards the hallway and the stairs.

"Well, don't soil the goods, will you? I'll be hoping for top dollar for a young blonde," Bernard called after him, and threw his head back laughing. He somehow managed to make a human being sound like a second-hand fur coat that couldn't be dry cleaned – he had a knack for not giving a toss about valuing a life. Rob watched his co-partner and, rather than raise suspicion, laughed along with him, though inside he was far from happy. But what could he do without getting himself killed? He was in too deep now. The floorboards above his head creaked as Martin made his way to Leanne's room.

"Come on, I'm not going to sit here and listen to him grunting above my head. Let's go grab some beers. I need some more ciggies anyway," said Rob, and Bernard nodded.

"Good idea. I'm half-starved anyway. We'll call at Macca's, eh?"

Rob didn't care where they went as long as he didn't have to listen to what was going on upstairs.

Chapter Thirty-Four

Chloe threw her arms up and cheered. "I won!" she shrieked, the glow of the candlelight reflecting in her eyes – not for the first time, Billy noticed. They were playing Scrabble back in 'their' garage, which made a pleasant change, something to do with their time together and take their minds off being cold.

"I'm not sure a couple of those scores were even allowed, that those were even real words," he chided.

"Such as?"

"Such as Nokia. It's a brand name, not a real thing," he said, laughing, "so technically, it should be me that won."

"Spoilsport Billy. I won fair and square," she said, putting the cream tiles back in the bag and folding up the board. "Where did you get this from anyway?" she asked, pointing to the game. They had precious little money for entertainment.

"I bumped into a guy going into the charity shop where I was passing. We chatted a day or two ago. It was him that gave me the money for your toothbrush and paste, so we ended up chatting a bit again. I think he was checking that I hadn't bought drugs or something. Anyway, he was dropping some boxes of stuff off and he gave me the Scrabble. For Christmas.

"That was nice of him."

"Yeah. Seems like a decent sort. He gave me his card," he said, reaching into his jeans pocket and pulling it out. "Said if we ever need anything, ever get in trouble, I should ring him." He looked at Chloe. Their eyes met and held.

"Why would he say that? Is he after something, do you think?" Chloe was uneasy. Why would a stranger make such an offer without wanting something in return?

"Nah, he's not like that, Chloe. More the opposite, I think." Reading the card out, he recited, "Jack Rutherford – Detective Constable Jack Rutherford, actually."

Chloe groaned. "You're kidding me, right? You bring a bloody copper into our lives? After what I've just had to do? Are you stupid?" Her voice gained volume as she spoke, and Billy reached out to calm her down.

"It's fine, Chloe. He's no idea, never seen you, so why would he connect us two, eh? All he knows is I have a female friend who likes clean teeth." He was trying to lighten the moment, put her at ease. The last thing he'd do would be to grass her up to the police. He held Jack's card out towards her. "Look, you keep hold of it, just in case, eh? I'm a little more street-smart than you are, and I've met him before, got his name should I need to use it. Keep his card with you, eh?" He pushed it at her further until Chloe finally took it and slipped it into her jacket pocket. With Jack's card safely in her procession, he changed the subject.

"So, are we off to a shelter for Christmas dinner, then, do you think?"

"Actually, we've got a dinner invite," she answered sweetly. "I was keeping it as a surprise but since you asked..." Chloe's eyes were gleaming as she delivered the news.

"Oh, nice one, Chloe. Where are we going?"

"Roy has asked us to join him in his flat. In fact, he's asked us to go around mid-morning, have a bath each and stay for dinner. How about that?" she said triumphantly.

"A bath? Whoo-hoo!" Billy said, pumping his fist in the air. "A bath! Imagine it, Chloe! And dinner!" His smile could have melted a frozen block of butter.

"It's so nice of him, isn't it? We should take the Scrabble round with us, have a game before we eat. Maybe I could thrash the two of you?"

"I suspect Roy might be a bit of a closet boffin, actually. He could probably thrash us both even if we joined forces together. I know he does the crossword each day. I've seen them filled in, and he doesn't watch TV much. Nah, I'd be surprised if either of us two wins, unless he lets us add dodgy words like you do," he said, laughing. "But we should take him a gift somehow. He's been good to us, to you particularly. But what, though?"

Chloe sat thoughtfully for a moment. Billy was right: they couldn't go empty-handed. "I'll think of something and organize it, a small gesture of our appreciation. First thing in the morning. We've only got tomorrow. It's Christmas Eve."

"Okay. From your face it looks like you have something in mind. I'll leave it in your capable hands, then," Billy said, lying back on the old bed and pulling a blanket up close. The small garage was beginning to look quite homely now with their few belongings; the extra blankets that Roy had dropped off helped tremendously. And so far, the old lady who let them kip there was happy with the arrangement, as long as her neighbours kept quiet. The moment they complained, Billy and Chloe would have to leave, and neither wanted that to happen. A safe and dry place to stay was a major coup for them. "But right now, I reckon it's time to get some shut-eye. I'm tired out – what about you?"

Chloe moved closer to him, and he wrapped his arm around her shoulder, pulling her close. While they weren't officially a couple, they cared for one another and looked out for one another and in the comfort of her friend's arms, Chloe let her mind wander off to her baby, Mary. She'd be wrapped up snug in a warm cot somewhere, safe and sound and hopefully loved already, a love that Chloe herself would never let fade, whether she was in the little girl's life or not. Giving her up had been the right thing to do. A newborn baby living on the streets with her was out of the question, and financially not feasible. So, it would be her first Christmas without her child, and while baby Mary fed on warm formula and was rocked to sleep on someone else's shoulder, Chloe hoped one day Mary would forgive her.

Chapter Thirty-Five

Christmas Eve or not, Chloe needed to work. Most wouldn't call begging 'work,' but nonetheless, generating an income off the streets was how she fed Billy and herself, and they both pulled their weight in that department. If they were ever going to get a little saved up so they could clean up and step up, every day counted. But begging could be cruel, they both knew, and pilfering could be risky. While it was quicker to do the latter, at least with begging they were receiving rather than taking. Either way, both would have preferred a proper job, but then both would have preferred a proper home, too.

While Chloe had told Billy a little bit about her previous life, he had shared nothing of his. She figured that the day he wanted to share with her would be the day she found out. He didn't pry into her background either; he had only touched on the subject the one time, and she'd clammed up anyway. Maybe with Christmas upon them and baby Mary safe and well somewhere, she'd tell him all about her life as Chloe Matthews, the girl her parents had rented out as a cash cow. Would he be disgusted at her, she wondered? She didn't think she could stand that. He was her only friend in the world right now and she couldn't imagine losing him and surviving on her own, didn't *want* to imagine.

She liked Billy immensely. And she hoped he liked her back.

And while Roy was on her peripheral, he wasn't a close friend, not like Billy. Roy was much older, a surrogate father on the edge of her life, keeping an eye on her when he could. He tried not to make himself responsible for her, and she tried not to need him to. He gave her space and kept her secret close to his chest. If he told the authorities it had been her baby found at the church, her life would be turned upside down yet again, and she wasn't capable of coping with it all again. The first lot of dust was only settling now. But she cherished his kindness, knowing he himself didn't have many friends. He was a bit of an oddball, and the sole inhabitant of the flat above his café, but he had a heart the size of a lion's. And she and Billy were spending Christmas Day with him. A hot bath, a hot dinner and a game of Scrabble – it was going to be perfect.

The clock on the outside of the old church in the distance read nearly twelve o'clock. No wonder her stomach was complaining. She reached into her pocket for the sandwich she'd made earlier. She'd made Billy one too, though 'sandwich' was too fine a word for the cheap bread smeared with beef paste from a jar. Still, it was salty and filled a corner of her otherwise empty belly. The thought of her belly made Chloe think again of what had been there, growing, unbeknown to her and those around her until it had been too obvious to ignore. She'd always been a slim girl; running had kept her strong and in shape. But eventually she'd been unable to conceal the pregnancy, and a few months later, baby Mary had materialized and Chloe had found her way to exactly where she was now – outside a storefront begging.

"Can you spare any change, please?" she asked the stream of blank, un-noticing faces as they passed her by. She repeated the same question, over and over like a recording, but was getting nowhere fast. With only £4 and some loose change in her hat out front, there wasn't going to be much to take home at the end of the day.

She noticed a group of five or six men in suits heading her way, laughing at something as they walked. They looked like wealthy bankers or lawyers, their tailored suits and thick overcoats like uniforms, only their ties setting them apart. Even the hair on their heads looked the same; they were like clones. She hoped one would stop. Surely at least one of them would have a couple of quid to help her out? Fastening on the friendliest looking clone, she tried to catch his eye as she spoke.

"Would you have any spare change, please?" she enquired politely. But the six men carried on past, not wavering from their jolly discussion, not hearing a word she said, their backs towards her as she followed them with her eyes.

"Even a little bit would help," she added fruitlessly, as her words fell on deaf ears. Then, to her surprise, the friendly clone turned and walked back to her. While he wasn't smiling, he wasn't threatening either, but even so, Chloe gulped a breath down as he approached.

"Hi. What's your name?" he asked flatly.

"It's Chloe. Why do you ask?"

"Well, Chloe, my sister is about your age and when she ran away from home last year, my parents went out of their minds with worry until she came home. I expect yours might be doing the same right now. I assume you're not living at home?" Chloe shook her head 'no' and let him carry on. If he was going to say something mean or spit at her, he may as well get it over with.

"Here. I'm giving you a couple of quid for the pay phone. Give them a call and at least let them know you're alright, eh? Even if you don't go home, give them a call, yeah?" His brown eyes pleaded with her silently and she knew he was telling the truth about his sister. The couple of coins in his black-gloved hand taunted her. What she could buy with them.

"How did she get back home? How did you find her?" she asked quietly.

"She got into trouble. The cops found her, thank god. It was hard on us all, but she's back safe and well now. It all worked out in the end."

"I'm glad she's okay. It sounds like she has a nice family, and that's where we differ. That's why I'm here." Chloe bowed her head, not wanting to say any more about her situation, and not wanting him to see the tears gathering in her eyes.

"Look, take the money anyway," he urged. "In fact, here's a tenner." He pulled his wallet from his inside jacket pocket and flipped it open. "Get something hot to eat, eh? And if you can find it inside of you, give your parents a call. Stop them worrying."

Chloe looked up again and their eyes met, hers wet with salty tears, his soft and kind. All she could do was nod; any words would have been strangled in her constricted throat. He nodded back, an encouraging smile on his lips, and then turned to catch up with his colleagues, leaving Chloe rooted to the spot, tears flowing freely down her cheeks.

It wasn't her parents she was thinking about though. It was Mary.

Chapter Thirty-Six

It was the click of the key turning in the lock that caught her attention. Gathering the thin blanket and pulling it closer around her shoulders, she pressed herself into the corner of the wall as best she could, in a vain attempt to disappear through it, like a small child escaping a monster in a nightmare. Unlike a bad dream, there was no waking up from this situation. It was her reality until she figured something out.

Or they let her go.

In her heart, she knew that would never happen. She'd seen one man's and one woman's face, though she doubted the woman was part of whatever it was she was involved in. No, she'd looked as miserable as Leanne herself, the abused rather than an abuser. Her eyes had held a scared, submissive message, a warning, perhaps.

Leanne watched, petrified, as a man she hadn't seen before entered the room and slowly made his way towards the bed where she was cowering in the corner. He was lanky and tall, with dirty blond hair and at least two days' worth of stubble. Strong as she was at home or with her friends, she didn't feel any of it now, her usual energy depleted from both lack of food and lack of sleep. Mustering the dregs of her courage, Leanne willed herself to look tougher than she actually was. Not saying a word, she waited to see what would happen next, what the man wanted. He sat on the end of the bed where the fat man had sat the previous day and reached a hand out towards her leg. She rapidly shifted it back, out of his reach. The man laughed, throwing his head back. The noise reverberated around the dim dank room, and when he finally stopped and turned to look at her properly, there was no joy in his face. What she saw there made her stomach lurch, and she fought to control the rising feeling of fright and panic mixed together with her last meagre meal. She swallowed it all down, vowing to carry on with her act of strength, not sure how long it would last, how long she could hold on for.

He reached out again. This time, his hand connected with her leg. There was nowhere for her to move to, to escape to, and she felt herself being dragged towards him. He put his other hand out now and grabbed her other leg, pulling her down the bed until she was laid flat. The man loomed over her.

If she closed her eyes, he'd won, she told herself. She vowed to keep them open, stare him in the face, try and make him understand that what he was about to do to her was wrong. So very wrong. Her bottom lip started to tremble as she watched him undo his belt and unbutton his fly. The zip slid down easily as he slipped his trousers off. His erection was visible in his boxer shorts.

"Thought I'd say goodbye to you before you go," he sneered as he tugged off her track bottoms and pushed her legs apart, leaving her exposed to his gaze. Still, she stared at him, her eyes starting to burn as the first tears stung them. She fought to keep them at bay, not wanting to show the weakness of every sinew in her body. There was no pleading, there was no fighting, there was nothing outwardly visible to her abuser, but that didn't mean it wasn't happening to her inside – in her head, in her heart.

As the man smiled his appreciation at her exposed body and moved to take his prize, she waited for her moment to come, the moment when she knew he'd be the least suspecting of her plan, the plan she was mustering all her inner strength for. The stale tobacco stench of too many cigarettes mixed with body odour assaulted her nose but Leanne focused above it; the smell she could deal with. It was what the pig lying on top of her was about to do to her that she couldn't deal with, not in the same way.

As the man fumbled with his shorts, Leanne mustered every gram of strength from the innermost parts of her body and slammed the sharp end of the teaspoon into the side of his neck with all her might. The outside of her fist connected with his skin as the point entered his neck, and she drove it home forcefully. Before he had a chance to react, Leanne yanked it back out and slammed it in again as he tried to gain traction and get back to his feet, holding his neck at the same time. The end of the spoon protruded from between his fingers. Blood shot in a jet up the wall as he held his neck; his shirt looked like it had been soaked in claret.

Leanne knew she had only seconds now. There was no time to see what happened to the man. It didn't matter. She had to leave the room, take her chances with what was on the other side of that door, and hope his screams of anguish went unheard. Perhaps they'd think they were her cries and ignore them; she could only hope. Her legs shook as she propelled herself across the room to the door. She yanked it open, grabbed the key, and relocked it behind her, leaving her captive on the other side. His shouts of fury and the sound of his fists banging on the door were audible to anyone in the building, but Leanne moved fast and quiet like a cat down the stairs towards the bottom, hoping she didn't meet anyone on the way down.

Once there, she could see an entrance door. She was in an old house of some sort after all. She glanced around the corner over the handrail. There was light coming from underneath one of the doors towards the back but there didn't seem to be any movement or noise. There was no time to spare, no time to stand and think, and as the angry shouts coming from the room upstairs grew fainter, she flew towards the main entrance and hoped it was her way out to safety and freedom.

Chapter Thirty-Seven

❧✿❧

It was nearly 4 pm by the time Jack managed to leave the station and seek out the young man he'd met only twice previously. He'd broached the subject of dinner with Janine, and while she'd readily agreed, Jack had picked up a question in her voice, one that she didn't actually ask: "Why this boy?" Why, then Jack? he'd asked himself. What was so special about this young man? It couldn't be his cheek alone. Did he see himself in the boy, perhaps, or was he getting soft in his not-so-old age?

The first place he headed was where they'd first met only a few days ago, not far from the station. Jack smiled again as he remembered the boy's Monty Python approach to begging, the reason he'd stood out in the first place, the reason Jack had stopped. With the last of the day's light, Jack got out of his warm car and set off in search of young Billy. If he and Janine could offer him and his girl a hot meal and a game of cards on Christmas Day, then they surely would. There was plenty of room for the four of them, and he hoped they would accept his invitation in the goodwill spirit it was intended and not fear that Jack and his wife were weirdos with an agenda. He hoped the card he'd passed on to the youngster would give him confidence and not scare him off; cops weren't always out to catch someone unawares.

But on Christmas Eve on a cold afternoon, there was hardly anybody out on the street. Most people had finished work much earlier and were probably now full of eggnog, sleeping the afternoon off on the sofa. The thought appealed to him, but with now three children missing, he'd be lucky if he got Christmas dinner himself.

After walking the same street for ten minutes or so and not seeing or hearing Billy, he was about to give up and try somewhere else when he saw a hunched form in a doorway up ahead, sitting on a piece of cardboard and wrapped in an old blanket. As Jack approached, he realized it wasn't Billy. It was a dirty-looking young man holding a cardboard sign.

"I'm looking for a young lad called Billy. About this height," Jack said, demonstrating with his hand around his own ears. "Fair curly hair, maybe seventeen-ish. A bit cheeky and maybe with a girl. Have you seen him recently? Today, maybe?"

The man's vacant eyes stayed vacant as he looked up at Jack and shook his head slowly.

"Any idea at all where I might find him?" Jack persisted.

The young man gave only a gentle shake of his head. Jack glanced down at the makeshift sign and read the words presumably he'd written himself – "Can you spare some change, please? I'd ask myself but I'm mute."

Abashed, Jack reached into his pocket for change. He tossed the handful of coins into the cap that sat next to the sign and won a nod of the man's head for his generosity.

"Take care, and Merry Christmas," he added as he turned and made his way back to his parked car. If only he knew where Billy called home, he could go round and find him, but he didn't, and with almost everyone gone from the streets as the darkness finally fell, Jack couldn't help thinking he'd left it too late, that the boy and his girl would now go without, or queue at a soup kitchen like all the rest. It was with a heavy heart that he drove on to the charity shop, his last chance of seeing the boy before he headed back himself.

As he pulled into an empty parking space, he wasn't too hopeful at his chances. The street was almost empty and most shops had closed. A handful of last-minute shoppers scurried from doorway to doorway.

Everyone had gone home. Perhaps Jack should do the same.

Chapter Thirty-Eight

Christmas Eve was not the most productive time to be coaxing change from strangers' pockets, and by 2 pm, both Chloe and Billy had called it a day. Frozen through like two popsicles, they found themselves back at the garage about the same time, each carrying a plastic bag. Billy slid his behind his back so she couldn't see what he had inside.

"Great minds think alike, eh?" he said, smiling warmly. "Not much happening for you either?"

"Nah. Thought I may as well freeze here in comfort. And I called and got Roy a gift for tomorrow. Hope he likes it." Billy detected a slight change in her, almost a sadness, and he wondered whether to ask after it.

"I'm sure he will. What did you get?"

Chloe pulled out a small paper bag, opened it, and carefully slipped the contents into her hand.

"I saw it in a charity shop window, and I thought it was appropriate under the circumstances. What do you think?" She held out a small glass paperweight; it had an old church inside the dome with snow on its roof. There was a man stood out front in a red suit;

Santa. Billy could see the hope in her eyes that she'd done the right thing, and that she wanted his approval.

"Chloe it's perfect!" he exclaimed, with a little more gusto than he intended, but what the hell, if that was what Chloe needed. He watched her face break into a smile, her eyes bright and excited again at his praise. He stepped towards her and gave her a one-armed hug, still keeping the other arm behind his back. The plastic bag rustled as they embraced, alerting them both to its presence.

"What's in the bag?" she asked.

"Nothing to concern yourself about," he said, mock-haughtily. "You'll find out soon enough." He guided her towards the side entrance of the garage, their home. He unlocking the door and stood aside to usher her in. He followed her inside and watched as she flopped down onto the bed.

"Is everything alright, Chloe?" he asked gently. "Only you seem a bit down about something. Was it a shitty day? Did you get loads of abuse?" He went and sat next to her and held her hand for a moment in comfort, as close friends do sometimes. Then he waited, giving her time to reply. Something was clearly bugging her.

"Not really," she said eventually. "No abuse, but a man stopped to chat with me. He wasn't that old, maybe about thirty, but he said his sister had gone missing last year, had run away, and his parents had gone nutty worrying. He asked me to call my own parents, let them know I was alright, even if I don't go back. Stop them worrying."

"Oh, I see. And what did you say?"

"Not a lot, except my parents wouldn't really care. It wasn't a good home. He gave me money for the phone, actually." Chloe paused for a moment and Billy sensed there was more to come, so he waited for her. With a big sigh she added, "He gave us a tenner to buy some food, which was lovely of him, but I can't ring my parents even if I wanted to. I've no idea where they've gone." She turned to him, her eyes wet again. "But that's not why I'm upset, Billy."

"Oh? What, then?"

"I got thinking about Mary. She'd be the one I'd like to call if I could, tell her I'm not far away. Tell her she's important to me and to stay safe at all times. To tell her I love her." Billy watched as a fat tear trickled down her cheek, and he caught it on a finger so it didn't fall any further. Then he took her in his arms and pulled her close, her chin over his shoulder, as her body quivered with grief. All he could do was wait until the worst was over and she stopped crying so hard. He passed her some toilet roll to blow her nose on when she eventually pulled back, her eyes looking sore and red.

"I know you miss her. Of course you do. And this man you met has brought it all to the surface again, but I'm sure he meant well. He obviously thought your parents would want to know you're okay. He clearly doesn't know your circumstances, though. And if truth be known, I don't know that much about them either." He gave her a small smile to show he'd like to find out more if she was willing to tell, but didn't hold up much hope. Her head was bowed and she stared at the floor.

"I haven't told anyone."

"I figured that. But whatever the reason, you know I'm here for you, right? It doesn't matter to me what happened. You're still Chloe, my mate." He squeezed her arm at the word 'mate' and she smiled though her head was still bowed. Billy saw the crease in her cheeks.

"Why don't you fill me in? Then I can show you that whatever it is, it doesn't matter to me. Because it doesn't. Maybe you murdered someone?"

Chloe shot her head up in alarm. "No! Of course not."

"Well, then, anything else is cool." He held her gaze while she thought it through. He could almost see the motion picture turning behind her eyes, the story playing out.

He watched her inhale and hold her breath a moment, then she began to tell Billy the whole sordid story.

Chapter Thirty-Nine

Someone had to man the station on Christmas Day, but that someone wasn't going to be Jack. Eddie had volunteered a shift, saying he'd go for dinner at the pub later, and Jack knew he'd wash it down with several pints of bitter and a couple of whiskey chasers. It was a bit of a sad existence for Christmas, but Jack didn't care what the man did as long as it didn't involve him.

When he'd left the station on Christmas Eve in search of Billy, he'd nipped back in to see how the investigation was winding up for the day. The three children were still missing. It was far from ideal, and everyone's thoughts were with the families of all three girls, none of whom would be tucking into roast turkey and wearing their new Christmas clothes. The only lead they had to go on was Martin Coffey's van, but whether the man had gone away for the holidays or was simply lying low, he was proving elusive to find and speak to. There had been no further sightings of the van in the massive amount of CCTV footage they'd sifted through, and even Mo, their most intense and dedicated researcher, had come up empty-handed. At shift changeover time, DI Morton had wished them all a wonderful Christmas and told them to go home to their loved ones, as he would be doing himself. Jack and Clarke had stayed on another hour or so, generally mulling over the case and the evidence. Neither felt they should be off consuming sherry and wine quite yet. It didn't feel right.

"You know what saddens me?" Clarke asked Jack during a quiet moment. The two were almost kneecap to kneecap at his desk, thoughtful.

"What's that?" Jack twiddled with his upper lip, his eyes glazed over.

"The lack of leads we've had from all the press coverage as well as the TV. We've sod-all to work with. It's like three girls upped and left in the night, and apart from two folks who mentioned a dark van, that's it. It's not enough, Jack," she said, raising her voice in frustration. "We need a break desperately, or we'll never see them again. Even worse, more could vanish the same way."

It wasn't a pleasant thought, but it was one that Jack had tossed around the inside of his own head for several nights while he lay in bed with Janine sleeping peacefully beside him. He rubbed his eyes.

"Maybe Eddie and the next lot on duty will have a lucky break. That is, if they're not too busy with the piss-heads tonight, though Christmas Day is normally quieter – once they've slept it off in a cell, that is." Jack stood and held his hand out to her as if to pull her out of her chair. "Come on, then. I'll buy you a swift one before we head home."

She took the hint to leave, though she didn't feel the need to take his hand.

He'd called home earlier and told Janine he hadn't been able to find Billy; it had been too late on the shopping front. Regardless, Janine had done their possible guests proud. As Jack looked in the fridge for the chocolate éclairs they always had on Christmas Eve, he saw that there was barely space left over to store a wafer-thin mint. There was enough food to feed half the street, never mind two more mouths, and he wondered what they'd do with it all. Standing there looking for the familiar white cake box that was probably hidden away behind Brussel sprouts and pork pie, he felt a bit lightheaded. He'd already had a pint of bitter with Clarke at the pub, then a glass or two of wine over dinner that had further softened the smooth edges of his nerves. He could hear Janine call him from the other room.

"Can't you see them, Jack? White box."

"I know. I can't see the bloody white box for everything else stuffed in here," he complained to the empty kitchen, and began to take packets and bags of Christmas indulgence out and put them on the floor. The desired box was right at the back and he pulled that out too, just as Janine walked through the door. A sprout rolled her way, sprung free from a hole in its net. They both watched it stop at her feet.

"Oh, Jack!" she exclaimed, trying not to laugh at the scene before her. "You look like a naughty boy who's been caught stealing the cakes and surreptitiously trying to hide the sprouts at the same time."

He struggled to his feet as another sprout fell from the net he was holding in his hand. It bounced a couple of times then rolled towards the other one.

"Ah, look," Jack said, smiling. "She wants to be with her friend."

"How do you know it's a 'she'? Could be a 'he.'"

"Nope, all sprouts are 'she.' Otherwise, you wouldn't serve them. I'm sure it's a girl thing. Forcing us men to eat them though we detest them. I don't know anyone that *likes* Brussel sprouts, yet we all have to eat them at Christmas." He bent to pick the two strays up and put one in his ear. Janine looked quizzically at him, waiting for him to explain. In a mocking doctor's voice, he said, "Mr Rutherford, you really must eat more sensibly." His eyes were full of mischief and the effect of the wine as they filled the kitchen with laughter.

"Ha-ha. Very funny, Mr Rutherford. You should be on the stage," she said, then changed the subject. "Perhaps your friend Billy will appreciate some leftovers anyway. We'll make up some sandwiches on Boxing Day, put a picnic together for them. I'm sure they'll enjoy them and we'll find a home for all this food. And if we can't find Billy, we'll give them to someone else in need. There'll be plenty of grateful souls in the usual places, I expect." Wrapping her arms around his middle, she pulled him close. "It always feels good to do some good, don't you think?"

"It does," he said, putting his arms around her shoulders and squeezing her tight in return. "Love you, Mrs Rutherford. Now about them sprouts."

Chapter Forty

They'd taken the van, since it was the least personal of the vehicles and not registered in either of their names. Rain pelted the windscreen like it was the monsoon season in Asia, transparent rods of liquid falling straight down from the black clouds that loomed over the south-east side of London, though officially they were in Kent. Bernard had the wiper blades working double time in an effort to see the road he was driving on.

"What the hell are we doing out in this shit?" Bernard complained.

"Well, I wanted a Macca's and you need ciggies, so unless you've got a secret stash of both, we have to go get them. That's how it works." Rob sounded facetious and stroppy as he said it.

Bernard was on the attack instantly. "What's up with you? Got your period, have you?"

Rob stayed silent, his mouth taut like a drum skin, while he seethed inside. What about, he wasn't entirely sure, but he knew he wasn't happy with the situation back at the house. How the hell he'd got mixed up with Bernard and Martin he'd never know. Actually, that was a lie. He did know. And he couldn't let on to Bernard that he was pissed and wanted out. They didn't do loose ends. He let out a sigh and made up a story he hoped was convincing.

"It's my old mum. She ain't well and I'm worried about her, if you must know. I was thinking I should drop in and see her over Christmas, play the good son for a while."

Bernard glanced across to the passenger seat. "Well, ain't that sweet, you great pussy. Wait till I tell Martin. He'll laugh at that one, all right," he sneered.

"Tell him what you want. She's my old mum. Don't you see your old mum? Don't you care much?"

"Don't really have one to care about, so no. Last I heard she was still inside. And my old man is definitely still inside, not that I know him much. He's been inside most of my life."

"What's he in for?"

"Murder. Killed a bloke during a robbery that went a bit haywire and he got sent down. The others grassed on him to reduce their own sentence. Stinkin' grasses. Nobody likes a stinkin' grass."

Rob wasn't sure if the message was directed at him or not, a warning should things come to it later on. There'd be repercussions for sure, and he wasn't interested in what they might be. Rob grunted by way of reply and stared straight ahead, watching the road for somewhere to put his eyes. It wasn't long before the familiar burger logo could be seen in the distance and Bernard pulled in to the drive-thru lane. He wound his window down to place his own order first.

"Quarter Pounder, large fries and an apple pie, large Coke."

Rob shouted across Bernard to add to their order and they pulled forward. Bernard sneered as they waited for their order to be prepared.

"What you sneering at now?" asked Rob.

"Apple pie?"

"I'm hungry. What's wrong with that?"

"Told you you're a pussy." Rob ignored him. It wasn't worth his breath. When they'd picked up their order, Bernard pulled into a parking spot and they tucked in in silence. Rob watched as the windscreen began to fog up like those of the other two cars in the small car park. Everyone was content consuming hot greasy food on a cold rainy day. Bernard noticed the fogging up and, with an overstuffed mouth full of burger, attempted to speak, particles of bread roll falling from his mouth as he did so. He held a fry between finger and thumb, waiting for a space in his mouth to come free so he could concertina it in. Rob looked away before he was turned off his own meal.

"I bet Martin is busy fogging up a window with that girl, eh?" he said and laughed. He caught a crumb in the back of his throat for his troubles and ended up in a coughing fit. The remains of a mouthful of burger landed in his lap. When he finally caught his breath, he took a long pull on his Coke. He brushed the wasted burger off his lap into the footwell. It would stink the van out for the next couple of hours until he kicked it out.

"There ain't a window in there."

"What?"

"There's no window in that room, so he won't be fogging it up."

Bernard could only glare. "I meant it metawhatsically. I know there's no window."

"Metaphorically," Rob prompted, his voice clear and even, and carried on with his own meal.

"Whatever," Bernard replied caustically.

They finished the rest of their meal in silence, then Rob took their wrappers to a bin nearby. The rain was easing a little. Noticing the burger remains in the well, he suggested Bernard kick it out before they left but Bernard ignored him. He didn't like anyone telling him what to do.

"I could do with a quick pint now. Want one?"

Since it was Christmas Eve and he was in no hurry to get back to the house, Rob accepted, vowing to set off back to his own place when they returned. They didn't need all three of them there at the same time, and since they weren't expecting any customers after tonight, they could surely spare him some time out. Perhaps he'd drop in on his mum and say hello. But Rob played along a while longer. "Let's make it a couple, eh? And we'll grab a bottle of spirit to take back. There's an Asda up there on the right. Look, they'll have cheap whiskey. Pull in, will you?"

So Bernard made the turn and waited in the van while Rob entered the store and selected a bottle, grabbing a box of Milk Tray for his mum while he was in there. Once he'd paid, he was back outside and into the van, headed for a nearby pub and a pint of bitter or two to pass some time.

They should have stuck to beer.

Chapter Forty-One

He'd always liked younger girls, though they had to be in at least double digits. Any younger was not his thing, though he knew plenty in his circle went in for it. He'd managed to keep his sexual preferences under wraps for the past twenty-five years, having discovered them not long after he'd lost his own virginity when the younger girls would flirt and give him the come-on. Then he'd met a woman who was quite a bit older than he was, and she'd introduced him to her friends. It had been at one of the 'parties' she held occasionally that he'd had his eyes opened to various sexual tastes and what could be supplied for those willing to pay. It was all normal to her, all she knew. When she'd eventually taken all that she needed from him and moved on to someone else, he'd stayed in the circle and found a taste for the younger girls, deciding he liked them the best. But along the way, he'd met his future wife and while sex with her was adequate, he craved the bodies of the young. So, he had carried out his secret indulgence behind her back. He'd been doing so for many years now, and with a job that took him both north and south as he travelled with work, he had endless opportunities to get his desires filled at the same time.

It had been while he'd been working and staying over not far outside Manchester that he'd found the perfect setup for his needs. He'd kept in touch with some of the regulars from those earlier parties he'd attended; they'd been sort of a club. A club that catered to people with particular wants and needs. And from that club, he'd found a private address where a young girl would be supplied. He couldn't call the others in the circle "friends," but they did look out for the group as a whole, not wanting the wrong set of eyes or ears to focus on them and curb their activity. And since they each knew of the other, they self-incriminated as a way of proving extreme loyalty. He had begun calling in whenever he was up there. The deal was that as long as he arrived in the evening, he was always welcome – for a fee, of course. It had all been working out fine; everyone was happy.

But suddenly his extracurricular sexual activities with a particular girl had stopped – for what reason he never did find out. On the second Tuesday of each month, he'd had a standing arrangement for 10 pm on the dot at the same address, but on his last visit, there had been no one there. The flat had been empty. And he'd had no way of finding where they'd moved to. So, he'd turned back to his acquaintances with his tale of woe and, kind-hearted as they were, they had fixed him up elsewhere with another youngster. But he liked the one he had been seeing regularly because she reminded him of someone special. The girl had always been quiet about him being there in her room with her, never made a fuss or a noise, and the parents had kept their distance too, so it was the perfect setup for them all. He'd miss seeing her, he knew, because she looked so much like his daughter.

Driving south now, he wondered about that, how he'd found comfort with this young girl for so long yet never approached his own daughter that way, knowing it wasn't right. She was too close. He missed Leanne desperately, as did Penny, and they both prayed for her to be reunited with them and be home in time for Christmas. But as time marched on without any clues coming to light, he doubted they'd ever see her alive again.

Meanwhile, he still had needs and desires, so with the help of his acquaintances, he had found himself another venue. He'd visited a couple of times and found it satisfactory; at least his needs were getting seen to.

Unlike his toothache.

He opened a fresh piece of gum from a packet that he kept in the centre console and gently chewed it, forcing it to the offending tooth and adding pressure, the relief like a rattle to a teething toddler's mouth.

He slipped off the M25 and on to the A20, thoughts of stress relief ahead, the feeling of utter peacefulness and contentment he'd experience after his long-awaited conclusion. All that had gone on of recent, including his toothache, would be banished for an hour or so and he could do what he wanted and answer to no one. It was his piece of 'me' time, a time he deserved.

He was a little earlier than his usual 6 pm, but hoped it wouldn't be a problem. His acquaintances didn't hand out telephone numbers, so there was no way to let the venue know of his earlier arrival. But since his money was as good as the next person's, what did it matter? He could see the roof of the property up ahead and took the long gravel driveway down to it until the house became visible through the copse of trees that surrounded it. To anyone looking on from the outside, it was a simple, quiet farmhouse with a couple of vehicles parked out front. On the inside, it was where pleasure and pain mingled together like lost souls at a cocktail party.

Dave Meadows made his way to the large front door and entered, making his way through to the lounge that he knew was the first door on the left. It was empty. Strange, he thought. There was always someone in there to pour him a drink and direct him to the designated room. So, he helped himself to the watered-down brandy that stood in a mock crystal decanter and threw a couple of fingers worth back in one hefty gulp. It had an almost instant effect on him and the warmth spread through his body like warm water moving through a cold .radiator. He was still puzzled that nobody had yet arrived to greet him, but he knew better than to call out.

There were cars out front and that meant other customers. So he waited a moment before pouring himself another drink and sat down on the sofa. At least his tooth was feeling a little better; the brandy was working its pain reliever talons on his mouth. He soon grew tired of waiting; he was anxious for pleasure. He took the cash from his wallet and slipped it under the cheap decanter. Someone would pick it up later. Opening the door and making his own way quietly up the stairs, he glanced at each door in turn to see which had a key on the outside and selected the one furthest away at the end of the hall. He turned the key and entered. The room, like the others he had been in, was dimly lit and contained a single bed and a small table.

And a girl.

He locked the door behind him. As he approached the bed, he removed the gum from his mouth and stuck it to the top of the cheap table. Then he began to undress.

Chapter Forty-Two

It was almost dark when he left the house for home. Bumping the car down the rough track, he was reminded once again it wouldn't be a Christmas to celebrate, not this year. In his mind, 1999 would always be remembered as the year that his daughter had disappeared, and he hoped that whatever happened, if she wasn't found alive and well, that she was returned to them so they could mourn properly. He knew he wasn't strong enough to tolerate the not knowing, the lack of closure. He could understand how families fell apart with such a tragedy in their lives. The pressure on bereaved couples was immense, he knew, and even now Penny wasn't coping particularly well. She and Leanne had rowed that morning, and she blamed herself.

The gravel track leading away from the house eventually joined the tar seal and he picked up speed, intent on not getting snarled up on the M25 during rush hour. He hoped that since it was Christmas Eve, everyone was already home starting their celebrations with their loved ones.

He missed his Leanne.

A handful of miles away in The Red Lion pub, Rob and Bernard were on their third pint each when Rob noticed the time. They'd been out far longer than they'd intended – they'd only nipped out for a burger and cigarettes – so Martin was sure to be pissed with them both for leaving him there on his own. Rob wondered why the man hadn't called them. Tough shit, he thought. Martin wasn't their babysitter.

Bernard scrunched up the empty packet of pork scratchings he'd devoured and turned to Rob. He too had noticed the time. A streetlamp nearby shone with a pale glow, making the twilight seem darker than it actually was. He drained his glass then stood up. "Better get our skates on. We've got a couple of punters coming through tonight. I'd have thought they'd have better things to be doing on Christmas Eve than getting their jollies."

Rob swallowed the last of his pint, stood and grabbed his jacket. They made their way to the back door and out to the van. The rain had stopped, but the air turned their breath to mist as they walked, making them look like a couple of smokers. Once in the van, Bernard turned the heater on full blast, and the windscreen began to fog up. The blast of cool air blew into their eyes as it bounced off the glass and Rob willed it to turn warm soon. On a freezing evening, a cold draft was the last thing he desired.

Content that there was a patch of glass big enough to see through, Bernard set off and joined the road outside, continuing to clear the windscreen with the back of his hand.

"Sod this weather. Has Christmas ever felt this cold before?" Rob moaned.

"That's 'cos you're a pussy like I said. Harden up, will you?"

"Not me, mate. I'm no pussy. Anyway, I'm not hanging around tonight. When the last one's gone, I'm off to see my mum. What about you?"

"Well, I ain't hanging around on my own 'cos Martin won't be. I'll tell you that now. I reckon we should lock the place up and leave 'em be. They'll be alright for a day or two. Give 'em a box of cereal each or something. They'll manage." Sneering, he added, "Getting fed is the least of their worries, don't you think? And they're about due to be passed on anyway. They're becoming a bit skanky. Don't want the punters complaining."

"When is that? Any idea?"

"Nah, that's Martin's domain, not ours. Grab and go, that's us," he said turning to Rob and smiling. "The hired muscle, the guys that get," he said proudly, and laughed at his own terminology. A sign up ahead directed them towards the house and they turned right down a narrow lane. Bernard was still chatting to himself about nothing. Rob closed his ears, not interested in what the fat man had to say, and silently wished he was someplace else. Even his own flat, as meagre as it was, was preferable to this man's company. And it was quiet.

"Look," Rob said. "I wonder where they've been?" A car was travelling towards them in the opposite direction. A sole occupant in the front caught Rob's attention. "There ain't nothing much out here, that's all. Wonder where they've been?"

"Home probably. People do live out here, remember?"

"Yeah, but I don't think I've ever seen another car on this road, ever."

"Well, how do you expect the punters get to the house, then? Fly in their helicopters? Dumb shit," Bernard said, shaking his head in disbelief. "You're usually inside the house, remember?"

Rob stayed quiet, realizing he did sound stupid. Eventually they turned into the gravel road and slowed down a little. The van tossed its occupants with each pothole they drove through; the suspension was working overtime to smooth their ride and not doing a good enough job.

"Need a Land Rover down here, not this great thing," Bernard added as the house came into view in the distance. "Still, it serves its purpose."

They pulled up out front next to their own vehicles, climbed out and walked up to the house. Rob opened the front door and Bernard followed him through. They headed for the kitchen out back where they usually congregated and smoked. Bernard called out to Martin, but there was no answer. He called again.

"Strange," said Rob. "He can't still be upstairs with the blonde, can he?"

"Probably getting his fill from the candy store on legs," Bernard jeered. "Dirty sod."

"Come on, best get set up. First one's due at six pm. I'll go up and see what he's up to," volunteered Rob, and headed for the stairs. He tapped on the door. The key was not on the outside. "You in there?" he called, careful not to mention his boss's name to overhearing ears. It was one of the house rules: no names of anyone at any time. He knocked again. "Come on. You've not gone to sleep on the job, have you?" he called but still there was no reply.

He went back downstairs to get the spare key.

Chapter Forty-Three

"Where's the spare key to that room?" Rob asked, pulling open a drawer filled with all kinds of odds and ends.

"Not sure if there is one. Why? He's fallen asleep, has he?"

"Dunno, but he's not answering and the key's not on the outside. The door's still locked. Nobody answering, either." He rummaged in the drawer some more, pulling out various other keys. None was the one he was looking for. When all the keys were on the table, it was apparent there wasn't a spare.

"No spare key."

Bernard looked perplexed and stood up. "Come on, let's go look," he said. They both went back upstairs to the offending door. Bernard banged hard and turned the door handle at the same time, but it was definitely locked and nobody answered. He thumped again and yelled, all to no avail. It was obvious Martin wasn't going to come to the door.

"What about the girl?" Rob asked. "Even if Martin isn't in there, she'll still be and if we break the door down. What are we going to do with her then?"

"We'll deal with her if we have to, but for now, we need to get inside and see what's happening. Martin must be in there; the cars are outside and we had his van, so he'll be here somewhere. Stand back, will you? I'll give it a shove."

Rob stood back and watched as Bernard did his best to shoulder the door in. He then tried to kick it in, without the desired result.

"You have a go," he instructed, and Rob charged at the door with his solid bulk. There was a splintering sound and a loud crash as the lock ripped through the frame and the door swung open into the room. Stepping inside, their eyes adjusting to the low light, they saw Martin lying face down on the floor, trousers around his ankles, looking for all the world like he had fallen asleep on the job.

Were it not for the blood-soaked floor. And the spoon sticking out of his neck.

"Houston, we have a problem," Rob said.

"Ya think?"

"The girl's gone too. She must have locked him in and taken the key." Bernard glanced round the room, confirmation registering. Martin was one thing, but a loose end of a girl who could identify him was another. And he wasn't going to be linked to this holy mess.

"What the fuck do we do now?" Bernard asked, touching the side of Martin's neck and feeling for a pulse. There was one, but it was faint. "He's still alive, barely." He looked at Rob, trying to read his face, see if he was thinking the same as he was.

"Loose ends get us caught," Rob replied. "The girl can tie herself to this place if she's out, and that means evidence of us. And this," he said, pointing to Martin. "We can't take him to a hospital. Too risky."

Bernard nodded in agreement. He ran his hand through the remaining fine hairs covering his bald dome and sighed heavily. "We have no choice. We'll have to torch the place. We'll dump the other girls. They're too young to know this place or us, and we'll burn it to the ground, destroy any evidence pointing back to us."

"And what do we do with him? And the woman?" Rob asked, not wanting to know the answer but figuring it anyway.

"He's almost gone anyway. He'll not feel a thing. We'll take the woman with us, dump her too." He looked at his fake gold watch. "We'd better hurry before the first punter gets here. We'll start it in the lounge. The sofa will go up quickly, and we'll secure the girls in the van. We'll have to torch the cars too."

"I've got a better idea. The van is his, and there'll be evidence in it, so that should go up too. We'll each take a girl in our own cars, stick them in the boots. Then toss them when we can. There's no trail back to us."

"Nah, way too risky. And we've no time. We'll take the van and torch the cars. Now let's get on with it. I'll start the fire; you get the cash and we'll shift the girls together. Or we could leave them too and drive off in our own cars, as you said?" A smile crept across Bernard's face as he said it. "Makes more sense, doesn't it? Then our cars are both gone."

There was no doubt it was the more thorough way to clean up for good, but Rob wasn't convinced. "Hey, I never signed up for murder. That's going too far." He started to pace nervously up and down in the small room

"You going all pussy on me again?" Bernard demanded. "You're alright with Martin here getting toasted, but not the girls, not the woman, is that it?"

"I don't want anyone being toasted, but we haven't much choice with him, have we?"

"Well, either way, I'm going down to get a fire burning. Time is running out, so I suggest that whatever you decide, you do it quickly because in about ten minutes, this place will be lighting up the sky, whether the girls are in it or not!"

Bernard stormed out of the door and stomped his way down the stairs, leaving Rob to make his mind up. While he knew Martin was a lost cause, he didn't want the girls on his conscience. He couldn't bear the thought of them being burned to death. With so little time, it was difficult to know which was the best option. Stick together and dump them out somewhere, or take one each and go their separate ways? Option two meant leaving evidence in their own vehicles if fingers got pointed back to them. But they could hardly leave their cars outside. Then an idea came to him: take the number plates off. That way, there'd be no way to trace two burned-out vehicles back to them. The idea was perfect, and he dashed down to the kitchen for a screwdriver. He could already smell smoke.

A couple of minutes later, he'd taken the back and front plates off both cars and put them in the van. He went back inside to find Bernard.

"Start the cars burning. I'll move the van round the back, then we'll grab the woman and the girls," he shouted, then ran back outside. Thick, grey smoke now filled the hallway.

By the time he'd returned, the two cars were already smouldering, flames licking the upholstery of the front seats. It wouldn't be long before they were fully ablaze and the petrol tanks caught, obliterating any evidence linking them to what had happened.

Back upstairs, they unlocked the remaining rooms and dragged the two petrified girls and the woman out to the van. There, they secured them with duct tape, added a piece across each mouth for good measure, and tied pillowcases over their heads. With only Martin left in the burning house, Bernard drove the van away, down the potholed track and out towards the motorway in the distance, the orange glow of the blazing building reflecting in the rear-view mirror.

"There shouldn't be much of that left to sift through," he said, with a touch of pleasure.

"No. But we've got to sort this little lot out, and the sooner the better," Rob said, wondering what they'd end up doing with the three of them in the back.

"I've got an idea," Bernard said.

Rob hoped he'd agree with it.

Chapter Forty-Four

Her eyes hurt with crying. Her feet were torn to shreds. Leanne crouched down low, tucked behind a hedge in the middle of nowhere. She had no clue where she was or where she was heading. All she knew was that the house she'd run from several hours ago was behind her. How long had it actually been, she wondered? With no sun to go by, she'd no clue when she'd set, out but as it was fully dark now, she knew it had to be at least 5 pm. Her teeth chattered from the cold. Her soaked sweatshirt keeping the chill fixed on her body, but she was loath to take it off and reveal her complete nakedness. In her frantic rush to leave the room, she'd left her track pants on the floor. It had been a blessing her fingers had found the strength to turn the key and lock him in.

She closed her swollen eyes at the memory of what she'd done, what she'd had to resort to get him off her and protect herself from a violent personal theft. There was no way she was going to let that filthy pig of a man do that to her. Slobber all over her. Run his grubby hands over her body and snatch her virginity away like a dirty tissue. That was one thing her mother had taught her – when she chose to give her gift away, it was to be to someone she loved. She hadn't been willing to give it up to anyone who felt they could take it. Leanne doubted she'd ever be able to wipe the experience out of her mind completely – the feeling of stabbing the soft side of his neck, driving the spoon handle in hard, and twisting it before finally tugging it out and driving it home once more. The feeling of shoving his sweaty bulk off her and clambering off the rumpled bed... His blood had spurted like a hosepipe turned on at the tap and shot across the room. God, how he'd bled . . . She glanced at her hands, knowing they were still red. His blood had long since dried on her skin; the rain had done little to cleanse them. Was he dead, she wondered? What about the others in the house – the girls, the woman? Had she now put them in danger somehow? Were the men searching for her, the thinner guy and the man with sausage meat for skin? They'd never have let her get away. She'd seen at least two of their faces, plus the woman, though she doubted she'd been part of things. That woman had saved her life.

As darkness had fallen, she felt safer to move, get herself to a road and find help, naked from the waist down or not. She couldn't worry about her modesty now. Leanne wiped her face on her sleeve in a vain attempt to focus her attention on her situation and figure out what to do next, where to head. In the far distance was the glow of streetlights and the muffled sound of traffic, and she rightly assumed it to be a motorway. But which one? She could be anywhere. She looked in the opposite direction; that way seemed black all over with a slight differential where the skyline met the ground. Behind her, it was much the same. But was there a glow of creamy light, the movement of headlights maybe. Could there be a local road to aim for? There was only one way to find out, and with thistles pricking at her feet and cold mud and what smelt like cow muck squashing between her toes, she padded her way as carefully as she could towards the light. With no stars or moonlight to guide her, she fixed her gaze forward, feeling for possible obstacles that might trip her up. She didn't think she could cope with any more pain.

She'd had time to think back in the room; there had been precious else to do, and she'd thought a lot about her family life and her relationship with her parents. She and her friends at school constantly moaned at the restrictions their parents put on their lives – not letting them go to concerts or see a boy who was a couple of years older or wear makeup. How she'd fooled them in the past, saying she was at a friend's house studying when in fact she was someplace else. And what a fuss she'd made of cycling on Christmas Day and on other days when her parents had encouraged her to spend time with them. She choked back a sob. It was all so pointless now, and she vowed that when she did get back home – because she would – things would change on her part.

What she wouldn't trade now to be safe at home with her mum and dad. Her tears were still falling; they had never properly stopped completely though they had slowed in pace. Fresh sobs caught in her throat. She wiped her nose on her wet sleeve again and pushed forward across the soggy grassland, hoping she was moving in the right direction, that the creamy light up ahead was a road or a house, somewhere she could get help, somewhere she could call her mum and dad and tell them she was alright. A house or a shop or somewhere, anywhere, with someone who would help her and take her home. She fell to her knees and wailed into the night, pouring out a torrent of grief and remorse from deep inside her soul.

At last, spent and shivering, she lay where she'd dropped and curled into a foetal position for comfort as the icy cold rain began to fall once again.

Chapter Forty-Five

By the time they'd heard the fire engines in the distance, the van and its occupants were heading west on the M25, though neither of the two men could agree on what to do and where to go, having rushed from the house in mayhem. In the back, the two girls whimpered. Nobody heard their muffled cries apart from the other occupants of the van. The woman stayed silent.

The air was filled with tension, and the smell of stale urine and filthy clothing.

"You stink," Bernard shouted back at the youngest girl. She'd been terrified by her ordeal and her clothes were sopping.

To Rob, he seemed to be unravelling a little. "Calm down, will you? The house and all evidence are gone, and these can't identify and find us," he said, pointing over his shoulder. "No names, and no idea where they've been all this time, and with the fear of god put into them, I'd say there won't be an issue. And in any case, I've been chewing through a plan while you've been stressing."

"Let's hear it then, bright spark."

"We drop them off individually, at different spots so they never see each other again. Drop one off somewhere here, another in another county and the last in another. The cops won't figure it out for a while. It's Christmas, remember, so they'll be on minimum staff and full of turkey if they've any sense. Perfect time to give them something to do. We'll be lucky if things get linked together by New Year, and we'll be well out of it by then."

Bernard sat and mulled it over in silence. "So, you reckon one around here someplace?" he said at length.

"I'd say so. We're not far to the next county, so we can do two quickly. Drop them on a quiet side road. There'll hardly be any traffic over the next couple of days, so it'll be ages before they're found."

Bernard liked the sound of it. It seemed the logical thing to do, and the smell was burning into his sinuses. A junction loomed ahead and he flicked his indicator to turn off. "May as well start here," he said, slowing down and pulling off the motorway. There wasn't another soul on the road but he took the first left down an equally quiet road, followed by a series of further left and right turns. He silently hoped he'd manage to navigate his way back to the motorway. When he was satisfied they were remote enough, he pulled into a layby. With no streetlamps, it was pitch black.

Turning to Rob, he said, "Get the smelly young one out of here. She reeks."

Rob opened his door and walked around the back of the van. As the hired muscle, he had a part to play. He yanked the door open and reached a strong arm out to the smallest child, pulling her forcibly forward. She did her best to scream from behind the tape covering her mouth, but Rob ignored her distress, pulling her towards the open door like she was an old suitcase.

"I'd have thought you'd want to get out," Bernard shouted spitefully as the child stood awkwardly at the rear.

Rob closed the doors. The girl stood shaking, obviously petrified, in the darkness. Icy rain pelted them both, and Rob didn't want to hang around any longer getting soaked. Bending down to her level to speak into her ear, he hissed, "And don't ever think about telling anyone where you've been or who with. Remember, we'll know where to find you again and come and get you. Now get walking," he added threateningly, before getting back into the van and leaving her standing there with her hands bound behind her back, the pillowcase sticking wetly to her head. If she was lucky, a car might be along later, though he doubted it. By tomorrow, Christmas Day, she'd probably have collapsed from exposure.

Back in the van, Bernard said, "Only two more to go. I'll be a happier man when they've both been turfed out."

They drove in silence as the rain lashed down, the windscreen wipers working double time. As they hit West Sussex, Bernard again spoke.

"We'll get rid of one here, then it's not far to East Sussex for the last one."

"They are the same county. That won't work," Rob protested.

"You thick or what? They are two different counties, dumb shit. We'll drop one here, then it's not far to East Sussex."

"I'm telling you, it's the same county."

"Well, since I'm driving," he spat "and since I'm the brains in this duo, I'm telling you it's two counties, and we'll drop one in each. Now shut the hell up!"

There was no point in arguing, so Rob didn't bother, and when the time came to turf the second girl out on a quiet, wet road, he left her with the same warning in her ear. Half an hour later, the third and last girl, the young woman had been offloaded and left stranded in the pitch black and cold rain to fend for herself. The van was empty now save for Rob and Bernard.

"Thank god for that. Apart from the stink, I didn't want a nosey cop pulling us over and taking a look. That would have been awkward," Bernard joked. The mood in the van was somewhat lighter now. "Now, where are we headed, oh bright one?" he mocked.

Rob really wasn't sure of the answer. "A cheap motorway stop with a Macca's, I reckon. I'm starved."

As the van drove on towards the north, well away from the house they'd left burning behind them, three frightened girls began to make their way along three dark, deserted roads.

The first child, Kate, struck lucky first.

Chapter Forty-Six

"Are you sure you know where you're going?" the woman asked, sounding dubious. She was starting to regret her decision to leave the party. They'd been flirting across the room at each other all night when he'd finally wandered over, wearing a cocksure smile on his face. With several vodkas in her stomach and not much to soak it up with, confidence had come more easily than normal, and they'd eventually found themselves entwined in a hot, sticky embrace. He'd suggested they get some air and find a nice secluded layby, and she'd agreed readily, both knowing exactly what was to come next, both up for it.

"This will do," he decided, and took a long pull on the vodka bottle they were sharing. He passed it back to his conquest to be, who politely laughed a little in return. He pulled off the road into the layby, loose gravel crunching under the tyres, rain soaking the windscreen. He'd no idea where they were exactly, but he'd figure out how to get back when they were done. He turned to the woman.

"Right, then. Where were we?" he asked encouragingly, lowering his face towards hers and opening his mouth in anticipation of receiving her tongue. She smiled at his words and though he couldn't see her clearly in the darkness, he felt her relax a little more, tasting lingering vodka as their mouths mashed together hungrily.

As their urgency progressed to another level, they were unaware of a small figure venturing towards them on the remote road, weaving unsteadily as it struggled to progress. It eventually made its way past the stationary vehicle, sobbing quietly, unaware there was anyone inside it who could help, ease its distress and pain, make its warm again. The little figure would have to wait a while longer.

When the young couple finally finished having their fun and were making their way back towards the party, it was the woman who spotted the figure in the headlights first. It was hard not to: it was wandering in the centre of the road.

"Look!" she exclaimed, pointing out through the windscreen. The figure could have been a ghost from a horror movie.

"What the . . .?" the man said as they approached it and slowed down. In the headlights it looked eerie.

"It's too short to be an adult. Pull over," the woman instructed. "It looks like they've got a bag or something on their head." She turned to open her door.

"What you gonna do?"

"Take a look, stupid. That's no practical joke," she said pointing at the figure, which had stopped in the near distance.

"You'll get soaked," the man protested.

Not waiting to give a reply, she climbed out of the warm car and into the icy rain, headed towards the figure, leaving him sitting in the driver's seat watching. She called out to the figure.

"Hello. Are you alright?" As she approached, she could see with the light from the car headlamps that the figure was no bigger than a child, a child with what looked like a bag of some description on its head, and who was soaked and visibly shaking. She ventured closer, doing her best to make her voice sound comforting.

"It's alright. I'm going to come a little closer, okay? I'm not going to hurt you." Rain continued to pelt down around them both. Her own clothes were soaked now and she wished she'd brought a coat with her. Instinctively, she put her arm out towards the small figure, as though she was enticing a dog to come closer, except this dog couldn't see her gesture.

"I'm almost there now. Don't be scared," she encouraged again. When her outstretched hand finally made contact with the small figure's shoulder, she heard what sounded like a muffled sob. Continuing to talk quietly, she gently lifted the soaked bag off the figure's head, then drew back in alarm. Two swollen and terrified eyes stared back up at her. Grey tape was fastened across the child's mouth. It was a young girl.

"Dear god," she exclaimed quietly to herself as she bent down to the girl's level. Gently she peeled the tape off the tiny mouth and spoke again.

"My name is Jess, and whatever has happened to you, you're safe now. Can you tell me your name?" Jess watched as the child's bottom lip trembled uncontrollably and she waited patiently. But the child was too terrified to speak and stood mute, petrified with fear, as Jess tried again to reassure her. Noticing the child's hands were bound behind her back, Jess removed the tape from her wrists and rubbed each one gently to return the circulation.

"There, that must be better. Let's get you out of this rain, shall we? Then we can get you warmed up and get some proper help, let your parents know you're alright, eh?"

Still nothing from the lips of the tiny child as Jess bent to pick her up and take her back to the car, talking gently as she walked in an effort to reassure the little one that everything was going to be alright. The man opened the rear car door and Jess and the child got inside. They were both soaked.

"Take your jumper off," she directed the man. "She's deathly cold, poor mite." He did as he was told and watched as Jess draped it around the child's shoulders.

"Police station, I think, or hospital? What do you think?"

"Hospital, I reckon. I don't want to go anywhere near the police. I'm over the limit by miles."

"Whatever. Hospital then. This poor girl needs some help quickly, so get your foot down, will you?"

And with rain lashing down from the blackness above, little Kate Bryers was taken to the nearest hospital.

Her nightmare ordeal was finally coming to an end.

Chapter Forty-Seven

"So where are we heading now?" Rob asked Bernard, who was busy steering with one hand and fumbling for his cigarettes with the other. The van swerved across to the next lane as he pulled them free from his inside jacket pocket. It was a good job the M25 was quiet for a change.

"Back home, I'd say. No point going back to the house. There's nothing there. You want dropping somewhere?" A plume of blue smoke filled the driver's side as Bernard took a couple of heavy drags on his cigarette.

"Back to my flat, I suppose."

"I ain't driving all the way over there at this hour. I'm not a bleedin' taxi service, you cheeky sod."

Rob figured as much, but thought he'd ask anyway. On Christmas Eve at such a late hour there wouldn't be much in the way of public transport, and taxis would likely be scarcer still. He'd have to chance the train. Or thumb a lift.

"Drop me at the train station, then. I'll get home from there. Leatherhead isn't far from here."

Bernard grunted in reply, sounding like the Neanderthal he was. It had been a stressful night and both men were anxious about what had happened. With no proper plan in place and having made it up as they went along, there was ample room for error, something neither of them was particularly happy about. But there was no going back and changing things now. It was way too late. They'd have to pray the trail didn't snake back to their front doors.

"Look," said Bernard, stubbing his fag butt out under his foot on the dirty rubber mat. There must have been at least another twenty more with it. "We should steer clear of each other for a while, lay low. I'm going to get the hell out of Dodge, maybe catch the train to France, hide out there or move further south. I suggest you do the same. It'll only be a matter of time before they find the house, and Martin's body."

At the mention of Martin, Rob waited a moment before adding, "Yeah, probably a good idea. What a bloody mess, though. It wasn't supposed to be like this. There wasn't meant to be any real trouble," he said, his voice rising with each word, his anger mounting. "That's what you both said: nobody would get hurt. But they did."

"Oh, stop being so dramatic, would you? We'll both be out of it soon enough. And Martin? Well, he was collateral damage, unfortunate, like. So stop blubbering and figure out what you'll do to keep clear of the shit that will undoubtedly start flying." Bernard reached into his pocket again for another cigarette and struggled to light it. The motorway was almost empty as he swerved out of his lane for the second time then corrected his steering. The pull on the wheel jolted Rob, who had been busy gazing through the side window, deep in thought.

"What the—?" he yelled as he righted himself in his seat.

But Rob wasn't the only one who noticed the van swerving. Two cars behind sat a motorway patrol car, the officers minding their own business as they made their way back to the station at the end of their shift. Rob spotted it in his side mirror, but it was too late. As he opened his mouth to tell Bernard, blue light reflected around the inside of the van as the patrol car gained, then pulled alongside them in the adjacent lane. Bernard glanced across at it. The driver signalled for him to pull over.

"You've no choice, have you?" Rob said, defeated. "We're hardly going to outrun them in this pile of crap. This isn't an episode of *The Bill*, more's the pity." Bernard wasn't convinced, however, and carried on, the siren from the police car sounding harsh to their ears as it reverberated around the tin can of a van.

Rob had another go. "Pull it over! Don't be a dumbass. We'll never get away, so let's see what they do. Might be nothing."

That seemed to pacify Bernard; they might only want him over for a rear light out or something equally trivial. He flicked his indicator to pull over and drifted to a stop on the hard shoulder. Both men sat silently, waiting. In the vehicle behind them, they knew the officer would be doing a vehicle check and both men hoped it didn't throw up anything that they couldn't handle.

They were correct. A vehicle check was indeed taking place, a check that showed that the van was a vehicle of interest to the Croydon police in a possible abduction case. The two traffic officers looked at each other and rolled their eyes.

"Better take a look then, hadn't we? I guess we'll not be getting back for a mince pie just yet."

As Officer Michaels approached the driver's side of the van, his partner slipped down towards the passenger side and waited, largely in case the passenger decided to make a run for it. He'd had it happen before and didn't fancy taking his chance with a chase in the wet so late on Christmas Eve. He should be on his way home.

"License, please," Michaels demanded wearily, and waited for Bernard to hand it over.

"Not with me. Sorry. I'll have to drop it in to you." Bernard was playing for time, with no intention of confirming who he was if he could get away with it.

"What's your name, sir?'

"Bernard Marks."

"Is this your vehicle, sir?"

"No, it's a mate's."

The officer nodded, like he'd heard it all before. "Well, Bernard, do you want to tell me why you were weaving across lanes on two separate occasions?"

"Ah, sorry. I was struggling with a packet of cigarettes, nothing more." Bernard tried a bright smile. It didn't work.

"Have you been drinking, sir?"

"I had a couple at lunchtime. Nothing since."

"Well, since we're here, it makes sense to double-check with a Breathalyzer." He looked at his colleague. It was the other officer's cue to retrieve it from the patrol car.

"What's in the van, sir?"

"Nothing. It's empty."

"Mind if I take a look?" Bernard's brain was thinking through the various outcomes at record speed, not sure which way to go.

"Sir?"

"Go ahead. It's empty." Bernard was starting to get warm under his collar, hoping there wasn't anything lying around in the back, something they'd missed.Something that could screw this up even more.

From their seats, Rob and Bernard watched as the officer approached the rear of the van and opened the double doors. In the low light available, there didn't look to be anything amiss. It was, as Bernard had said, empty. Rob slowly let his breath out and relaxed a little as the officer closed one door and started to close the other.

But something had caught his eye.

Chapter Forty-Eight

Billy and Chloe lay beneath their blankets, their breath visible on the air in the small garage, morning light filtering in through a triangle of bare glass where the old curtains didn't quite meet each other. It was another grey-sky day, but at least it wasn't raining. Chloe watched Billy as he lay sleeping, his mouth open a little, deep in a warm dream. He looked so peaceful. There wasn't a sound outside their garage; the streets were quiet on Christmas morning. As if he sensed someone looking at him, Billy opened his eyes and stared straight up into Chloe's.

"Morning. Merry Christmas," she said, smiling down at him, and watched him further as he returned a smile and wished her the same.

"What time is it?"

"A little after seven o'clock. I didn't mean to wake you."

"You didn't really. I was coming to anyway," he said, struggling to sit up and wrap a blanket around his shoulders as he did so. With no heating, it was cold in their setup, but at least they had privacy and safety. Chloe sat up with him and he pulled the blanket around her too.

"And what would you like to do today, Chloe Matthews?" he

asked, smiling, knowing whatever she said would be make-believe.

"I think I'll take a hot shower, then I fancy smoked salmon and scrambled eggs with a pot of hot coffee. What about you?"

Playing the game, he carried on with, "I fancy bacon and eggs for a change today, on a couple of soft white rolls, if I may. I'm sick of salmon."

Chloe smiled at his sense of humour. "Well, I can't help you with everything you desire this morning. sir, but I can provide you with the next best thing."

"Oh? What's that?" He watched as she rummaged in her bag and pulled out a familiar printed brown paper bag. She handed it to him.

"Merry Christmas! Open it."

Billy peered inside, and his face broke into a smile again. Inside was a cold Bacon and Egg McMuffin. She'd bought it with the money from the stranger who wanted her to call home – she'd put it to better use.

"Chloe – thanks! How thoughtful. Let's share it, though."

She shook her head. No. It's yours. I've got my usual. Plus, the fact we have a nice hot dinner to look forward to later. I don't want to spoil my appetite, now, do I? You eat it. It's your present." She watched him unwrap the greaseproof paper and, even though she could have ripped it from his hands, enjoyed watching him devour it hungrily, grease shining on his lips. When it came to the last mouthful, he offered it to her.

"Please, take it," he insisted, and she opened her mouth to receive it without him having to ask twice. It tasted like heaven, even cold.

"Now it's my turn," Billy announced, slipping his hand into his own rucksack and pulling out a small bag. When he'd been in the charity shop, he'd seen it and knew Chloe would have liked it. He handed her the small white paper bag.

"What's this?" she enquired, surprised.

"Open it and see, silly."

With delight and surprise, Chloe tore into the bag like she was six years old again. Inside the bag was a square of printed silk, baby pink with pretty, tiny flowers on it.

"Oh, Billy. It's beautiful! Thanks."

"It's real silk. I thought you might like to wear it to lunch, have something pretty for a change. I know girls like pretty things." He was smiling broadly, hoping she really did like it and his words didn't sound condescending.

"I love it, Billy. I'll treasure it – thank you!" she said, and leaned over and gave him a big kiss on the cheek, taking him a little by surprise. For a moment he wasn't sure what to say, and the pause between them was awkward, neither knowing what to say or do next. Billy broke the silence.

"That was nice," he said quietly, almost inaudibly, then reached out to pull her back inside his blanket, planting a kiss on her cheek in return. "I like you, Chloe Matthews."

"And I like you too, Billy Peters," she said, smiling warmly as she snuggled in close. The smell of the McMuffin still lingered on the air of their small space.

"I'm looking forward to a hot bath and dinner, aren't you?"

"Definitely,' he agreed, pulling her closer.

And there they stayed for a few more minutes, enjoying the warmth of their friendship and the warmth of the blanket they shared between them.

A couple of hours later, they were making their way to Roy's place. Chloe's gift for him was tucked in her pocket, along with her new scarf to wear during dinner. As they walked arm in arm like the two close friends they had become, Chloe reflected, and not for the first time, on how her life had been catapulted into something so far away from what she had known only a few months ago – how she'd discovered she was pregnant, and that her parents had effectively been renting her out for money while she'd slept. What kind of unhinged parent did that to their child? No, she was better off without either of them, living like she was with Billy.

Chloe wondered if, someday, Mary would ever think about her own mother.

Chapter Forty-Nine

She awoke to a strange shuffling nearby. Weak sunshine was forcing its way into her swollen eyes, making her wince with pain as she let the morning into them. As she realised she wasn't waking in the dimly lit room where she'd been held, the memories of the previous day rushed through her head like an old mail train, pockets of information making her relive the experience all over again.

But she wasn't in the room, not now. She was outside and the sun was in her sore eyes as she forced them open to orientate herself. How long she'd lain there she'd no idea. She figured she'd passed out from exhaustion in the hammering rain the previous night. She was conscious of movement behind her head somewhere, but as she tried to turn and look, a stab of pain in her neck made her gag. Bitterly cold, her body seemingly frozen to the spot, she forced herself to awaken properly and look what was making the strange noise, hoping she wasn't in trouble again.

Tentatively, she pushed herself up to a wobbly kneeling position and turned towards the noisemaker. A small congregation of half a dozen or so cows stared at her nervously, ears twitching and glistening mouths chewing thin air as they watched her with trepidation. Relief washed over her at the realization she was in no danger.

After all she'd been through, Leanne found the little energy she needed to smile for the first time in a week and relax for a moment. The cows were more frightened of her than she was of them.

"Hi," she said feeling she should say something. "Where am I?" she asked, though she expected no reply. Covering her eyes with the side of her hand to make a shield against the sunshine, she looked around. There was grass as far as she could see, but she could hear the sound of distant traffic, although it was much quieter than the previous night. She gave herself a quick once-over. Blood was still visible in patches on her shirt and hands; her bare legs were filthy with half-dried mud; and her feet were red and sore from stumbling about in the dark with no protection for her tender skin. Raising her hands to check her head, she could feel that her blonde hair was matted. The ends she could see were tinged with more red – his blood. Feeling conscious of her nakedness out in the open, she dropped her hands to cover herself, more out of instinct than necessity. She knew she needed to keep moving, find a way to safety, let her mum and dad know she was alive, then wait for a ride home.

Home.

It could now be a reality, something while locked away in that room at the house she thought she'd never see again.

A male voice from behind startled her, and she instinctively hit the ground again as if to hide in the grass which was, of course, no use, but she lay there any way curled up, listening, as he repeated his call.

"Hello there. Are you alright, miss?"

She wracked her brain to see if she recognized his voice, not wanting to sit up and look who it might be. Was he from the house? He called again. No, she didn't recognize him.

"Hello, miss. Don't be afraid. I won't hurt you. But are you okay?" Scrambling on to her hands and knees but still staying low, she raised her head and looked at the man with terrified eyes. He was about twenty feet away. Every inch of her body trembled uncontrollably as she watched him get a little closer, taking his work coat off as he progressed in her direction. He tossed the coat her way, missing by a couple of feet.

"Please, take my coat. I'll turn around for you. Put it on. It's good and warm," he said. Leanne watched as he turned away, grateful for his consideration and the bit of privacy, grateful for the bit of warmth. She realized the man was likely the owner of the field she was in, the cows his; he wasn't the enemy. The man turned back around and started towards her, and Leanne's tears began to fall all over again. She began wailing like a banshee. The man rushed to her side and scooped her up in both arms and she let him, her whole body going limp with exhaustion. Slowly he picked his way through the field and back towards a vehicle that she hadn't even noticed was there. Just being in the stranger's arms felt a blessed relief to her soul, and she cried like a baby into his shoulder, spilling words out that didn't make any sense to either of them. Manoeuvring her slightly to free his hand, he opened the passenger side door and gently placed her inside on the seat. He closed the door and then hurried around to the driver's side and started the engine. The vehicle began to move forward and she found herself rocking slightly from side to side, too drained to support herself.

"You're safe now, miss. Whatever has happened, you're safe." He smiled warmly; his cheeks were rosy red from too many years working out in all weather. On any other day, he'd have looked a lot like a garden gnome. "What's your name?"

"It's Leanne. Leanne Meadows. I need to tell my mum I'm alright. I've been gone a while; days, I think."

"Where is home, miss?"

"Near Croydon. Where am I?"

"A little way from there, in Kent. Swanley is the nearest town. How about I take you to my home, make you something hot to drink and call the police and your mum? Is that okay?" he asked politely.

"I can't think of anything I'd like better," she said, mustering a small smile.

"I'll turn the heater up for you. You must be frozen – maybe a touch of hypothermia even. I expect the police may want you to go to the hospital and get checked out and whatnot. But first, hot drink and the phone calls, eh?" He smiled cheerily again, and Leanne was grateful for his warm spirit. "It's all happening round here at the moment."

"What else has happened?" she enquired wearily.

"Big fire last night. I guess you didn't hear the fire engines? A big old house over there," he said, pointing. "Up in flames."

Leanne instantly knew it had to be the same place. The hairs were standing up on the back of her neck. Gone up in flames, eh? Along with the man she'd stabbed. She wondered about the others she knew were kept there.

"I must have passed out. Was anyone hurt?"

"Not heard, miss. I dare say it'll be on the news. By the way, Merry Christmas. Best present ever for your parents, you coming home, I'd say."

"Sorry? What day is it?" Her sense of time had disappeared with no way of seeing the outside world.

"It's Christmas Day, miss. It's Christmas Day."

Chapter Fifty

A Christmas Day tradition in the Rutherford household was crumpets for breakfast, with lashings of melted butter. And it had to be butter, not margarine, not on Christmas Day. And when they'd finished a pack between them, they'd make coffee with warm milk and Janine would add a slug of rum for good measure. Crumpets and rum in his coffee were always the best way to start the day's festivities. Sitting in his chair as content as a cat by an open fire, he smiled at Janine as she collected the cups and plates away from the table. She caught him looking.

"What?'

"I was just admiring the view," he said cheekily, a twinkle in his eyes. Probably the early rum, he thought.

"Well, don't be getting any ideas if you want turkey and all the trimmings at lunchtime, else it will be bedtime, knowing you." There was laughter in her voice as she gently reprimanded him; she cherished him and his wicked thoughts dearly.

"And nothing shall stop Christmas lunch being served at lunchtime, let me tell you. It's the best day of the year," he said. He lifted his hand and counted off on his fingers as he spoke. "One: I have you all to myself. Two: I have a fat and rather full stomach to ache later while we watch Noel Edmonds give out his presents. And finally, three: there's always sherry trifle left over for before bed, just to top me back up again in case I was feeling peckish. It's the perfect day in every way," he said, getting up and following her with the remainder of the breakfast things balanced in his hands.

"Well, that's good to know. Now, I'll give you the veg to start peeling and I'll get on with the rest," she said as she loaded carrots, sprouts, potatoes and parsnips onto a tray along with a knife and vegetable peeler. Jack picked up a sprout and put it to his ear and waited for her to notice.

"And that, last night, was the worst joke I've ever heard. There'll be better ones in the crappy crackers we pull later on, Jack Rutherford."

"Possibly not." Jack took the tray from her and headed into the lounge to peel the veg in front of the television. As he left, he quipped, "Mr Rutherford, you really must eat more sensibly," loud enough for Janine to hear back in the kitchen. He could almost hear her roll her eyes. Still, the veg in front of the telly was all part of Christmas, he thought contentedly as he turned the set on and made himself comfortable. It was still early, and *Live and Kicking's Christmas Cracker* was in full swing. He settled in to watch, fascinated by the seasonal silliness of it all and the heart-throb band of boys crooning – Westlife, they were called. God, he felt old sometimes. At least *Morecambe and Wise* were on later; they were a bit more his thing, though, really, Westlife should have been for his age group. He concentrated on the potatoes as the boys sang their Christmas hearts out and Jack was surprised to feel himself nodding a little in time with them. In the hallway, the phone started to ring.

"Jack, can you get it, please? My hands are covered with stuffing mix," Janine shouted down the hallway. "It's probably for you anyway."

Grumbling that he hoped not, he answered it anyway, hoping it was a relative passing on festive cheer. He was wrong.

"Sorry, Jack, but I have some news for you." Jack recognized the voice of Pete Abbott, the sergeant who manned the front desk.

He'd obviously pulled the short straw and was on duty Christmas morning. Jack felt dread creep up his spine like a tarantula. Not in the mood for small talk, he dove straight in without the pleasantries.

"What is it, Pete? What's happened?"

"It's good news, Jack. The girl, Leanne Meadows – she's been found. And she's okay."

It took a moment to sink into Jack's head. Westlife wound down in the lounge as the news finally registered. "What happened? When?"

"Kent police called a moment ago. Seems the girl escaped. A farmer found her and called the police. She's in hospital being checked out for possible hypothermia as well as cuts and bruises, but otherwise, she's unharmed. Frightened, but okay. Her parents have been contacted and they're on their way to see her. Obviously, Kent police are keen to speak with her, find out what's been happening, where she's been kept."

"Well, that's excellent news, Pete. I'd like to know myself." Jack's brain was in a tizzy as he tried to think what to do next.

"Any news or sign of the other two missing girls?"

"Nothing else to report, Jack. Sorry."

"Is Eddie aware?"

"Can't raise him to tell him. Thought I'd best tell you directly."

Some things never change.

"Thanks for letting me know. Any idea when Kent will be able to speak to her?"

"Not at the moment. Sorry."

"Keep me posted, will you?"

"Of course, Jack. Good news, though. Nice for them all to be reunited for Christmas."

"Yes, it's great news, really great news." Jack finished the call and stood looking at the phone in his hand like it was going to morph into something special. He sensed Janine behind him and turned.

"Don't tell me you have to go ...?" The look of disappointment on her face bit into his heart.

"I don't think so. But I may have to later. One of our missing girls has been found safe and relatively well. They've taken her to hospital."

"Well, that's great news!" She dried her hands on her apron as she spoke.

"Yes, it is, it is. I could do with talking to her, though. I'd like to be there when she's interviewed."

"I understand, Jack. When will you know?"

"Soon, I hope. I'd better not drink anything over lunch. Don't want to be done for drink driving. Wouldn't look too good." He turned and headed back to the lounge and his half-finished tray of vegetables. For someone who had received news that one missing girl had been found, he didn't feel much like celebrating. The other two girls were still missing and the time lapsed so far didn't bode well for their survival.

He focused on peeling the potatoes.

Chapter Fifty-One

He was as stuffed as the turkey he'd eaten. Jack sat restlessly on the sofa beside Janine; a rerun of *Morecambe and Wise* was about to start on the TV, and a half glass of wine sat on the side table.

"No point me getting it. It'll be for you," Janine remarked for the second time that day as Jack struggled to his feet to answer it. "You get off. I'll sort the kitchen," she called as he made his way to the phone. While he'd been waiting for the call to come through, he'd been dreading it too, not wanting to let his Janine down on Christmas Day. Unfortunately, crime never took a break. It didn't celebrate Christmas.

"Jack Rutherford," he answered.

"DS Tom McCormick, Kent police. I believe you might be expecting my call?"

"Yes, thanks for ringing. What's the story? How's Leanne?"

"I believe not bad, all things considered. I'm hoping to talk to her in the next couple of hours, hence my call to you. Fancy a drive?"

"Tell me where to meet you."

After he'd noted the hospital address down and said his see-you-laters, Jack headed back to the lounge to break the news to Janine.

"Just get back when you can. I'll make some sandwiches for supper later and we can eat them in front of the TV. *The Vicar of Dibley* is on at nine o'clock. Try and be back for then if you can, eh?" Janine pecked him on his lips and smiled. "I hope the girl is alright. Now go and see how you can help get the others back."

Jack looked down into her forever sparkling eyes and lightly pecked her lips back.

"Janine Rutherford, what have I done to deserve a woman like you, eh?"

"You picked a good'un, didn't you?" she said softly, reaching up to adjust his shirt collar slightly, not that it needed it. It was more a touch of love on her part. "Now go and do your job and I'll see you when you get back. Drive safely."

Jack opened the front door to leave. "See you later, then."

Janine waved through the window as he started the Taurus and pulled out of the driveway.

Jack took the opportunity to try and raise Eddie, wherever he was, but came up short. His calls kept going through to his mailbox. He wasn't officially on duty so he could be forgiven, but there was rarely rest from a case like they were working on. Christmas Day and its skeleton staff fell at the wrong time for three missing girls. He called DI Morton, more out of duty than necessity; Morton was as much use as a chocolate fireguard. Like Eddie, there was no response.

"Best I sort this myself, then," he said to himself, feeling like he was the only person who cared about what happened to the girls. He pushed the CD into the player and ELO started out with "Hold on Tight," which seemed fitting for the drive. His dreams at that moment were that Leanne was alright and that the other two girls would be found safe and well. After that, he dreamed of heading back to the warm fireplace, Janine, and supper. That would make his Christmas, alright. He turned up the volume and sang along with ELO. He knew every word of every song on the album and when it switched over and "Horace Wimp" started, he thumped the steering wheel in time with the lyrics.

With almost clear roads ahead of him, he headed around the M25 towards Kent, and thought about how lucky Leanne had been to escape. He hoped the others could be so lucky. Fifty minutes later, the red brick hospital building came into view and he swung in, immediately finding a parking space near the front entrance. He marvelled at how easy the drive and parking had been; perhaps every day could be like Christmas Day. Life would be a little easier. He put his foot out onto the damp tarmac; the rain was long gone and the afternoon sun was doing its best to dry the earth beneath it. There were lighter patches where it had succeeded, but the sun was not hot enough to cause steam to rise. Maybe on another day. Heading inside, Jack made his way to the ward and the room number he'd been given by Tom McCormick, and wasn't surprised to see a uniformed officer by the girl's door. "Looks like someone else cared too," he thought with relief. Tom was a decent bloke. He showed his warrant card to the officer on duty and then poked his nose in. Leanne was with a nurse. He withdrew it again.

"I'm looking for DS Tom McCormick," he said to the officer, retracing his steps back out to the corridor.

"Just gone for a coffee. He'll be back soon, I expect."

"Thanks. Are her parents here?" Jack asked, nodding towards Leanne's door again.

"Yes. They are with Tom getting coffee while the nurse is in."

"Any other visitors?"

"Not that I've seen, and I've been here pretty much since she came in. Good news she's here, though, made it out alive."

"Certainly is. Now we have to find the others."

"Well, if they were in that house too, they'd be lucky. Leanne got out before the fire."

This was all news to Jack. "What fire?"

"A fire was reported nearby where she was found by the farmer. We think it could be connected, might be the place where she escaped from, though until we've spoken to her, we don't know much. Speculation on our part for a while longer. Anyway, Tom will tell you more," he said, pointing down the corridor at a group heading their way. "He's here now with her parents."

Jack watched as a weary Dave and Penny Meadows walked towards him with Tom McCormick. Since he'd last seen them, they looked like they had aged twenty years. He put out his hand to greet them both when they reached him.

"Good news for you both. I'm so glad she's back," Jack said compassionately, his eyes meeting Penny's. Hers looked sore from crying, but she was happier than the last time he'd seen her. He had hated asking if her daughter had been pregnant, and he'd left their house feeling like he'd made matters worse.

"We just want to see her, see our baby girl."

"Then let's go and do that," Jack said.

Tom nodded.

Chapter Fifty-Two

It felt good to be safe and warm again, and even hospital food was better than what Leanne had been eating over the last few days. *Christmas Top of the Pops* was on the TV and she was half-watching that. She'd been examined by doctors, examined by forensics, and had briefly been questioned by police, though the doctors had put a stop to it until she'd rested a while. Right now, Leanne Meadows lay deep in thought and feeling thankful to be alive while she waited for her parents to arrive. Then, she'd talk to the police properly. The police, she knew, were extremely anxious to get moving.

A nurse put her head round the door of her room.

"Your parents are here now, Leanne. Do you feel up to seeing them?" she asked kindly. Leanne nodded, a weak smile playing on her lips. She wished she could muster a little more energy but exhaustion was weighing her down. The nurse approached her bed and helped her to sit up, fluffing her pillows behind her like a mother hen.

"I'll show them in. The police are here too, so I'll give you a minute together, and then I'll let them in. The sooner you get it over with, the better, I say. Then it's a good night of rest for you. Okay?"

Leanne nodded. A moment later, she heard her mother before she actually saw her. Mrs Meadows gave an excited cry and rushed to her daughter, arms wide and tears of joy rolling down her cheeks. She took her daughter gently in her arms and sobbed her relief. Her father joined in, wrapping his arms around them both, squeezing a little harder than perhaps he ought to have. When, finally, they both pulled back, Leanne was crying with relief too, and all three collectively wiped their eyes with the back of their hands.

A detective hovered at the doorway, waiting for permission to enter. Leanne waved him in; his colleague followed close behind him. Leanne's mum glared for a moment.

"It's alright, Mum. The sooner I get this over with, the better."

"Are you sure, dear? Don't you want to rest more first?"

"No, I want to get it out of my system, and then I can forget it. It's best, I'm sure." The detective took a seat by her bed, the old plastic chair creaking under his ample weight. Would it hold out while they talked? Leanne wondered, trying to prepare herself for what she had to say, to find a little humour in the horror of it all. She also knew it could have been a good deal worse for her than it had been. She'd never forget that bit, she was sure. The other detective stood next to him, a pleasant-looking man, she thought. He had kind eyes, though he looked a little nervous fiddling with his top lip like a child. Both her parents stayed close by, Leanne's mother holding her daughter's hand, stroking the back of it gently, careful not to touch the drip that was inserted a little higher up. The seated detective introduced himself.

"Hi, Leanne. I'm DS Tom McCormick, Kent Police. And this is DC Jack Rutherford, Croydon Police." Jack nodded and smiled without actually showing his teeth, just enough to acknowledge her. "Do you feel up to answering a few questions?" Tom continued.

"Yes, I want to get it all over with. Ask whatever you want."

"Well, I find the best place to start is at the beginning, so why don't you tell us what happened on Monday and we'll take some notes. Sound okay?"

Leanne nodded, thought for a moment, and then, taking a deep breath, recalled the whole story from when she'd left work – the puncture, the van, the younger girl being kidnapped, the house and how she'd managed to escape. Tears flowed as she spoke, not only her own but her mothers, and when she told them of her room visitor and what he'd been about to do, Mrs Meadows cried out loud with anguish. Her husband comforted her as her lower lip trembled uncontrollably. When the room had quieted down again, Leanne finished her story with the farmer finding her, taking her back to his house and calling the police. Then she had a question of her own.

"Am I in trouble for stabbing the man?"

"No, you're not. It was brave of you, but no, you are not in any trouble." It was the seated detective and he had a question in return.

"Let's start with the house where you were kept. How far from where you were found do you think it was, and what can you remember about it?"

"It was two storeys, old, cold and in the middle of nowhere. When I ran, I didn't know where I was going; it was dark and raining. I'd say I'd been running for at least an hour when I fell, but I couldn't be sure. It was so disorientating. I hadn't a clue where I was going. I'm sorry. I tried to keep moving but ..." When her voice trailed off, both detectives looked at one another and something passed between them, something that Leanne also saw.

"What is it?" she asked.

"There was fire reported late last night, not that far from where you were found. An old property, in the middle of nowhere. It might be the same building. We'll know more when forensics have finished with it." Dave Meadows cleared his throat, perhaps a little too loudly, and Jack looked his way. Their eyes met for a second then Jack broke away.

Leanne carried on, "What about the others? There was at least a young woman. I don't think she was part of it. She couldn't have been much older than me. She brought my food. She was the one that brought the spoon. If she hadn't done that, I daren't think what I'd have done when he came in." Her voice broke. She owed her life to the young woman. With the back of her hand, she wiped the big tears that had started to fall again. Her mother passed her a tissue.

"We have only found one body in the house, and right now we're assuming it's the same place you were held. Again, we'll know more after forensics have finished. The house was gutted. If the others did get out, they could be anywhere. Who are the others you definitely know about, other than the girl, and the man who attacked you?"

"I only met one other man, but I heard screams in the distance so I couldn't say who else. I only heard the screams." Leanne described the other man in some detail. The fact he'd been so repulsive made it easier to remember what he'd been wearing, his pudgy face and sausage-meat stomach. Maybe if she let it all out she could be cleansed of the vision of him taking up space in her head.

When all the details were down, Tom McCormick closed his notebook. "Leanne, you've been extremely helpful. Thank you. I'm sure we'll have a few more questions, but we've plenty to work on for now, so I suggest you get some rest. I'll call back, probably tomorrow. I believe you'll be going home soon?" He looked at Penny Meadows for confirmation.

"When the doctor has done his rounds tomorrow – fingers crossed," she replied with a hopeful smile.

"What happens now, then, Detective?" Dave Meadows asked after clearing his throat again.

"We see what that house tells us."

Did Jack imagine it, or did Mr Meadows blanch?

Chapter Fifty-Three

It was almost dark when Jack got to the scene of the fire. He'd followed Tom McCormick out so they could each go in their separate directions afterwards, and even though it was getting late, Jack was interested to see what was left of where Leanne had been held. Mobile lighting shone brightly up ahead, highlighting the spot they were travelling to. The bumpy track played havoc with the old Taurus's suspension. He really should get a new car. They pulled to a stop and headed over to the makeshift tent that had been erected. The crime scene investigators were taking a break. They were dressed in hooded white paper suits, face masks pulled down under their chins while they chatted. Tom introduced Jack to the team, whom he knew well; there were collective nods all around. Behind them, the remains of a blackened, wet, stinking building were lit up like a museum on a gala evening. Smoke hung in the air, making it smell like a November bonfire night rather than a jolly festive Christmas evening. A lone firefighter was dampening down hotspots; the others were packing away their tools, their sooty faces looking exhausted. Jack would have a word with the forensic investigator in charge in a moment, but now he turned his attention to a man who was walking purposefully towards them both.

"Jack, this is my DI, Graham Brooks," said Tom, introducing them. "Anything for us yet, Guv?" Tom asked.

"Surprisingly, yes, actually. A couple of things of interest. From their initial examination, it looks like the fire started in a downstairs room, middle of the house. Accelerant residue suggests arson, and there's accelerant out front also, by the two burned-out cars. The building partly collapsed over the seat of the fire," he said, pointing. "That part went down first and that's where they found the body, but luckily not all of the building has gone, as you can see. Whoever started this fire wasn't too lucky if they were hoping for it all to burn. Fire service got here pretty quickly, so there's something left to work with. Hopefully, forensics will come up with something useful."

"Well, the VINs should be a useful start. Those two cars will tell us something. I wonder why they were left?" said Tom.

"My guess is someone thought taking the reg plates off would be enough," Brooks said, nodding over to the burned-out cars. "There's usually remains of a plate left, but both plate holders are empty on both vehicles, so I'd say they were a bit thick in that respect."

"Let's hope they weren't stolen vehicles, then – dead ends. We could do with a break. Anything else so far?" This from Jack.

"Not much yet. Crime scene techs haven't been upstairs yet. It's too dangerous."

Jack hoped there weren't any more dead bodies up there, namely those of the missing girls. The DI read his mind.

"Fire team went up initially, and there were no other bodies found. Just the one, which is on its way to the morgue, but we think it's too big for any of the missing girls. For now, we're suggesting that it's probably the man who attacked Leanne. There's nothing but charred remains, so we can't be totally sure as yet. Maybe dental will help us there, and the VINs with a name."

Jack looked at the blackened mess up ahead. How the hell they'd get much else from the burned-out building he'd no idea, but he knew there were ways. He'd stay hopeful.

Tom's phone rang, and he moved away to one side to answer it, leaving Jack with his thoughts. If the girls were not in the building, what the hell had happened to them? And where had the other men gone? There had to be others. Leanne had said there was another male in the van; surely, one man couldn't have set this up all on his own.

He turned to the DI. "What's being done to find the missing girls. Is there a search in process locally? If they were in this house, they could be on foot, as Leanne was. Any signs of anything?"

The DI shook his head. "We only found out about the girl that escaped a short time ago, so no, not as yet, but we have a team on their way out. It's possible they could have been moved somehow, which is what I'm suspecting. Given the two cars parked out front, I'm betting there's another mode of transport – a van, maybe."

"Well, that fits with what we have already: a van owned by Martin Coffey, one we've been looking for since this all broke loose. He did five years in Strangeways for kidnapping, so he's someone we'd like to talk to. I'm also wondering if that's who Leanne stabbed, and whether he's the charred individual found inside. In which case, someone else is driving that van, and a couple of very frightened girls could well be inside."

Tom rejoined the conversation. "Then that van is our priority. We need to find it and fast. When the team arrive, I'll get them focused locally in case they are nearby, but we need that van."

Jack's phone began to ring and he excused himself, leaving the two men to talk. The call turned out to be music to Jack's ears. When he'd finished, he filled the two detectives in with what had happened.

"That was Sussex Police. Seems a young couple picked a girl up late last night near Maresfield, wandering in the road, bound and gagged and severely distressed. Had a bag of some description over her head. She was taken to a nearby hospital and the local police attended, and they have since connected with our investigation. Her description fits one of the missing girls apparently, hence their contact."

"Which one is she, do you know?" asked Tom.

"They think maybe Kate Bryers. Apparently, she's too traumatised to talk. Hasn't said a word since she was found. I'm going to shoot over there now, see if I can confirm it's little Kate and let her parents know she's alright." Jack was already on the move towards his vehicle, hoping he could find his way back out to the motorway without getting lost in the maze of narrow lanes. He didn't fancy an unnecessary detour. It was late enough already.

"Let us know, eh, Jack?" Tom shouted after him, and Jack waved his arm in the air in acknowledgment. He hoped with all his heart it was one of the young girls they'd been looking for.

And that meant there was only Lesley left to find. What a Christmas this was turning out to be.

Chapter Fifty-Four

Jack had arrived back home to Janine just before midnight, missing not only *The Vicar of Dibley* but turkey sandwiches for supper with the woman he loved. How his wife stayed so understanding he'd never know. She really was a gem, and he admired her resolve to be as supportive as she was every day of his life. Still, he'd had the pleasure of confirming it had been little Kate Bryers that had been found and had informed her parents, who had then leapt into their car and met him at the hospital. Not wanting to intrude on their time together, he'd waited patiently while they'd sat around the child's bed and offered their love and support. When he couldn't wait any longer, he'd sat with all three of them and gently tried to pose his questions, but Kate hadn't spoken a single word. It had been a nurse that had put a stop to it, conscious of Kate's need to rest. She'd then given the little girl a sedative, making any further questions pointless.

As for Kate, she had a long road to recovery ahead of her, to repair not only her physical injuries but her mental scarring, too. Her ordeal would take some considerable time and patience to heal from.

There was still at least one more girl to bring home. Where they would now start looking, he had no idea.

The crime scene investigators came up trumps the following day. After the fire brigade had finally left and they'd got the scene all to themselves, they had conducted a thorough examination of the burned-out remains. It had been filthy work, particularly in the downstairs rooms where the ceiling had collapsed onto the floor below. The team had had a couple of feet of charred timber and other building materials to sift through. It had been hard going looking for clues as to what had happened prior to the fire, but they'd found items of interest. The upstairs, or what was left of it, had been particularly fruitful, though getting results from the items they'd retrieved would take a while longer. The remaining upstairs rooms had suffered from mainly smoke and water damage, so there was little chance of fingerprint retrieval from any of the remaining surfaces. Still, there were small pieces of what could be bedclothes, and the crime scene investigators hung their hopes on getting some usable DNA on the fragments they'd bagged.

Other than that, there wasn't much else to find, even though each room had been searched with a magnifying glass. Then, as a technician was on his way out of the remains of the last room, he had spotted a small, smooth lump on the edge of a table. Why it caught his attention he'd never know. It was merely a small black lump on top of a sooty surface, and it looked like everything else in the room – black. But sometimes fate was on your side, so he took a closer look. Peering at it, he still couldn't figure out quite what it was, so he had taken his tweezers and picked up the tiny object, slipping it into an evidence bag and labelling it to be processed along with all the other items the team had retrieved between them. After one last look around the charred room, he had made his way carefully back to join his colleagues who were working downstairs.

At the rear of the property, another crime scene technician was painstakingly going through the remains of the rubbish bins; there were dozens of discarded take-away trays in a bag beside him at his feet. Further along, another technician was on her hands and knees removing gunk from a grid cover where a pipe emptied out, more than likely from a basin or bathroom somewhere in the house. Mixed in with leaves and other detritus could be human hair, and if there was even one strand, preferably with its root intact, it could be vital to telling them who had frequented the place. There was barely a sound as everyone concentrated diligently on their work. Life as a SOCO was not as sexy as it was on the TV.

"Bingo!" said a voice excitedly.

Everyone's head popped up to see what was going on, who had found what.

"Look at this beauty!" the voice said. It belonged to Louise, one of the more experienced techs. She was holding up something familiar to all, a smile on her face the size of a watermelon slice. "And it's not empty," she added gleefully. In her gloved fingers, she held the top edge of a used condom, its contents perfectly preserved in the bottom of it.

"Now that's what I like to find – an easy bit of the puzzle. Let's hope he's in the system and he can tell the police exactly what he was doing here and when," she said, then slipped it carefully into yet another evidence bag to be examined in greater detail at the lab.

By the end of the day, they were almost done photographing, videoing and packaging items of interest. The crime scene vans were packed with items for closer analysis later. It was tough and monotonous work, but important work that sorted the guilty from the innocent.

And they wanted the guilty.

Chapter Fifty-Five

Billy and Chloe were back at work on the streets begging, though with Boxing Day shoppers in a hurry to get to the next bargain, there wasn't a lot of charitable donating going on. Not even Billy's cheery way of persuasion was working, and by lunchtime he felt like calling it a day. He wondered how Chloe was faring. Was she having better luck than he?

"Spare a coin for an old ex-leper?" he repeated to passers-by. He sat wrapped up warm against a cold breeze that felt like it was blowing from the North Pole. He hoped snow wasn't on its way, though it would stop some of the drafts in the old garage if a few inches fell, and it would add to the festive cheer, a cheer he wasn't witness to right now.

"Spare a coin for an old ex-leper?" he chanted, almost on autopilot now.

"Hello, Billy," said a familiar voice. He turned and was happily surprised to see Jack, the man who'd given him money, the man he'd helped in the charity store and the man who he knew was a police officer.

"Come to arrest me for deception, Mr Rutherford?" he joked. "Not being a leper and all."

"Well, I wouldn't know about you being an ex-leper, now, would I? Though I can clearly see you aren't currently suffering from the disease. And it's not even called leprosy anymore."

"No? You mean I have to call it something else, change my marketing strategy?"

"Possibly, but asking for a shekel for an old ex–Hansen's disease sufferer doesn't have the same ring, in my book." He grinned down at Billy, who smiled back. Billy put his hand out to shake and Jack obliged.

"Did you have a nice Christmas Day?" Billy asked.

"We did, thank you – when I wasn't working, that is. And you? What did you and your girl do?"

"We got an invite to a friend's place – dinner and a bath, actually," Billy said in mock smugness, touching his coat collar like he was royalty. "It was a real treat. Played Scrabble, would you believe."

Jack smiled at the mention of the game he'd given the boy, glad they'd had fun with it. He hated wasting anything.

"Well, I'm glad you had fun. Janine and I were going to invite you to come to ours but I couldn't find you."

"Well, that was nice of you both. Thanks."

"As it turned out, Christmas Day was a bit of a write-off. I had to go to Kent, then Sussex for a case I've been working on, and I didn't get back until almost midnight. But it was good to reunite two missing children with their parents. So, it all turned out well in the end."

Billy lost his smile for a moment, deep in thought at something. Jack picked up on it.

"Hey, I wasn't making a point at your story – not that I know what your story is. This was a child. She was only twelve." The two looked at one another, neither sure what to say next until Jack remembered why he was out looking for Billy in the first place. He handed over a bag.

"Janine and I thought you'd appreciate this since we didn't make a get-together. She's made a stack of turkey sandwiches. There's pork pie and Christmas cake and a couple of packets of crisps. Oh, and I slipped a couple of cans of lager in too." Jack beamed. "Please, take it. She makes the cake from scratch herself. It's the best there is."

Billy reached out and took the bag. "I don't know what to say. Thanks. Thanks very much. Chloe and I will enjoy that later. Please thank Janine for us both."

"You are more than welcome. Now, I'd better let you get back to work. I'll see you around, then?"

"Thanks, Jack. You will, I'm sure," Billy said, and watched him walk off into the distance. He was heartened that there were still some decent folks in the world, folks who wouldn't judge his lifestyle or his circumstances. Chloe had found Roy from the café, a man who had helped them enormously, and Billy was glad to have met Jack Rutherford, police or not.

On the other side of town, Chloe was finding trade slow too. Her begging technique was somewhat different to Billy's, and again with distracted Boxing Day shoppers in a frantic hurry to either shop or go home out of the freezing cold wind, she was about to give up herself. Her stomach rumbled. Roy's Christmas dinner was ancient history and the mince pies she'd eaten for breakfast had long gone. She yearned for a hot mug of tea and a bacon butty. And a friendly face. After a particularly nasty experience, when a shopper had spat at her and hissed, "Why don't you get a job? Scum!" she decided she'd had enough for one day. She packed her few things together and set off back towards home with tears threatening. She fought to contain her emotions and not let them show. Blaming it on her mixed-up hormones after giving birth and the added stress of abandoning her baby, she braved it out, not letting one salty drop slide down her cheeks and betray her. She would not let herself be undone by the words or actions of a stranger who knew nothing of her or what she was going through.

Nor cared.

The change she'd gathered rattled in her pocket as she walked along the pavement, and while there wasn't much, there'd be enough for a can of Coke. Chloe slipped into a small corner shop and browsed the shelves for what she could afford. She was conscious of a set of brown eyes watching her from behind the cash register but carried on browsing, deciding how best to spend the money she had earned. She selected a can of no-name cola, which was cheaper than Coke, then made her way over to the fridge. There might be a sandwich going cheap, close to its use-by date as they sometimes were. But she was out of luck; they were all full price, a price she wasn't prepared to pay. A packet of six sausage rolls caught her eye. At least if she had them she could save a couple for Billy for later – he'd like that – and eat the others with the cola. But the price was too high. If she purchased them, there'd be nothing left, and since she didn't know what kind of day Billy was having, she couldn't chance it. There was only one other way. She'd have to steal them.

Checking that the clerk was busy with another customer, she slipped the packet of sausage rolls inside her coat and took the can of cola up to the counter to pay. She was almost clear and walking out the door when she felt a strong hand on her shoulder, pulling her back. It was enough to unbalance her and loosen her grip on the packet within her coat, and the sausage rolls fell unceremoniously to the floor.

"Thought so, you thieving little cow," snarled another brown-eyed man, and roughly pushed her towards the small office area at the back of the store. "Let's see what the police have to say to your thieving, shall we?" he said, not expecting her to answer.

There was no escaping for Chloe, though it was the perfect end to such a rotten day. She slumped down into the proffered chair and kept her head hung low, staying silent. If she didn't say anything, she wouldn't get in any more trouble.

Or so she thought.

Chapter Fifty-Six

Just outside of Horsham in West Sussex, Beryl and Malcolm, along with their dog Brandy, were taking a welcome Boxing Day walk in the late afternoon before the little sun there was finally disappeared for the day. After another big lunch of leftovers, they'd played hide and seek with the grandchildren until the children had grown tired and cranky. Feeling a little old for such constant entertainment needs, Beryl and Malcolm had breathed a sigh of relief when home time had finally been announced and both sets of children had headed off to their own homes. The pair were heading home now for some peace and quiet, and to plates of leftovers for supper should they fancy a bite to eat. Malcolm belched contentedly.

"That was a bit loud," Beryl admonished as they walked out towards the green fields and the few trees beyond.

"There's no one out here to hear me, B, and it's not good to hold it in," he reasoned, taking her hand in his as they strolled. Brandy dashed around them as dogs often did.

"She's probably sick of being indoors too," Malcolm said, nodding to the beagle. "I love the children to bits, but they're a bit young yet to know what's what, and they wind her up terribly. I fear one day she might snap back at them. Won't you, Brandy?" he added, in that cutesy voice dog owners always seemed to use. The dog sensed she was being asked a question and gave a single bark in reply.

"See? Even Brandy agrees with me."

"Don't be daft. She'd bark like that if you asked her the lottery numbers. It doesn't mean she has them."

Malcolm squeezed his wife's hand lightly. "Now wouldn't that be nice, B? What would you do with all that money, at our age?"

"I'd book a cruise, for starters, then figure the rest out while we lay in the sunshine somewhere a long way from here."

Brandy ran on ahead, sniffing the ground as she went, searching for something of interest known only to her as they headed closer to the trees. Beryl and Malcolm followed slowly behind, bantering companionably.

Suddenly Brandy gave two sharp barks.

"What's she found now? A poor rabbit or something?" said Beryl. Neither she nor Malcolm could see the dog now.

"I don't know," said Malcolm, sounding curious. "It doesn't sound like her normal rabbit bark, though, does it?" He turned to Beryl and they stood still for a moment to listen. Brandy obliged them with a few more barks.

"I wonder what's upsetting her, then. She sounds insistent at something."

Beryl called the dog back, but Brandy stayed put. "Now that's strange. She always comes,' she said, and they both took the cue and headed towards the sound of the dog's barks. When they'd pushed their way through the lower branches and brambles of the small copse, they could see Brandy ahead, but nothing else was obvious. Brandy was sitting still, barking constantly now and looking at both Malcolm and Beryl as they approached.

"What is it, Brandy?" Malcolm asked, Beryl close behind him. Twigs snapped under their feet as they made their way forward. The carpet of fallen, sodden leaves covering the sticky ground made it difficult to see where they were stepping. When they finally reached the dog, it was Beryl who saw what was exciting Brandy, and she gasped and covered her mouth with her hands. Malcolm followed her horrified gaze. Partly covered with leaves was a body. Malcolm stepped closer and brushed the hair from its face slightly. It was a young girl. Her face was as white as a bedsheet and she had bruising under her eyes. Instinctively, he knew she was dead, but he put his fingers to her neck anyway.

And waited.

And waited. Beryl stood silently nearby, Brandy now quiet at her heels, and then reached for her cell phone to call the police, thanking their son silently for having given her such an extravagant Christmas present. 'To keep you both safe should you need it," he'd said. Well, they needed it right now, and as she pressed for emergency and waited for a connection, Malcolm shouted three little words that would stay with them for the rest of their lives.

"She's still alive!"

Chapter Fifty-Seven

It had felt good to drop a bag of food off to Billy and his girl, not that Jack had managed to meet her yet, but he doubted she was a figment of Billy's imagination. He might beg like someone from a Monty Python sketch, but he seemed genuine enough. And cheeky. Jack smiled again just thinking about the young man. Janine would like him too, he was sure. Jack looked across at DI Morton's still-empty office and wondered yet again how he managed to keep himself out of events, and how the brass higher up never seemed bothered. Eddie was obviously taking a leaf out of his book, and since Morton was hardly there to witness what his team were up to, that also never got dealt with. Jack and a handful of others were the only true coppers in the squad that gave a damn.

News had spread that Leanne and Kate had been found, alive and relatively well, and the morning briefing had been completed for those present. Jack was heading for the coffee cupboard when Mo, the civilian researcher, caught up with him. Even the small journey from her desk to where they both stood made her breathless and she stood for a moment trying to gather some control before she spoke. Jack waited patiently for her to say whatever it was she wanted to tell him. The woman could do with losing three or four stone to get down to a healthier weight, he reflected. There were biscuit crumbs stuck to her ample cleavage and Jack tried not to notice.

"What's up, Mo?"

"Christmas Day evening, late on," she panted, then carried on. "Traffic cops on the M25, Sussex. Stopped a van. Our van. Nothing inside. The driver wasn't Martin. He wasn't there. A man called Bernard, with no papers on him, and another guy, a passenger. The driver said he'd drop them into a station soon."

"Right," said Jack, waiting to see if there was any more. When it was clear she'd finished, he went on. "So, they let the van go?"

"Yes, no reason to hold it, or them. One thing, though. I spoke to the traffic officer. Says there were a couple of sets of vehicle reg plates sticking out from under the passenger seat. The men said they were off a couple of old vehicles back at home and that was the end of it. Unfortunately, the officer didn't make a note of the plate info. Shame, really." She was able to speak normally again now. "It was late. Shift was nearly over and they had nothing else to report, but I wondered."

"I see where you're going, Mo. You're thinking about the two burned-out vehicles that were at the house. The plates were off them. Shit! So close. Damn it!" shouted Jack, making the few in the room stop and turn their way. Mo's neck reddened for no reason other than the outburst from Jack.

"And no, there's no CCTV footage from that area that night. The cameras were off; there wasn't enough traffic to warrant them. When will the day come when they are on full time, eh?" Jack stood, thumb resting between his lips, thinking. "The area could fit too. They might have dropped little Kate off and carried on. Which part of the motorway were they stopped at?"

"Not far from the Horsham area, so West Sussex. She was East Sussex. Still would work, though."

"Right. See if any cameras were working, further along. We could do with a break, though I expect the van's long gone now. It's nearly twenty-four hours ago. If they've any sense, they'll have ditched it somewhere and burned it. Can you let the local police know to be on the lookout, or see if they've already found it and not realised we're after it?"

"Right, yes. I'll get on to it."

"And Mo?"

"Yes?"

"Good work. Thanks."

Mo's neck turned an even deeper shade of red.

He turned his focus back to making his mug of Nescafe and piled in a couple of sugars for good measure. Breakfast seemed like an age ago and the instant kick of caffeine and sugar would carry him through a while longer. A sausage sandwich would have been perfect right about now. He was about to return to his desk when the phone in his breast pocket rang, He jumped, slopping coffee over the rim of his mug and on to the stained carpet tiles below. He'd had the phone a while, but still, it gave him a fright when it went off. He cursed under his breath.

"DC Jack Rutherford."

"Jack, it's DS Mark Tomlinson here, Merevale Police up the road."

"Yes, hello. What can I do for you?"

"Well, we brought a young lady in for shoplifting earlier, and when we were processing her, we found your card in her pocket."

"Oh? What's the young lady's name?"

"It's Chloe Mathews, of no fixed address. I thought you might like to know, since she's dealt with you in the past."

The line was silent as Jack searched the memory banks in the back of his head for where he might have come across the girl.

"Right," he finally said, stumped. "Well, I can't think who she is. Has she asked for me at all?"

"No, just me thinking I should call you. Anyway, that's all I wanted."

Suddenly it dawned on him. "Chloe. Homeless, you say?"

"That's right."

"I'm on my way over for a chat. Make her a mug of tea, would you? And find her a couple of biscuits."

"Eh? She's been caught nicking sausage rolls, for heaven's sake."

"As a favour, then. Tea and biscuits. See you in a few minutes."

Jack smiled at the phone. She sounded like Billy's girl, all right, and just as cheeky.

Chapter Fifty-Eight

As Jack turned into the Merevale station yard, he wondered what this Chloe Mathews would be like, and how she'd got hold of his card. Yes, she was probably Billy's girlfriend, he thought. He pulled his jacket close, climbed out of the car and headed towards the back door as a bitter wind caught him around the ears. Maybe it was time to start wearing a woolly hat, he mused, like an old boy would. He pressed the buzzer and waited for the door to open then made his way in to meet DS Mark Tomlinson. Tomlinson met him halfway, striding towards him with an outstretched hand and a friendly smile.

"Nice to meet you, Jack."

"And you. Thanks for calling me. I think I know who she is now, though I was struggling to remember her right then and there. How's she doing, and what's happening?" he asked as they entered an empty interview room. It looked as comfortable as any other interview room up and down the country – made for criminal confession and not for comfort. Jack took one of the plastic chairs and sat awkwardly.

"She's been arrested before, but since she had your card, I figured you might like to know that there may another connection someplace. Shoplifters don't normally carry detectives' cards about their person – not in my experience, anyway." He smiled as he said it, and Jack warmed to the man. "She thanked you for the tea and biscuits, by the way."

It was Jack's turn to smile. "May I chat with her, off the record?"

"Be my guest."

"Where are you up to now with her? Has she been charged?"

"Yes. Had to."

"Right, yes. Okay, if I can see her that would be great."

"I'll bring her in. We won't be listening."

While Jack sat waiting, he wondered exactly what he was going to talk to her about. He only knew her through Billy, had never met her before now, and of course couldn't do a fat lot for her at this point since she'd already been charged. Figuring he'd work it out as he went, he turned as the door opened and a young woman walked in.

"I'll be outside if you need anything," Tomlinson said, and then he was gone.

Jack studied the girl until she sat down, her head falling forward, making it difficult to see much of her. What he could see of her face looked defeated. He waited, hoping she'd say something to kick the conversation off, but after a full minute, it was obvious that was going to be Jack's responsibility.

"I'm Jack. A sort of friend of Billy's. I'm assuming you're Billy's girl?" He kept his voice light, hoping to encourage her confidence in him. "What's your name?"

Silence.

"Look, I may be able to help here. I told Billy to call me if he was ever in trouble, and since he gave that card to you and you are right at this moment in trouble, well, why don't you help us both out?"

Quietly, she said, "I'm sorry for nicking the sausage rolls. I was hungry. And I thought Billy would like some for later. I hadn't enough money for them and the cola."

It was a start; the girl was speaking.

"I understand, Chloe," said Jack.

"Can you get me off, Jack? I didn't mean any harm." Her voice was barely audible; she still had not looked at him.

"It's difficult now you've been charged, but why don't you tell me the whole story and I'll put a word in for you." He waited for another beat before adding, "What have you got to lose?"

And so, still without raising her head, she told Jack the brief story of how a rotten day begging had ended her up at the police station, and how she'd been processed like a criminal for a few sausage rolls that had been stolen out of desperation, not malice. Had she had the money, she would have gladly paid for them. Stealing was wrong, she knew.

"What will happen to me now?" she asked, a tear dropping off the end of her nose onto the table in front of her. Idly, she placed a single finger over it and played with the tiny puddle. Jack felt his heart catch in his chest as he watched.

"Well, you will appear in court, and the judge will decide. I doubt you'll end up inside. Stealing sausage rolls does actually carry a six-month custodial sentence because the value of the item was under two hundred pounds, and of course, you'll carry a criminal record. Good job they weren't really expensive ones; that would have meant even more jail time. Even if you only get a caution from the police here, it's still a criminal conviction, which doesn't look good for your future. Employers hate criminal convictions."

"But if I get a caution, I won't go to court and people won't see me?" There was an ounce of hope in her voice.

"That's correct. You still have the conviction, but no court appearance." He narrowed his eyes, puzzled. So her need for privacy was more important than jail time. "Is that important to you, that you don't go to court? Does it have something to do with why you live as you do, with Billy? Maybe away from your parents?"

At the mention of her parents, the girl visibly recoiled, hugging her arms around her, and began to cry in earnest. So this was why she was living almost alone, away from home, Jack thought unhappily.

The girl had been abused.

Jack slipped her his handkerchief and she blew her nose.

"Hey, it'll be alright. Let me have a word, eh? But why don't you tell me a bit more about yourself, if you can?"

Chloe blew her nose and looked up at him quickly, then down again. "I'm from Manchester. My parents went to live in Scotland. I live with Billy in a garage on Pitt Road. That's all I can tell you."

At least it was something, Jack thought. She lifted her head now and looked him in the eye. He thought she looked familiar somehow but couldn't place why. He stood to leave.

"Look, I'll see if they are happy to caution you and leave it at that. Will that suit you?"

"Yes, thank you."

"I've not managed it yet so don't thank me quite yet, but I'll try. And if I do get them to agree, you can't go nicking stuff again or you will end up in custody next time. Do you understand me, Chloe?"

"Yes." She sounded brighter already, and he watched as she dried her eyes and handed him his handkerchief back.

"Sit tight. I'll be back in a minute."

As he walked in search of the DS, he tried again to figure out why Chloe Mathews looked so familiar.

Chapter Fifty-Nine

To Jack, it didn't seem fair that the young woman would do time for trying to feed herself and her boyfriend, and it appeared the powers that be agreed with him. So now she wouldn't have to. The DS had taken Jack's word for it that she wouldn't be shoplifting in the future, had learned her lesson – and Jack hoped she wouldn't let him down. He was on his way to see if he could find Billy, taking Chloe in the car with him for a lift back home. At least this way, they could pick him up too and Jack could check out where they were both living. He hoped Billy still had the picnic Janine had wrapped up for them both. It would make a nice surprise for the girl.

As he crossed town towards where she had suggested Billy was working, he reflected on why he was taking such an interest in the pair of them. He wanted to find out more, but was reluctant to pry. He also knew that excess interest on his part would look odd – Billy and Chloe would wonder why he wanted to know.

Chloe was gazing out the window in silence as they drove.

"So, you think he's on the high street, you say?" Jack asked, hoping to get the girl talking a bit more. "What's he wearing?"

"Same thing as every other day: jeans and a sweatshirt and his black parka." Jack knew what he was wearing. He'd seen him earlier but didn't let on.

"There he is," she said pointing across the street. Jack glanced across to confirm and quickly pulled into a space that wasn't really a parking space. Anyone else would have got a ticket. Chloe looked at him accusingly.

"Perks of the job. I'll only be a minute. Sit tight."

Chloe watched as he crossed the street heading towards Billy. When Billy saw him approach, he raised his hand to wave. Chloe couldn't help but smile, and she watched as a brief conversation took place and Billy collected his things together and picked up an odd-looking bag she didn't recognize. They both walked back to the car. Billy was smiling broadly as he clambered into the back seat.

"Hi, Chloe. Had a rough day, eh? I see you've met Jack, the friendly detective."

"Yes, I have. To both."

Jack and Billy exchanged a look in the rear-view mirror as if to say "Oooh, touchy," and smiled knowingly. They knew Chloe would come around later when she'd calmed down and stopped feeling so sorry for herself.

"I'm only giving you two kids a lift home before it gets much later. Thought you could do with a long chat together, or else I'm going to be in the poo if Chloe ends up back at a police station. Plus, it's cold as all hell now."

"We appreciate it, Jack. Thanks. Don't we Chloe?" Billy prodded her.

Chloe offered a begrudging "Yes, thanks." It was clearly going to take a while for her to thaw out and relax before their talk could begin. Jack turned up Pitt Street.

"What number?"

"Here's fine, thanks," said Billy, and Jack got the hint. No matter. He could find out which garage if he needed to. He could only see half a dozen in total. He pulled over and let them both out.

"Now remember, as much as I'd like to see you both again, let's not meet at a police station, eh?"

Billy saluted and Chloe kept her head hung low, and again Jack wondered what the girl was hiding. He watched them for a moment as they made their way down the pavement before he turned and headed back towards the station. At least he had a warm house to go home to later, and more than likely Janine would have cooked something hot to tuck into. He hoped it was a turkey supreme or a curry, and he hoped for a quiet night. After missing most of Christmas Day, he could do with a break, a quiet night in with Janine and whatever was on the TV. Perhaps they could watch the recording of *Morecambe and Wise*, and make a start on that box of Quality Street – yes, this sounded good. He was almost back at the station when his phone rang again.

"Oh, what now?" Scrambling before it rang off, he retrieved the phone from his inside pocket. "DC Jack Rutherford." He pulled into the curb.

"Jack, it's DS Julie Ford, Horsham, Sussex Police. Sorry to bother you on Boxing Day but thought you'd like to know."

"No problem. I appear to be working anyway." Jack could see his evening about to slip away into the distance like a twig on the surface of a river. "What do you have?"

"A young girl was found today by dog walkers, half buried in leaves and whatnot and barely alive. She's in the hospital here in Horsham, but she matches your description of a missing girl. Lesley Raby, possibly? She's heavily sedated but we could do with someone to tell us if it's her first off, then we can notify her parents. I'd hate to get their hopes up and drag them out here if it's not her. I'll fax you a photo over."

"How badly hurt is she?" Jack asked, with his eyes firmly shut in an effort to keep the barrage of horrible images out of his head.

"She's suffering from hypothermia; there's evidence of sexual abuse and she's pretty banged up. The doctors say they're hopeful she'll come round and make a full recovery, but they're keeping her sedated for now. She needs rest."

"Well, that's a good thing then. Poor kid. Fax it over. I'm nearly at the station now so I'll call you straight back."

In his heart, he already knew it was Lesley, and while it was a good thing she was alive, having seen little Kate and Leanne, he knew it would be a long journey to recovery for Lesley too.

Now all he had to do was figure out exactly what had happened and find the animals responsible before anyone else got hurt.

Chapter Sixty

With both Kate and Lesley now reunited with their parents and being cared for in hospital, things were looking up. Kate was still unable to talk about what had happened. The trauma of it all was too much for her to cope with, and a team of professionals were on standby to aid her recovery. It was going to be a long journey for her and her parents.

Lesley was also extremely lucky to be alive. By the time the dog walkers had found her and called the ambulance, it was estimated she'd only had a matter of hours left before her body would have finally given out. Luck had been on her side but, like Kate, she was unable to speak and give the police any information whatsoever. While it was frustrating that the culprits were still out there, more than likely getting out of town, there was nothing much the police could do. They really had nothing to go on.

Jack fixed himself another mug of coffee and headed to his desk. Surely SOCO had something by now from the burned-out building, something they could use. He dialled and waited. When he finally got through, there wasn't too much to tell.

"It's a bit early yet, Jack," Janice Coop told him. He'd met her at the burned-out house that night though he hadn't been able to talk with her for long; the call about Kate had come through. "As you can imagine, the fire being extinguished compromised the scene, as always happens with fires. It can't be helped. But we did manage to get some items of interest. We're waiting for results on them."

"Anything you can tell me you're working on?"

"Two main things – prints and DNA. I reckon we'll be extremely lucky to find any of either with the amount of soot and water and ash. But we did find what looks like a piece of gum. Now while I don't expect any usable DNA to be left on it now, there is an interesting imprint on the surface. Can't say much more except it will be processed soon and I'll let you know. The condoms we found in the bins outside again should tell us something. There were also a couple caught in the toilet drain, but I'm not optimistic that we'll get anything useful from them. They may have been flushed clean over time. We'll see, though."

"And the body. What does the pathologist say? Have you heard?"

"No, you'd need to speak to her on that."

"Right. Yes, of course. Keep me posted, won't you? Those three girls need some good news."

"Will do. And Jack?"

"Yes?"

"Get the animals that did this, won't you? My niece is the same age as little Kate and I couldn't repeat what I'd do to those men if it was her in a hospital bed."

"Oh, I intend to, Janice. You mark my words."

Eddie approached his desk as he was hanging up. Jack figured he must have had a guilty conscience and decided to check in and do some work. He'd probably heard down the pub that Jack had missed most of his own Christmas. The smell of stale whiskey wafted into his airspace, and Jack held his breath for a moment. Eddie slapped his back like an old chum, or someone pretending to be one.

"What about the starting line-up for Chelsea then, Jack? Not a single British player amongst them in a Premier League side. What is the world coming to? Wish I'd been at The Dell to see it."

"I've not been to a game in a long while. Don't seem to get the time," Jack said pointedly. "I always enjoyed a bag of chips afterwards. Used to go with my dad. He was a Red Devils fan, and Manchester isn't exactly local. I hear it worked out for Chelsea, though. Maybe they could spread some luck on our case."

"Well, I've just heard back about the body in the burned-out house. Seems it is a male, and by the age and height, it could be our Martin Coffey, though we're still waiting for confirmation from the pathologist. Bloke was almost burned to a crisp. Did you see it?"

Biting back his distaste, Jack ignored the question. "Well, if it is him, that's both good and bad. It leaves us sod-all now if he's gone. All we had on him was a van, and the traffic cops let that drive off with two blokes in it. Numpty lot. Probably wanted their Christmas pies at the end of their shift and couldn't be arsed doing anything useful about it."

"That may be so. The van was empty. But it's not over yet. There's no fat lady singing in my ears." Eddie was doing his best to sound positive, because it was obvious Jack wasn't.

"No. I suppose not."

"Well, then. That van might still be out there. All three girls are back to safety, albeit in hospital. Our wanted man is possibly dead, and we know there were two men in that van when it was pulled over. But we should get some DNA evidence from the house, so even if we get a match there, we have someone to talk to. So there's still plenty to go on, Jack. Plenty." He slapped Jack's back again making him lurch forward slightly.

"Now why don't you go round to Leanne's house and see if she's up for a few more questions? Something may have jogged her memory since you saw her yesterday. Then go home, get some rest. You look like you need it. Tomorrow, we'll both go over and see Lesley in the hospital. She may be awake and talking."

While Jack hoped so, he didn't fancy their chances. And he certainly didn't fancy taking Eddie with him. The man was like a bull in a china shop.

Chapter Sixty-One

It was almost dark when he pulled up outside the Meadows' place on Cedar Road. A creamy glow emanated through the net curtains from a lamp in the front room. Jack glanced up at the upstairs window above it and noted it was in darkness. But that wasn't unusual in this style of house. It was more than likely the parents' room; the children's rooms were usually at the back of the house. He wondered if Leanne was awake and ready to chat some more, preferably without either Mr or Mrs present. If something had gone on in that house that Leanne didn't want them to know about, she certainly wouldn't say so in front of them. Right now, Jack needed every morsel of information there was to have. He was about to push the buzzer when the door opened. Someone must have seen him arrive.

"Hello, Detective," Penny Meadows said politely. She sounded a good deal cheerier than the last time he'd seen her. "Come on in."

"It's good to see you looking happier," he commented as he stepped into the hallway.

"It's so good to have my baby back home. I can't thank you enough, Jack."

"Well, I'm glad she's back and in one piece. It's what we always hope will happen. And the best Christmas present for you all, being back together. How's she doing?"

"Really good. No real injuries, thank goodness, but some emotional scars to contend with, I expect. But one day at a time. She'll be back on her cycle before we know it. Would you like to pop up and see her?"

"If I may, thanks. You may have heard we have the other two girls from the house. They weren't quite as lucky as Leanne, but they're recovering well in hospital."

"Well, that's good news, then. I'm glad their parents have them back with them. These last few days have been the hardest days of my life. I wouldn't wish them on my worst enemy, I can tell you. But you didn't come to listen to me prattling on. Go on up. She's awake. First door on the right at the top." And with a flick of her hand, she encouraged him towards the staircase while she made her own way back towards the kitchen.

Jack detected the warm, comforting smell of something sweet baking in the oven, a cake maybe. He could hear the low murmur of a TV as he approached Leanne's room at the back. The door was partly open, and a pink china nameplate was stuck to the outside of it; it read 'Leanne's Room.' He knocked lightly on the frame so as not to make her jump and smiled her way. She was sat up in bed, her blond hair looking darker as it fell around her shoulders. She looked somewhat different from the photo they'd pinned up on the board back at the squad room.

"Hello, Detective." She managed a smile. "Come on in." The room was pink, but not chintzy. At fifteen, she'd gone for a more modern twist on her room décor; miniature bicycles were dotted here and there on various surfaces, as well as paraphernalia from famous cycle races gone by. There was a pink cycling jersey in a frame hung on the wall, and Jack ventured closer for a better look. It was signed with a black squiggle from a marker pen.

"It's the Giro d'Italia shirt, signed by Gotti himself after winning the 1997 Tour, though it's only a replica. I won it at an event last year," Leanne offered.

Jack searched for something light-hearted to say in return, keep her chatting. "Gotti, eh? He doesn't sound like he's from around these parts – south London, I mean. Where's he from, then? Up north?"

She laughed at his naivety. "He's Italian, actually. Won it a couple of times. But you're right to an extent. He's from up north, but the north of Italy, not the UK."

This seemed to brighten her up, anyway; she was clearly happy to talk cycling with anyone who took an interest.

"Will you compete in the Tour one day?" he enquired, glancing at the framed photos of Leanne on her bike. In some, she wore medals around her neck.

"Doubt it. You have to be male, for starters, and a pro rider, so I'm out on both fronts. And I suspect you didn't want to look at my room, Detective. What do you want to ask me about?"

Jack grinned at her, "Well, if you don't make it as a pro cyclist, perhaps think of becoming a detective eh?" He pulled up a chair that was by her bed and sat down. "First, I wanted to check how you are doing, and I see you're well on the mend, sharp as a paper cutter, in fact. And second, the mind is a funny thing, and I wanted to give you the opportunity to tell me if anything else has surfaced about your ordeal since we last spoke. A smell perhaps, or the faint sound of something – anything at all. Anything."

He let the silence stretch for a minute without filling it himself, hoping she was regurgitating something from her own files in the back of her head. This tactic usually worked, and he waited patiently for her to speak. He tried not to look at her too intently while her brain was hard at work; instead, he returned his attention to some of the photos dotted about her room. In them, her summer tan, natural smile and almost golden hair made her look like a young actress from the seventies. The Americans would have called her an 'all-American girl.'

"Have you found the others yet? Lesley and Kate?" she asked instead.

"We have, yes. They are both in hospital, though they will need a little more recovery before they will be allowed home yet. But they are safe now, in good hands."

Leanne nodded her approval. "I'm glad. Poor things. Were they found nearby where I was, or at the house?"

"Neither, actually. But I can't tell you much more than that for the time being."

"And what about the third one, the young woman? The woman that gave me the spoon? Have you found her yet?"

Jack blinked. With everything that had happened in the last 48 hours, he'd not given the woman another thought since Leanne had mentioned her back in the hospital. How the hell had that happened? "We haven't found her as yet, no. Can you tell me about her again? There may be something new you remember."

"There's very little to tell, but I'll try."

Obligingly, Leanne went through all she knew about the other young woman, Jack making notes as she spoke. By the time they'd finished and he looked up from his pad, Leanne looked like she'd gone backwards a little; the memory of her ordeal was clearly a little too painful for her to relive yet again. Her head was bowed and she seemed to be struggling not to cry. He turned to see Penny Meadows watching at the door.

"I think it's time for you to go, Detective." Her voice had lost its friendly tone. He nodded; there was no point asking Leanne anything further. He stood and said his thanks and goodbyes, and wished Leanne a speedy recovery. He was halfway down the stairs when he saw Dave Meadows at the bottom, about to climb them himself. He let Jack descend and said hello as he arrived at the bottom. He was chewing something, wincing slightly as his jaws moved.

"Tooth still bugging you, Mr Meadows?" Jack asked brightly.

"I really should go back to the dentist and get it re-filled. Hurts like hell."

"They should all be back to work now Christmas is over. I'll see myself out," he called as he vanished through the front door.

Back in the peacefulness of his car, he sat there thinking about the third missing girl and recalling Leanne's face as she spoke. It reminded him of something. Or someone.

Where had he seen that look before, he wondered?

Chapter Sixty-Two

Eddie was back at the helm again, and much of the team had returned from holidays. This was a welcome change from the smattering of resources over recent days. Jack was glad things were returning back to normal. He felt like he'd been running the show on his own. When he'd grumbled about it to Janine, she'd told him it was because he had been, then pecked him on his cheek as a sign to get out the door and solve the damn case.

While Eddie made a start now, Jack smiled to himself about his wife. Not many coppers had a marriage as good as his, a woman as understanding as his. It made all the difference. He scanned the faces around the room, watching their body language, their facial expressions, their interest, and was glad to see the focus they showed after the brief holiday break – a break Jack was still to get in. Movement in the corner of his eye made him turn his head. DI Morton entered the room behind him and stood with his arms crossed.

"And of course," said Eddie, "we believe there is still one girl, said to be around eighteen years old, out there somewhere. From how Lesley and Kate were found, she is more than likely bound, gagged and with a pillowcase or similar over her head." He pointed to the map, which was dotted with red pins. "These pins indicate where the three girls we've found so far were located. As you can see, they were all not far from the M25 in an area that stretches east and west of it." He pointed to the house's location. "If Leanne was found here after escaping on foot, and the house was here, and the other two were here and here, it seems reasonable to assume the other girl will also likely be around here." He was pointing to a wide area southwest of London. "And since the van we'd been looking for was stopped here," pointing to a blue pin at Cobham, "we again can assume she could be around this area here."

While it was still a huge area, at least it had been narrowed down by the position of the empty van. "I know," he went on, "that she could be anywhere, and since nobody has reported seeing her, that's not good. It's been as cold as hell. We were lucky to find Lesley alive, so let's pull out all the stops and bring this girl home too.

"Jack, I'll leave you to organize liaising with the local stations out there. Do what you need to do and delegate accordingly. Mo, get on to what CCTV there is available. You may have to use the private feeds from businesses nearby; petrol stations are a good start. Get Clarke to give you a hand. Tell Jack what else you need, manpower-wise."

Jack watched as the poor woman turned scarlet again at being singled out in front of the rest of the team. Even a positive mention seemed to embarrass her.

"Right, that's it then," Eddie concluded. "Get to work."

Jack felt Morton shuffle off from behind him and, yet again, felt like he himself was the single driving force for the investigation. It was beginning to bug him. Eddie slapped him on the shoulder as he walked past on his way to the coffee cupboard. That was beginning to bug him, too. He followed him in.

"And what will you and Morton be doing while Mo and Clarke are sifting through footage and I'm liaising with the locals, eh?"

Jack's tone was civil, but there was no mistaking his meaning. Eddie picked up on it at once.

"Hey, hey, Jack – why the aggression? What's bugging you?"

"I'm not being aggressive, but I am feeling a bit alone in all this. And since you ask what's bugging me, you are actually, Eddie, as is Morton." Exhaustion and frustration, mixed with the sense that no one else seemed to give a damn about the fourth missing woman, were knocking the lid off his temper. Raising his eyebrows, Eddie closed the door to the coffee cupboard. The air smelled of the remains of a greasy bacon sandwich and cheap instant coffee.

"Come on, Jack. Spit it out."

"You and Morton. You're supposed to be leading this thing, but it's been me running about all Christmas. Seems like both of you went to ground, and there's been no sign of any real help from either of you. There's still at least one girl out there. There could be more; we don't know. But you need to take charge, Eddie, as does Morton. It's not up to me to do all this."

Jack waved his arms out to emphasize the enormity of it, sending a packet of biscuits flying across the small space. It hit the opposite wall and fell to the floor with a crinkly thump. Normally, Jack would have made a joke about it, but he wasn't in the mood for frivolity this morning.

He picked up his coffee mug and left Eddie open-mouthed in the coffee cupboard.

It was almost 6 pm when Jack finally had something to report back on, though there was nobody around to actually report it to. A young woman's body had been found floating in a pond. She was bound and gagged as the others had been, and had been dead for several days. A fisherman had called the Elmbridge police and reported his horrific find. She matched the description of the fourth woman in almost every way; it had to be her.

Eddie had been right about the location. It was moments away from where the van had been stopped on Christmas Eve. If only those traffic cops had been a few minutes earlier in pulling the van over, thought Jack bitterly, she may have been somewhere safe for Christmas.

Instead, she was lying in a fridge the morgue.

Chapter Sixty-Three

❦

Jack arranged to meet the local DI at Epsom the following morning and go over the links to the case. The girl was already dead, he reasoned unhappily, and zooming off to Epsom during rush hour was not going to bring her back. He read over the information he'd received so far. The woman's body was badly bloated from her time in the freezing water, and was wearing a sparse amount of clothing like the others had been. The initial findings indicated she had drowned; her hands had been bound and she had been unable to save herself. Whether she'd fallen in or had been thrown in, they couldn't say, not until the pathologist had finished. They'd know more by the time he arrived there the following day.

With a heavy sigh, Jack retrieved his coat and headed home.

"I'm home, love." Seeing his drained face, Janine collected his coat from him and guided him to his chair in the lounge, where a bottle of beer stood waiting for him on a side table.

"Sit," she instructed. "Dinner won't be long, so enjoy your beer and try to unwind a little. Then we can talk when you've eaten, if you wish."

She wore her no-nonsense smile as she spoke, and Jack was reminded again how much he loved the woman he shared a home with. She left him sat contemplating and busied herself back in the kitchen. Jack was grateful she gave him space when he got like this, got so involved in a case that it consumed every ounce of his energy, leaving nothing behind. But they both knew it never lasted for long. Cases got solved, or closed, or moved, and something else took their place. There was always another set of victims or culprits waiting around the corner.

The beer began to soothe his nerves, and after a while Janine came in to fetch him. Together, they sat down to enjoy the last of the turkey that Janine had made into a pie, along with Christmas ham and leeks from the garden, all topped off with a crust. She'd even put a couple of pastry leaves on top. The pie was deep golden in colour from the egg wash, and looked and smelled magnificent.

"My god, Janine, that's a work of art. It's almost a shame to eat it." He peered closer as Janine took his plate and cut into the pie; creamy sauce oozed out like a pale landslide moving slowly over the cut leeks. Steam drifted upwards. She handed him the plate back and he helped himself to mash and mixed veg with an extra helping of sauce from a jug. When she'd served her own, they ate in silence for a couple of minutes. Jack would speak about what was on his mind when he was good and ready, she knew; they'd stick to more mundane topics, in the meantime. It was nearly the end of their meal before he spoke about what was niggling him.

"I had words with Eddie today," he started. "Told him I was sick of doing it all on my own and that he and Morton needed to give the team more of their attention and resources. I ended up smacking a packet of biscuits up the wall. Better than smacking him I suppose, that wouldn't have done me any good."

They both sat quietly for a moment digesting what he'd said.

Then Janine said, "Did they break?"

"Eh?"

"Did the biscuits break?" Janine was smiling, knowing the worst was over for him now and normal service would resume shortly. He couldn't help but smile back and, feeling more relaxed and rested than he had for days, picked their empty plates up and took them through to the kitchen. There was a trifle sitting on the kitchen side.

"You really have been busy," he called back, but Janine was already standing behind him.

"I'll bring us a bowl each. Go and sit down."

And so he did, and when he'd devoured the sherry trifle on top of the pie, he'd almost forgotten he'd missed Christmas at all. An hour later, he was sound asleep in his chair in the lounge while Janine cleared away in the kitchen.

Somehow later that evening, he'd got into bed, and it was nearly 7 am when he finally awoke to the sound of Terry Wogan chatting quietly to his audience across the length and breadth of the UK. The pips signalled the time on the hour, and he sat bolt upright with a start. Next to him, Janine stirred slightly at his sudden movement, then rolled over on her side without saying a word. Jack rubbed his hands over his face before flinging the quilt back and heading to the bathroom. The previous evening was a complete blank, save for the pie and trifle.

He slipped inside the shower curtain and turned the taps on, and waited until the water ran through warm. As steam started to fill the small room, he stood underneath the jets, the warm needles of water feeling therapeutic on his head and shoulders as he lathered shampoo onto his head. The sleep and the meal had done him a world of good, as had unloading his day on Janine, though he'd only told her about his lazy colleagues. There was never any need to bore or burden her with case details. It wasn't necessary. With the fragrance of a pine forest filling his nostrils, he dried off, quickly dressed and headed downstairs to make Janine a cup of tea before heading out. He was almost done when he heard the phone in the hall ring and hurried to grab it before it rang off.

"Jack Rutherford."

"Jack, it's Pete Abbott here, on the desk. I've got a message for you."

"Yes, Pete. Good news, I hope?"

"Well, that depends on who you are and what your view is, I

guess. We now have DNA confirmation that the body in the burned-out house over at Swanley was that of Martin Coffey."

Jack let the news sink in a moment. "Thanks, Pete. Yes, good and bad, indeed. Is Eddie aware?"

"Not managed to get him."

Why bother asking?

Hanging up, he reflected on what the news really did mean. If Coffey had been involved in a sexual abuse ring of some sort, the world was better off with him dead. But that left them with yet another piece of the puzzle: what kind of horrors had been going on in that house?

They needed more, so much more. Maybe the day ahead would bring them something useful. He could only hope.

Chapter Sixty-Four

Jack had arranged to meet the local Cobham police sergeant at Epsom morgue, where their assumed latest victim had been taken after being found in the pond. It wasn't a long drive down, only fifty minutes or so in easy traffic, and Jack made use of the time on his own to reflect on the task ahead while listening to some music. Never a Spice Girls fan, he enjoyed the rougher sounds of mainly male rock and roll, namely his beloved ELO. He pushed the start button on the CD player and waited to be transported to another place while he drove. "Last Train to London" spilled into the car, and he sang along in an attempt to make the task ahead more bearable, moving his head from side to side in time with the music, strumming his hands on the steering wheel, his imaginary drum kit. He'd been to many of their concerts and enjoyed the peace and energy the band gave him, particularly when he needed to think. Next up came "Mr Blue Sky," and he let the words roll over him like a therapeutic massage. He knew every word by heart, and warbled away happily as he made his way down the A232 towards the hospital.

A mobile food van came into view and, checking his watch, he decided there was time for a quick bacon butty. If he was going to do a spot of thinking; he could chew at the same time. The food van looked like any other roadside convenience. A queue of four people waited to place their orders, attesting to the quality of the food. He indicated left and pulled into the layby.

Ten minutes later, he was back on his way towards the hospital at Epsom, one hand on the steering wheel, the other nursing his sandwich, and "Mr Blue Sky" on repeat play for his thinking time. He sang along to the words between bites, his mind working over the lyrics.

Please tell us why ...

You had to hide away for so long ...

Thoughts of the girl he was about to meet, though in death rather than in real life, filled in within the words of his private concert, the faces of the band members clear in his head as they sang and posed the question to only Jack.

Tell us why ...

Why had she died? What had been going on in that house? And why had she helped Leanne escape but not escaped herself?

You had to hide away for so long ...

Where had she been hiding? And how had she become embroiled in whatever it was? She was only a young woman herself, not much older than Leanne. He wondered where she was missing from. Leanne had said she'd sounded foreign, so maybe from somewhere across the eastern bloc. Maybe she was Polish, or Albanian even. She'd had a look about her, Leanne said, and had told him it wasn't French or Italian or Greek even. Her colouring had been all wrong. In another few minutes, he'd see for himself, though the fact that she'd been in the old quarry pond for so long meant the colour of her flesh would have altered dramatically. In cases such as this, it was hard for even parents to identify their own children.

Jack entered the hospital building and followed the signs to the morgue where he was due to meet both the pathologist and the local DI. Had the young woman died before she'd been thrown into the water, he wondered, or had she drowned? Because if she'd already been dead, that added a new dimension to the case – two dead bodies under suspicious circumstances. If she'd been alive when she'd entered the water, that meant she could have fallen in herself. He wasn't thinking suicide, though he wasn't ruling it out either.

He entered the office space and the clock on the wall told him he was bang on time. Two men turned his way at the sound of his shoes on the tiled floor. Jack assumed one was the local DI and the other, the smaller man in surgical scrubs, was the pathologist. He introduced himself.

"DC Jack Rutherford, Croydon," he announced with an outstretched hand. The taller man, about Jack's age, stepped forward.

"DI Peter Woodhouse. Good to meet you, Jack." Standing back a pace, he introduced the smaller man, who Jack thought looked a little like a mad professor, thinning grey hair standing up on end like he'd had an electric shock. The man could have only been about five feet tall in his shoes. "And this is Dr Charles Winstanley," Woodhouse said. The second man stepped forward slightly and shook Jack's hand.

"Any relation to Dr Barbara Winstanley, by chance?" Jack asked.

"My daughter, Detective." Winstanley's smile was gentle and his eyes glinted at the mention of her name. He was obviously a proud father. "And Stanley, my son, is almost a pathologist. He will graduate later this year. You know Barbara, then?"

Stanley Winstanley, Jack thought, trying to keep the smile from his face. It was almost child abuse.

"Yes," he replied. "She's been helping me on another case with a DNA puzzle – which reminds me: I should give her a call. With all that's been going on and Christmas coming at the same time, it's been on the back burner a little. Missing girls and dead bodies take precedence over most other cases." Jack hadn't given a great deal of thought to Mary. He'd hardly had a moment to himself of recent, but he made a mental note to call Barbara and follow up.

Pleasantries over, the doctor suggested they get to it, and both detectives followed him through the swing doors to a smaller room where a sheet-covered body lay on a gurney, only its face exposed. As Jack approached, he could see the brown straggly hair that would have fallen to her shoulders, a pale and rather thin face pointing straight up towards the bright lights of the room, eyes closed. The water had done its worst to her skin, and he closed his eyes for a moment out of respect. The young woman laid out in front of him was indeed young; her thin frame looked more like a twelve-year-old's. It never got any easier seeing a body in this condition, and Jack only hoped she hadn't suffered in death.

"Did she definitely drown, then?"

"I'm afraid she did," said Dr Winstanley. "Her lungs were nearly double in size. We usually see that with a freshwater drowning, and there are traces of pond vegetation in her airways. She has bruising to most of her body, some old, some more recent. Both arms have also been broken in the past and healed again; I'd say within the last five years. I'd estimate her age to be around eighteen."

Jack closed his eyes again to shake the images of her abuse from his mind, but it didn't work.

DI Woodhouse took over now, with a question of his own.

"Do you think her death was deliberate, or could this be an accident? Did she fall in, for example?"

"Given she was bound and gagged, I'd say this wasn't an accident on her part. What I can't tell you is whether someone placed her at the pond knowing she'd fall in, or whether she made her way there of her own accord. Her feet are badly cut up, so she'd walked barefoot over rough terrain for some time, but again, she could have been going around in circles without realizing it, only to end up falling in."

Both detectives were now looking at the young woman's face, deep in thought. Neither said a word.

"I did find something of interest for you both, though, something I've never seen in all my years of working with the dead."

"Oh?" they responded in unison.

"It was inside her stomach, actually, along with the meagre

remains of her breakfast cereal. And I found a similar example tucked into the cuff of her track bottoms."

Jack looked at Woodhouse and they both followed Winstanley over to a table where he had set out his findings in plastic evidence bags.

The first bag contained small pieces of paper that had been reconstructed, like a puzzle, back into a single piece. On it were several words written in what looked like blue pen. In the second bag were the remains of what appeared to be cardboard from a cereal box, again with words written on them in blue pen.

"I'd say she was trying to send a message," said Winstanley.

"Holy shit," Jack exclaimed.

Chapter Sixty-Five

Hey you, pretty face...

"Is that what I think it is?" asked Jack incredulously.

"It is, or so I believe," said Woodhouse. "Though it's going to need some work, it's definitely a list of names."

Both men looked at each other as if the answer, the confirmation they needed, was written on the other man's face.

Inside the simple plastic bag Woodhouse was holding was a list written in blue pen, but what did the list refer to? Customers? A business network? Victims, even? There were large parts missing where the ink had soaked away, as well as gaps where sections of paper were missing, but there were the bones to work with. The machine printing on the reverse of the paper in the first bag looked like a flyer of some sort.

Jack had the other evidence bag in his hand, containing the cardboard from her tracksuit bottoms.

"And I'd say this is a duplicate, looking at the bits still visible."

"Looks like we have a puzzle to do," Woodhouse announced. "I take it you have copies of this for us, Doc?"

"Of course. From my observation, if I may?" he enquired.

"Please do," encouraged Jack.

"She must have known she was going to die to have done this. Something happened for her to do this only once, because there were no older particles of paper in her system. They were all from this one ingestion. If she'd done it repeatedly – say, in the hope of one day getting this information, whatever it relates to, out in the open – there'd be more. My guess is something went down to encourage her to do this. She was a smart girl to hide whatever it is in this way. It can't have been easy. And having a duplicate could have put her life in danger. She was extremely brave."

Her life had been in grave danger anyway, it seemed, but Jack kept it to himself. He was thankful for her efforts.

"How long ago would you estimate that she went into the water?"

"Two days; three absolute tops."

Jack reasoned that would tie in nicely with the events of Christmas Eve, the house fire and Leanne escaping. All hell must have broken loose and, somehow, this clever and no doubt terrified girl had managed to leave them something to work with in her death. Jack walked back across to where she was lying. The two other two men joined him.

"You said she'd had both arms broken in the past. How about sexual activity?"

"I'm afraid there's been plenty, and for some years."

"Any clue as to who she is? We have reason to think she wasn't from the UK. One of the victims told me she had an accent, so she may have been from somewhere in Eastern Europe."

"There was nothing on her to indicate who she is, and no DNA match in the system. Dental is no use unless she matches a missing person's listing. We may never know her identity," Dr Winstanley said gravely.

Jack let the words sink in. Another lost soul, name unknown, life extinguished. Someone's daughter. Mary flashed into his mind for the second time that day. He needed to focus on her again as soon as he could and help get her young life back together before she too became a lost soul.

DI Woodhouse broke into his thoughts. "Do you think this young woman is part of your case, then, Jack?"

"I do. It's too much of a coincidence. I'm loath to show her photograph to my only witness, a girl a handful of years younger, but I may have to take that chance. I've no other way. And if that list we have is customers or the perpetrators, I want to find every one of them. And damn soon."

"Need some help?"

Jack knew the man didn't have to offer; resources were always tight in every force. "I'd appreciate that, thank you. Yes."

"Right, then. Well, if we've done here, why don't we head off for some lunch and you can fill me in with what you know so far. Then we'll head back to the station and see what we can put together. The sooner we can fill in some of those names, the sooner we can start looking into them and see where they fit into this mess."

Back outside in the cold fresh air, DI Peter Woodhouse steered them in the direction of the town centre. Jack was glad he'd kept his jacket with him and not left it in the car.

"So, I'm wondering," Woodhouse asked, "if you were in the young girl's shoes and being held against your will at that house, what list would you make to help the police after your death? What would be the most valuable information you could share?"

"Well, the most valuable would be the ringleaders, the organisers. But let me ask you a question. Which list would she *know* about? How would she know either category's names? That makes me wonder if she knew the *customers'* names, those who desired what the house was peddling, took part in what went on in those rooms?"

"I get you. Though I'm wondering how she could have, unless they're well known, of course, like off the TV or something."

Jack didn't fancy the idea.

"It would be too risky to check wallets, but credit card transactions?" Jack inquired.

"Now that's a thought. Would they be stupid enough? Cash surely."

"You'd think so, but it's worth a try. It's the stupid things that get people caught, right?"

"Indeed."

They turned off the main road and down a narrow alleyway.

"It's only a short walk from here," Woodhouse told him. "I expect you like curry?"

"Fine by me."

"I know a place that does a great lunchtime buffet, quick and cheap. Then we'll look at those names. A bit of digging and I reckon we'll have something to work with."

"I damn well hope so. With our prime suspect burned and crispy like a lamb tikka, and a young woman trying to talk to us from the grave, a real live interview with someone on that list would make my week."

"Then let's make your week." Woodhouse opened the door, and they went inside. The aromatic smell of curry and garlic was pleasant and warming to their nostrils after the chill of the morgue.

When they were seated, Woodhouse turned to Jack with a grin and said what Jack had been thinking earlier: "Stanley Winstanley? What a terrible thing to do to a kid. I can only imagine the poor child's nickname – Stanley Stanley."

"Like New York, eh? So good they named it twice."

Chapter Sixty-Six

Lunch had been a welcome change, and both men sat nursing bellies full of spicy chicken tikka and naan bread. Woodhouse had had a pint, but Jack had stuck to water. With a drive back and plenty to think about, he wanted his wits about him. Having seen firsthand the horror the victims had gone through, it was high time the culprits were brought to justice, both the ringleaders and those who had frequented the house – they were all guilty.

Jack sorted the bill out – it was the least he could do after Woodhouse's offer of resources – and they walked back to the station together. They'd spent their lunch hour filling in some of the more obvious blanks, but many gaps remained. They had decided to work on one puzzle each and see what they could find out with the few scant letters that were still visible. They would also give copies of both puzzles to their teams to take a shot at. The more brains working on this the better. It reminded Jack of the Zodiac murders in the US, where the police had asked for the public's help to solve the puzzle the perpetrator had left them by printing it in the newspaper. It was a shame they couldn't get the list of names printed in the same way. Now that would be a triumph for any paper, though a right royal lawsuit in the making if they exposed those names, not to mention the vigilante spinoff.

While he was a decent detective, puzzles were too frustrating for him to tackle as a hobby after he'd been working a case all day – he preferred to rest his brain to music, thank you very much.

Hey you, pretty face…

He didn't doubt that the young woman in the morgue had once had a pretty face before she'd died in the freezing pond water.

It was nearly 2 pm already and even at this hour, the sky seemed to be closing in, losing its energy like a dimmer switch was slowly turning the light down to nothing. In another couple of hours or so, it would be fully dark. He'd be late home again. He needed to let Janine know but he'd call later. He was keen to get a move on with the local resources before they were turned off.

Jack was making his way with Woodhouse to the side entrance when his phone rang, making him jump. Woodhouse smiled at his reaction as he walked.

"I'll never get used to it. Makes me jump every damn time," he moaned as he went to answer it. "Jack Rutherford."

"Jack, it's Eddie. I've news on the van. It's been found abandoned near Waterloo station."

"Empty?"

"Yes, but SOCO are heading out there now to see what they can gather. My guess is the driver got on a train somewhere. We're checking the CCTV that's available, but since it was down a side street, I don't hold out much hope. I'll keep you posted. Where are you?"

"I'm in Epsom. I've been to the morgue to look at the young female victim from the pond. Looks like she was one smart girl. She somehow swallowed a list of what looks like names, and the pathologist found the remains of it in her stomach contents, along with another list in the cuff of her track suit bottoms."

"Whoa!"

"We're thinking a list of customers rather than culprits, maybe off credit cards?"

"Who's we?"

"The local DI, Peter Woodhouse, met me there. I'm back at his station now to make a start, see what we can decipher, then I'll head back with the rest. I reckon Mo could be the right person for this. I'm pretty sure she's a puzzle master."

"Right. Okay. Look, I'll let you know what forensics come up with, whenever that might be. See you later, then."

As Jack hung up, he thought about the van and its driver. Waterloo. That meant trains to the south, to start with. It also meant trains to the continent, to France. And from France, Europe was practically borderless. The perpetrator could go undetected almost anywhere, and that gave Jack and his team a problem all in itself. Sure, there was Interpol, but without a name or a photo they were no use at all.

Names. They needed names.

"News?" Woodhouse asked, breaking into his thoughts.

"Oh, kind of. The van we think the girls were moved in has been found dumped. Looks like our driver could have left the country. It was near Waterloo." Jack rubbed his face with both hands, feeling his energy levels dimming like the daylight around him, and wished he was closer to home than he was. But more than that, he wished he had an answer for the poor young woman in the folder he had under his arm.

Names. We need names.

"Come on, let's get this show on the road, then, see how far we can get. SOCO will find something for you to go on, because my bet is this outfit are a stupid lot. They're bound to have screwed up inside the van. From what you've told me so far, they could be sat around at their mums' now, sipping tea and eating ginger-nuts, and not on a train to anywhere. The job now is to find the names of these two men, and fill in the blanks on this list, of course." Woodhouse smiled as if it would be the simplest task in the entire world.

They both knew it would be anything but.

Chapter Sixty-Seven

By the time Jack had set off for home, rush hour was well under way, and he inched his way forward to insert himself into the traffic headed north. It was going to be a slow journey home. His eyes stung from staring at the computer screens and the photocopied puzzles, but their efforts had been fruitful: they now had a partial list of names with only a handful still to be filled in. It seemed the names belonged to customers: none of them had matched names in their database in connection with other sex-related cases. With hundreds of people with the same name, it could be a slow job tracking down the right ones, but not impossible. At least with a crossword, you knew how many letters you were searching for to complete the word.

He glanced across to the passenger seat, where her lifeless face stared back at him from a glossy 10x8 print. Her mousy hair fell in lank strands, fine like a baby's, and there were dark circles under each eye. She looked tired. Had she looked so tired in life, too? What had her role been in all this, and what was her name? She needed a name.

He dialled Eddie to tell him how they'd fared and get an update at his end. It went straight to voicemail – no surprises there. He dialled the station and was put through to the only person in the squad room – Mo.

"Where is everyone, Mo?" He could almost sense her turning red at his question.

"Gone home, I expect."

"So why haven't you?" He regretted the question as soon as he'd asked it, suspecting he already knew the answer. He felt foolish. And a bit sad. But if he retracted it with an apology, he'd only draw attention to his faux pas. Best leave it be. An empty silence filled the car while Mo must have been thinking about an answer. Finally, she spoke.

"Thought I'd try and find the poor girl in Epsom morgue, her real name. No one deserves to be nameless. It's bad enough she was disposed of like that."

Jack pressed his eyes shut for a second, long enough to feel the pleasure of the pressure but not long enough to run into the back of the vehicle in front of him.

"And how did you fare?"

"I have twenty-seven missing girls' descriptions to choose from." There was satisfaction in her voice.

"That's wonderful news, Mo. Can you get the details down to the morgue, to Dr Charles Winstanley? Apparently, the girl he has there has had both arms broken in the past, and of course there's dental to look at, so with twenty-seven possible names, this will make it a whole lot easier, not to mention quicker. Good work, Mo. Thanks."

"I will," said Mo after a pause, during which Jack could almost hear her blushing. "Is this doctor any relation to Dr Barbara Winstanley, by any chance?"

"Yes, he's her father. Oh – one more thing before I go, Mo. Any news on those VINs? Those two vehicles at the house have to have belonged to someone, though I'm betting they were stolen, which would be another dead end."

"I'll chase them up in the morning. They'll all have gone home too, I expect. I'll keep you informed."

The traffic in front of him was starting to speed up and thin out a little, requiring him to put both hands on the wheel and get rid of his phone.

"Thanks. Right, I'd better concentrate now and drive. See you tomorrow."

He hung up and pressed the on/off button on the stereo system, and ELO once more filled the car. While Jack didn't bother to sing along this time, he listened to the words he knew so well. If the group ever needed a replacement singer at a concert one night, Jack figured he could fill the role easily, though the audience might not appreciate his tone. Two more songs came and went and as he approached Sutton from the south.

His phone rang, making him jump again.

"For heaven's sake, Jack! Get a grip," he reprimanded himself as he answered it, trying to calm his nerves. "Jack Rutherford."

"Jack, it's Mo again. There *was* still someone in the office." She sounded excited, like a kid on Christmas morning, and for a split second, he wondered who'd she'd spent her own with.

"What you got, Mo?"

"Two names for two vehicles. And lucky for us, neither has been reported stolen." He sensed her beaming smile at the other end of the line.

"And I'm guessing you've run the names already."

"Indeed. The names are Bernard Evans and Robert Stiles. Both have records. And get this – Bernard's mother is a convicted paedophile, released only recently to an approved premises here in Croydon. Father's inside for murder."

"Oh lord, this is too easy. They can't be the ringleaders, can they? Could they be so stupid as to leave registered vehicles there, parked right outside?"

"Customers, maybe?" Mo offered. "Though still stupid."

"Right – exactly. Do me one last favour before you go home, would you?"

"Of course. What is it?" There was excitement in her voice now.

"See if there is anything else from SOCO on the van found at

Waterloo station. If we can link either of these two to the van, we'll be pretty certain which part of the puzzle they belong to. Then we can move in a little closer." He thought for a moment before adding, "And do a passport check too, please, if you can. If they have left the country, I want to know about it."

"I'm on to it."

"And thanks, Mo. I know it's not strictly your domain. If you need my login, let me know."

"Already have it from last time, Jack."

Jack smiled at the phone. Thank goodness for the woman's commitment to the job, unlike some he could mention. When this was all over, he was going to have to do something about that, take it further up than DI Morton, since he was part of the problem.

"See you in the morning, Mo."

When he'd hung up, he drove the last part of the journey home in silence, thinking about not only where he was up to with finding the girls' captor and killer, but about how he might move Eddie and the DI out of the way so someone who gave a damn could lead the team. While he could do so much on his own, he couldn't do it all, and relying on Mo's generous nature was not the solution. Nor was giving her his login details. That alone could come back to bite him in the ass if anyone found out.

But that was for another day. Tomorrow, he felt sure, would bring the positive news he craved.

As it turned out, that was only partly true.

Chapter Sixty-Eight

The case had more loose ends than a plate of spaghetti.

By the time Jack arrived home, *Coronation Street* was just starting, the familiar theme music playing in as he walked in the front door. Janine greeted him as he slipped his overcoat off.

"You look worn out, Jack Rutherford," she said gently. "Do you want a beer before your dinner, maybe?" He watched her as she hung his coat up on the peg, admired the curve of her body in the deep pink wool dress she was wearing. Janine was a woman who took pride in her appearance. He slipped his arms around her waist from behind and gently pulled her close, nuzzling into her neck.

"Mmm. You smell good, Mrs Rutherford."

Smiling, she turned around to face him, still enclosed in his embrace.

"And you look lovely, as always," he added. "I'm a lucky man to live with you."

Holding his gaze, she replied, 'That you are, Jack," and leaned in to peck him on the lips. "Now let me get you your dinner before I ravish you here in the hallway."

Jack smirked; she'd read his mind.

"Well, since you mention ravishing, don't let me stop you. I'm all for a spot of ravishing." Eyes twinkling, Janine mock-slapped his shoulder and squeezed out from his arms in an effort to get to the kitchen before Jack decided dinner could wait.

"You need to eat, and rest. I'll ravish you later," she kidded as she walked off, leaving him standing with his hands on his hips, smiling broadly. "I'll bring it into the lounge," she added over her shoulder, so Jack obliged and went through.

He sat down in his chair, half an eye on the TV while he waited. On the screen, Roy Cropper was serving breakfast to someone he didn't recognize and Jack was reminded of his new friend Billy and his girl Chloe. Hadn't they gone to someone called Roy for their Christmas dinner? And didn't this Roy have a café somewhere? The thought tickled him and he chuckled to himself as Janine walked in with a tray set with his dinner. She placed it on his lap.

"What's amusing you? You hate *Coronation Street*."

"I was just thinking about Billy and Chloe. They know a man called Roy, and he even has a café somewhere. They went for Christmas Day – not sure if I told you. I was wondering if the two Roys were similar."

"Why, because they each own a café?"

"Pretty much." He stabbed a sausage and bit into the end, leaving the rest impaled on the fork.

"Well, that's that, then. If they each have a café, they must be the same through and through," she mused. She sat down on the sofa opposite him while he ate.

"How was your day, then? Any closer to solving your case?"

"It's coming together." But he didn't feel like discussing it. He'd had enough of grisly endings, and his morgue visit had topped it off. He changed the subject subtly. "Did I tell you I met Chloe, Billy's girl? She was arrested for shoplifting. Had my card in her pocket so they called me in to see her. Nicking sausage rolls for dinner."

"Poor thing. What happened?"

"She ended up with a caution and a promise to me she wouldn't do it again. Sad though, eh? Stealing for food. Seemed like a nice young woman too. I dropped them both back to their garage, along with your picnic – which, by the way, was greatly appreciated."

"Oh, I'm glad. I've not really seen you much to catch up and ask." It wasn't a dig. It was a reality they lived with.

"She reminds me of someone, though, and I can't get it out of my mind. She seems so familiar, though I know we've never met before. She's from up north, Manchester way. Not somewhere I get to."

"Maybe your paths have crossed and you don't realise. Maybe you've seen her around here?"

"Well, that's just it. She's not been this way long, only a couple of weeks, so I doubt it. But you remember when the older girl in this case went missing – the one called Leanne?"

"Yes."

"She's a lot like her. When I was at her house the other day, I noticed the similarity of her chin, actually."

Janine laughed lightly at what he was saying. "There are plenty of people who are similar to others in terms of parts of their body. Same style of mouth, for instance. That doesn't mean anything apart from the fact that they have the same style of mouth."

Jack forked mashed potato into his mouth. A blob of gravy fell to his chin and he wiped it with his finger.

"Seems like yours needs to be a little bigger," Janine said, smiling.

"I suppose. On both counts." He glanced at the TV screen, and they settled into a comfortable silence while Janine watched her soap. When Jack had finished his sausage and mash, he took his tray into the kitchen and rinsed his plate, leaving it on the drainer. He could hear the phone start to ring in the hallway.

"I'll get it," he called to Janine, and picked the handset up. "Jack Rutherford."

"Jack, it's Eddie. Look, I know you've finished for the night, but I thought I'd fill you in." Jack could hear voices in the background, and music. Sounded like Eddie was in the pub. "Are you in the pub, by chance?"

"Never mind that now. Forensics found a till receipt between the two front seats of that van, from the Asda at Swanley. Looks like the occupants of the van went shopping on Christmas Eve, according to the date stamp."

"I'm listening. What's relevant?"

"Well, not the box of chocolates they bought, but more the fact we know what time they were in the store."

Jack didn't need Eddie to spell the rest out. "So, we can check their CCTV cameras and see who made the purchase. Nice one, Eddie."

"We're already on it, and I've got a blow-up here in my hands. I've already run it and come up with the name of—"

Jack broke in. "Let me guess. Robert Styles or Bernard Evans."

"How the ...?"

"Because the two vehicles that were left abandoned and burned out at the house in Kent belonged to those two cretins."

"Shit almighty."

"They might have removed the registration plates, but you can't remove the chassis number quite so easily. Looks like we have ourselves a couple of pillocks, and we can place at least one of them in that van now. And we know we are looking at culprits, not customers, which means we need to move fast.

"Swig your beer back, Eddie. I'll meet you back at the station."

Chapter Sixty-Nine

Eddie stank of booze. Jack leaned over him as they stared at the computer screen on Eddie's desk, which, as usual, was a shambles, littered with Post-it Notes, dog-eared files, coffee cups with deep caramel stain rings and copious amounts of biscuit crumbs. It looked as organised as a jumble sale. He really was a slob, and not for the first time Jack marvelled at how he managed to pull so many women. He must have a secret weapon. He shook the notion off as quickly as it had come and tried to concentrate on what Eddie was saying.

"So you're also figuring that, since the van was at Waterloo, they've buggered off, then?"

"I'm saying it's an option, that's all. Think about it. Your venture gets turned upside down and burned out, so you ditch the girls and flee as far away as you can manage in the time you've got. Once you're out of the UK, the continent is your oyster. That's what I'd do."

"It does make sense. I asked Mo to put a trace on their passports, though – before we knew how they were connected, mind – because their cars were at the house. Now we know for sure, we can bring them both in. If we can find them."

"Do we have addresses? I mean, in case they have simply gone home – not that I'd expect them to still be there."

"They are stupid enough, from what I know of them so far. But I doubt it too. And yes, Robert 'Rob' Styles is local, actually. Croydon thinks Bernard Evans is the other side of London, in Watford."

"Then let's get a car round to Styles' place and see if he's in. I'll contact Watford to drive round to Evans' in an unmarked for now. We've no proof Evans was in the van yet, remember – only his car at the burned property. And a lowly receipt doesn't *prove* Styles was in it either, but it's more likely. There's nothing else to connect them – yet."

"There'll be private cameras near the store, and maybe near the car park and on other businesses. I'll get Mo and Clarke on to it first thing. At least we have a timeframe to work with now, so that'll cut some needless footage and wasted time out."

"Right. Yes. Okay, let's see if either of them are in. I don't want to spook them if they are daft enough to be sitting at home watching the telly. Not until we have a bit more. The CPS won't go for a receipt on its own."

"I'll do a drive-by of Styles' place. He'll not suspect my Taurus. Then we'll see what tomorrow brings before we pounce. Now we've got Styles' and Evans' names, I'll take their photos round to Leanne's and see if either was the man she remembers in her room. If it is, that'll do the CPS; they like an eyewitness. Then we'll swoop."

Jack checked his watch. It was gone 8.30 pm, a little late for house calls to Leanne, but this was important.

"I'll pop round now and let you know. Let's keep the panda car away from Evans' and Styles' places for tonight until we know they're involved for sure."

Jack was already heading out to his car, leaving Eddie alone in the squad room. Jack knew he'd be back inside the pub within the hour. Well, stuff him, he thought bitterly, and stuff Morton too. His direct superiors were a joke. As he slipped in behind the wheel, he resolved once again to do something about it when he had more time.

Oh, the irony of it.

He revved his engine and let his clutch out a bit too quickly, sending the car speeding towards the car park entrance somewhat faster than he usually did, but that was adrenalin building. And annoyance at his work situation. The case had fallen back on his shoulders again, and his evening was a write-off once more.

Ten minutes later, he was on Cedar Road and pulling up outside the Meadows' house. Glancing up, he noticed the front bedroom light was on, which meant either Mr or Mrs was in there.

"I'm coming in whether you're reading in bed or not," he said to himself as he opened his door to get out. An icy chill nipped at his nose as he slammed the car door shut, and the curtain in the lounge window twitched. A moment later, Dave Meadows opened the front door. He looked none too pleased to see Jack.

"This'll only take a moment, Mr Meadows, if I may."

"You'd better come on in, then," Dave Meadows said resignedly, which Jack thought was a little odd. Surely, he'd want to see Leanne's captors caught? So why not add a bit of enthusiasm, then? He followed him inside and they stood in the hall. An invite through to the lounge was clearly not on offer.

"I have a couple of photos here I'd like to show Leanne. We think they could be linked to the house, and one of the men could be the one Leanne spoke to in her room that day. Her confirmation will help get the man, or men, charged – if it's him, of course. May I go up?"

"She's sleeping, Detective, and I'd rather not disturb her." The man seemed a little nervous, not the concerned father he had been of recent. Was Jack imagining the man's lack of co-operation? It didn't add up.

"I realise that, Mr Meadows, and I wouldn't ask if this wasn't of the utmost importance." Jack smiled hopefully and watched Dave

Meadows' jaw move silently, tossing the ever-present gum in his mouth, no doubt, like a rapper. Their eyes met and Jack held his gaze. Reluctantly, Dave Meadows stood aside. Jack hadn't left him much choice.

"Let me go first and wake her. Wait here."

And so he did, though Jack already knew she was awake. He could hear her TV clearly from the bottom of the stairs. He didn't think whoever was in the upstairs front room would be watching "Top of the Pops." He couldn't see that being Penny Meadows' thing.

But it would be Leanne's.

The sound was suddenly turned down and Jack smiled to himself as he began to climb the stairs. There was no way he wasn't going in there tonight. As Dave Meadows was leaving his daughter's room, Jack was outside her door ready to nip in.

"I thought I asked ...."

But Jack was back inside the pink room already. Leanne was sitting up in bed with no obvious signs of having just been woken up – as Jack had suspected.

"Hello, Detective. Dad says you have a picture to show me?"

He could feel her dad hovering behind him and sensed something he couldn't put his finger on.

"Yes. I have more than one, actually. I know this could be a little distressing for you, Leanne, and I am truly sorry about asking. You're our only witness currently able to help, so once again, I'm really sorry."

"It's fine, really it is. Let me see."

Jack put down the picture of the girl lying in the morgue first. She looked so peaceful, and so young. There was no need to ask the question he wanted answered.

"Oh no," was all Leanne said. Then, "She wasn't lucky enough to get out, I take it?"

"You recognize her, then?"

"Yes. She saved my life. That's her." Leanne looked up at Jack with watery eyes, and he felt her pain.

"I have a couple more here, if I may."

He laid another two pictures down on the bed for Leanne, then stepped back, leaving her to look and hopefully confirm without interruption.

What he heard wasn't quite what he expected.

Chapter Seventy

Behind him, Dave Meadows gave an audible gasp. Leanne was looking at the photo of Bernard Evans.

"Yes, I recognize this one," she said.

Jack turned to her father, who stood in the doorway, his face pale. He watched the man for a long moment, though Dave Meadows didn't notice. He was far away, deep in thought about something. And Jack suspected he knew what that was. There was only one reason for Meadows to react as he had at seeing the photo of Evans.

Because he knew the man. *Dave Meadows knew Bernard Evans.*

The hairs on Jack's neck stood up involuntarily as the pieces of the puzzle slotted into place inside his head. Could he be involved? Could he have had a part in the kidnapping of his own daughter? Or had he been a paying visitor to the house? Either scenario was repulsive, incomprehensible, yet it had to be one of them. He thought forward to the avalanche of mayhem that was about to engulf the innocent members of the Meadows family.

Welcome to the human race...

He turned his attention back to Leanne, who was still staring at the 10x8. Remembering recent horrific events, no doubt. He felt sorry for the girl but was glad she'd been able to identify the man in the photo. Jack hoped both she and her mother would be strong enough to cope with what he predicted was to fall upon them in the not too distant future. He made the decision to keep what he'd witnessed to himself – for now.

Dave Meadows tried to take control of the situation now.

"Leanne needs her rest, Detective. Time for you to leave," he said firmly.

Jack took the hint and nodded at the man slightly, then gave a brief smile to Leanne as he took the photo from her. She was a brave young woman.

For now, with Leanne's confirmation, they had an eyewitness, which meant they could pull Evans in for questioning and the CPS would be happy. It would prove to be another nail in his coffin when it came to trial – once they found him.

Back outside, Jack called Eddie on his mobile. Unsurprisingly, Eddie was back in the pub; Jack could hear the clatter of glasses and distant jukebox music.

"How's it going, Jack?"

"A positive ID from Leanne on the girl and on Evans, but she doesn't recognize the other one, Rob Styles. Never saw him. Doesn't mean he wasn't there, though."

"No. I'll give the boys at Watford a call now, make sure they're still watching."

Jack doubted he would, but kept his opinion to himself.

"Any news as to whether he's buggered off to France then? I've not seen or heard anything," said Eddie.

"Me neither, but I think now we have a positive identification, I'll alert Interpol in Manchester and get a Red Notice set up. They have better access to things than we do, so if he's taken the Eurostar train, they can be on the lookout as he crosses borders and whatnot. Those scum involved in child abuse rings are a good deal more important to find than a diamond thief, so hopefully they collar him quickly. Let's hope he isn't travelling on forged documents under another name." Jack heard Eddie take a drag on a cigarette and pictured the blue haze around him as he spoke. He wanted to cough for him. "And what about Styles, then?" he went on. "Bring him in for questioning?"

"We have him in the van via a receipt," Eddie replied. "Nothing else as yet. His DNA isn't in the system."

"You've had results back from forensics? Was Evans' DNA present? He's definitely in the system, been inside." Jack knew Eddie wasn't sharing, and it bugged him. But then he hadn't shared his suspicions about Dave Meadows either.

"Yes, it was, as were several other sets, likely the girls'. And Martin Coffey – his prints were there. Thought I'd mentioned that, Jack."

He let it go. Battles and all that. "And I'll get those traffic cops to ID those photos, see if they were the two men in the van. That's another set of witnesses. Anything else you haven't told me?" Jack struggled to keep the annoyance from his voice, though if Eddie heard it, he wasn't going to lose sleep over it. Eddie was in the pub. Jack was the one still busting his backside.

"Get some rest, Jack. Leave Interpol to me. We'll see what the private CCTV cameras give us, then get Styles in too. I don't want to spook either of them. Both addresses are under surveillance for now."

That was something at least. Jack checked his watch. It was approaching 10 pm.

"See you tomorrow, then," he said, yawning, then hung up. If Evans had fled, there was precious little he could do about it on his own.

It was time to go home. To bed.

Leaving his mobile phone on the hall table with his keys, he climbed the stairs towards the bedroom. Janine was already in bed reading. He poked his head around the door and smiled. She looked so studious in her reading glasses. The dusky pink of the room's décor reminded him slightly of Leanne's room, though Janine had opted for a floral motif in theirs. He'd lost the battle on bedroom décor too.

"You look tired, Jack. Are you done for the night?" she enquired, peering librarian-like over the rims of her glasses.

"Done as a kipper, Mrs Rutherford," he said, and threw himself down on to the flowery quilt. "I'll grab a shower, and then, if I've still got any energy left, there was the mention of ravishing on offer." He smiled up at her, waggling his eyebrows comically.

She laughed out loud. "You look like Benny Hill doing that!" she exclaimed.

"Well, here's a fun fact for you, Mrs Rutherford. It was always the women chasing *him* to that stupid music, never the other way around."

"Really?"

"Yes, really. You watch next time he's on TV. He never chases anyone."

"Well, that's good to know. Now go and get a shower before you fall asleep where you are."

He wriggled off the edge of the bed and did as he was told, grinning like a love-struck teenager. He was a lucky man, indeed. Their relationship was as strong as a heavy-duty chain, and he wondered about Dave and Penny Meadows for a moment, and all that had gone on in their household recently. For a family that had gone through hell, they didn't seem particularly close, but then people coped with trauma in many different ways. Stripping off and standing under the warm jets of water, he suspected there was more to come for them. Dave Meadows' obvious gasp had been a dead giveaway that he knew Bernard Evans, though luckily Leanne hadn't picked up on that. For now, at least, that spared her from even more anguish, and Jack raised his head heavenward in a silent 'thank you.' Whatever the mess to come, it would be up to Jack to deliver it, no doubt.

By the time he'd finished in the bathroom, he could have slept bolt upright. Exhaustion enveloped completely him he returned to the bedroom. Janine pulled the covers back and he slid into his side. Within five minutes, he was snoring gently.

The ravishing would have to wait.

Chapter Seventy-One

Where the hell time went, Jack would never know, but damn it, it went quickly. He looked across at the alarm clock by the bed – it was after 8 am and Janine was already up. He stretched his arm out to her side of the bed, where she'd lain next to him all night, but it felt cool to his touch. She must have got up a while ago. He strained to hear her moving around downstairs, but the house seemed silent. Perhaps he was all alone.

Feeling more awake and noticing he felt more refreshed than he had done in a while, he grabbed his robe from the floor where he'd left it the previous night and went downstairs in search of Janine. He was almost at the bottom of the stairs when he heard the low sound of the radio coming from the kitchen. Terry Wogan's voice was a British morning staple – bacon and eggs for the soul. He pushed the door fully open and Janine looked up from her spot at the table, toast in hand.

"Morning, sunshine," she said brightly, as she did each and every morning. "Tea?"

"Love some, thanks. Why didn't you wake me?"

"You needed the rest, Jack, and I bet you feel better for it too."

He had to concede; he did indeed. He watched her as she flicked the kettle on and put fresh teabags in the pot, and was reminded again what a fine-looking woman she was. Perhaps a spot of ravishing could be on the cards later if he got home at a reasonable hour and didn't fall straight to sleep. He was vaguely aware of her speaking.

"Jack?"

"Sorry. I was miles away."

"Obviously. I said the lab called you a bit ago. Call them when you can."

"Did they say what they wanted?"

She placed a plate of hot toast in front of him and poured the tea. "No, never do to me. But I hope it's some good news for you for a change."

"I'll call them when I've eaten this. Thanks. I'm half-starved."

She watched as he pushed most of the first triangle into his mouth and smeared strawberry jam on the second piece, ready to follow the first. There were two more pieces on his plate, so she stood to put two more slices into the toaster – it looked like he was going to need them.

When he'd finally finished his breakfast, he called the lab back. The name and number she'd written down was not one he recognised. A woman answered. Her name was Janice Coop.

"It's DC Jack Rutherford here, Croydon. You called me earlier?"

"Yes, Jack. Thanks for calling back. We met at the burned-out house over Christmas?"

Ah, so that was it. "Yes, I remember, Janice. A damn cold night, and a wet one, too. Not the best conditions for your crew, I expect. What have you got for me?"

"Something of interest. One of the lads found a clump of something in one of the upstairs bedrooms towards the back of the house. He wasn't entirely sure what it was but had the brains to bag it anyway."

"Oh?"

"Well, it turns out it's a piece of gum."

"That's great! DNA. Who's the hit?"

"Not so fast, Jack. It was contaminated, covered in soot and ash, but the fire did a good job of setting it, you could say. And there's an impression on it, like when you have a crown made."

"So no retrievable DNA, but it's got an imprint of a tooth?"

"Correct. And it shows that whoever left the gum in that room has what we call a Carabelli cusp, or an extra cusp to you and me. And the filling has come out. It's extremely distinctive and not at all common." She let that sink in for a minute before carrying on. "So you're looking for someone, probably male, who needs a dentist. Sorry I can't give you more to go on as yet, but it's a start. Maybe try local dentists first?"

Jack stared at the phone. He could think of someone straight away who fitted that description, and he chewed gum.

Dave Meadows.

Could it be so simple? It didn't make sense. Leanne was his daughter. She'd been kidnapped and kept in a house where he'd visited. Had he known she was there? Jack's stomach rolled at the thought – his own daughter, for heaven's sake.

You know he knows Bernard Evans, Jack.

"Are you still there, Jack?" Coop asked him.

"Sorry, Janice. Yes. That's actually rather useful. Today could be my lucky day."

"Then buy yourself a lottery ticket. Glad to be of help. I hope you get the sick creep."

"I'll let you know when we do, and thanks again."

He couldn't believe it. Dave Meadows? But in order to prove it, that gum imprint needed to match the man who had now become a prime suspect in the case. He needed to talk to Morton and get a search warrant for Meadows' dental records. He also wanted to find out if Meadows' car had been caught in the vicinity, somewhere between his home and the crime scene, which was going to take hours of searching through CCTV tapes. There had to be a more efficient way to place him there. But then what? How was he involved, Jack wondered again? Customer or culprit? And now Jack had another problem – had Meadows alerted the two men? Was it too late? There was only one way to find out.

He dialled Eddie. No answer.

"Damn that man!"

Chapter Seventy-Two

He'd made it to the station in double-quick time. Eddie still wasn't in, but most of the team were, including DI Morton; this in itself was unusual, but at that moment, Jack didn't care. He stuck his head around the door. Morton was focusing on a pile of documents in front of him and, from where Jack stood, they looked like crime reports. And the handwriting looked familiar – it was his own.

Without looking up, Morton said, "Just the man, Jack. Come in. Sit down."

"I need you to authorize a search warrant actually, boss."

"That can wait a minute. I want to talk to you about your incomplete reports." Morton picked a selection up from the pile and pointed at blank spaces and crossed-out passages. "These really aren't good enough, Jack. They tell us bugger all, and, quite honestly, they look like a ten-year-old has filled them in."

"I'm a tad busy at the moment, as you know." Jack was doing his best to stay calm, but he was in a rush. He wanted that warrant, and paperwork was not a priority. Not right now. It would be best to agree and move on. "I'll do better. Once this case is done and out of the way, I'll pay more attention to it."

"I need to finalise my own month-end reporting, Jack. I need the info promptly. Can you get it done today?"

"In all honesty, no. I've bigger fish to fry. I've got a real lead on who else was in that house with the girls, and I want him in for questioning but I need a warrant first for his dental records."

Morton sighed, focusing again on the reports in front of him like they were the most important thing in the world. Paperwork was the bane of many officers' and detectives' lives, and while everyone knew it needed to be kept on top of, everyone really had better things to do with their time. Like catch paedophiles.

"I understand that, Jack. And I'll get you the warrant. Then will you give me properly completed reports?"

It was easiest to say yes, so he did. Strictly speaking, Morton hadn't stipulated a deadline.

"So tell me the story. What are you and Eddie up to?"

Jack resisted the urge to roll his eyes at the mention of Eddie's name, and set to with a progress report, concluding with the fact that the case was close to coming to an end.

"Good. That's what I like to hear. And breaking a ring like that – that's marvellous news. The chief will be pleased. Well done, Jack. Pass on my thanks to Eddie, will you?"

Jack nodded, biting back a retort. The man was a buffoon; he'd no clue what was going on outside of his tiny betting world. Wordlessly, he headed to the coffee cupboard to fix himself a strong one and try and calm himself down, not that caffeine would do that. The room was empty, so he pushed the door closed and stood resting his forehead on it in an attempt to regulate his breathing. That turned out to be a stupid move. A moment later Mo barged in, sending the full force of the wooden door into his nose and making Jack yell out in pain.

Mo was the colour of a Valentine rose in seconds as blood streamed down Jack's chin. He grabbed the grubby tea towel nearby to catch the worst of it as Mo shrieked into her hands and flitted from one foot to the other, unsure how to make the situation right. When she'd calmed, she apologised and swapped Jack's drenched towel for a fresh but damp one in an effort to clean him up.

When he could finally speak and Mo stopped dithering, he told her about the development and the need for CCTV footage, something to place Meadows at the scene.

"I'll get right on to it. Now, are you sure you're alright?"

Jack stood with his head tilted back slightly, his fingers pinching his nose. He nodded slightly, then asked, "Were you looking for me before you beat me up, or was you wanting a coffee?"

"Both. But please don't tell everyone I beat you up." Mo looked panic-stricken at the thought.

He let her off his hook. "I'm having you on, Mo. Of course, I won't tell people that." He did his best to smile and make her feel better. "Tell me, then. What did you want?"

"Remember the young girl done for shoplifting the sausage rolls, Chloe Mathews?"

How could Jack forget? "Yes? What about her?"

"Well, they processed her as they would do, so her DNA is now in the system."

Jack was beginning to feel exasperated as he took a deep breath.

"Mo, this is like a conversation by crossword puzzle. What are you trying to tell me?"

"That her DNA matches another case you've been working on," she blurted. "Baby Mary. Chloe Mathews has the DNA to be the baby's mother."

"I thought we had a match for that, although Leanne Meadows hadn't been pregnant and couldn't possibly be the mother. So, has there been a mismatch somewhere?"

"Well, it looks like there is another explanation – I checked back before coming to you. Both Leanne Meadows and Chloe Mathews have the exact same DNA. They are identical twins, Jack. So Chloe must be the mother, not Leanne."

Jack stood stock still, trying to process what she was saying. Yes, it made perfect sense, but Penny Meadows had told him that although Leanne had indeed had a sister, she'd died. Nobody had mentioned her being a twin. Jack had assumed the child has been born after Leanne, and had then died somehow. Shit! Why had he assumed and not asked?

"Crikey. How about that? So Leanne's identical twin is still alive! Holy shit."

He and Mo stood in silence, absorbing the news and what it meant, not only for Chloe but for Leanne and the wider Meadows family too.

They'd regained a family member. Two if you added in baby Mary.

"That will be why I recognized they both had the same look when they were upset, because they are sisters, and if Chloe grew her hair and lightened it . . ." He paused. "Yes! I see it now. How could I not see it before?" He slapped his forehead with the palm of his hand.

"You've been caught up with the bigger case, Jack, not looking at finding Mary's mother," Mo reminded him. "It wasn't your priority."

Then the rest of the puzzle fell into place, and Jack groaned out loud. "Oh, hell, no! It couldn't be!"

He stood and started to pace in the tiny room as best he could without bumping into Mo. Her face had gone pale, and he saw she'd come to the same horrific conclusion.

"So Dave Meadows *is* the father after all, only he doesn't know that Chloe was, *is* in fact, his *other* daughter, because he believed she'd died. The girls must have been separated early on, then, at birth maybe."

"Exactly. What a bloody mess. Not only is Dave Meadows the baby's father, but that makes the three girls sisters and half-sisters, as well as Leanne being Mary's aunt. Dave Meadows should be the *grandfather* to Chloe's child, not the bloody father!"

How the hell was he going to handle it from here on in, Jack wondered miserably. Poor Penny Meadows. She had more than a few shocks coming to her, as did Leanne and Chloe. Mary would be oblivious for the foreseeable future, thankfully. But Dave?

He was in deep shit no matter how you looked at it. And he deserved every sloppy ounce of it, right up past his ears if Jack had his way.

"Don't say a word yet, Mo," Jack said, collecting himself. "I need some air. You get on to the CCTV footage for Meadows' car while I think on the next move. Lips sealed, eh?"

"You can count on me. I won't say a word."

Jack wiped his nose with the back of his hand and made his way to the back door, avoiding the looks he knew he was getting. He looked a state. His shirt was splotched with blood, though at least it was his own.

He stood in the cold air, breathing evenly. He needed to plan his next steps carefully.

Chapter Seventy-Three

The walk did him good. As did the bacon sandwich from the food van up the road. But his waistline wasn't his concern at the moment and neither was his paperwork, so both would have to wait. His bloodied shirt, however, was a different issue, and he figured he'd better get changed into a fresh one before he did much else. So, instead of going back into the station, he slipped into his car and headed into the town centre. In the back of his mind, he had an inkling about what to do first, and that involved finding Billy. He hoped he'd set his stall up somewhere close to the charity shop.

Sometimes the gods aligned and things fell into place, and as he pulled into the curb a couple of doors down from the shop, he could see Billy up ahead chatting to an older woman. He sat and watched her body language, the way her head was cocked to one side listening intently to what he was saying. After a few moments, she broke out into a smile that matched Billy's. She handed him something, probably some change, Jack figured, and Billy shook her hand. A moment later, she was on her way, pulling a shopping trolley along behind her like a tired old dog.

Jack got out of the car and made his way over. Billy saw him and waved excitedly, then changed his expression when he noticed Jack's shirt.

"What happened, Detective? Someone get a bit feisty this morning?"

"You could say that. I had an altercation with a door in the coffee room and got myself a nosebleed."

"You want to get that changed, my friend," Billy suggested. "Not a good look for a copper. You look like you've been fighting." He added his cheeky smile and Jack tried one in return. "But you didn't come here to talk about your nose, I'm thinking," Billy went on. "What's up?" His face had turned serious now.

"Let me buy you something to eat and a coffee. I need to ask you something."

"I won't turn that down," Billy said, gathering his few belongings and putting his hard-earned change into his pocket. "There's a place around the corner," he said, indicating the direction they should walk in, and they set off. As they approached the café in silence, Jack realized where they were headed. Up ahead was a greasy-spoon – Roy's Café. He must have thought long and hard to come up with such a clever name for his business, Jack thought sardonically. He half expected to hear a bell tinkling above his head when he opened the door, but there was none. He closed the door behind them and they headed for a table. Decorated sometime in the eighties, the café was due for a repaint at least, but it was warm and the aroma of cooked bacon hung in the air. Jack was tempted to have another sandwich.

"Right, Billy, Big Breakfast, I'm assuming? Pot of tea?"

Judging by the boy's smile, there was no need for another form of confirmation, so Jack made his way to the counter to order. A man in his forties wearing an apron greeted him. The name "Roy" was embroidered on his shirt pocket, telling Jack he was the owner of Roy's Café. The man glanced at Jack's bloodstained shirt but didn't comment. He really must get it changed soon.

"Hello. A friend of Billy's?" Roy enquired, somewhat suspiciously, Jack thought. Or protectively.

"I like to think so," said Jack. "Thought I'd feed him up a bit. You?"

"I look out for him a bit, and his Chloe too. A nice young couple."

"So you must be Roy, the owner," said Jack, holding his hand out to shake. "Billy said he was spending Christmas Day with you. I've just put two and two together," he said, smiling, though he'd already deduced as much when he'd first seen the café.

"Didn't like to think of them both alone, and I'm on my own, so it worked out."

"And with Chloe having given birth not long ago, she in particular would have appreciated that."

It was a daring move on Jack's part, but one that paid off. Roy stared straight at Jack, a look of "How did you know?" on his face, and that was all he needed for confirmation.

Neither man spoke for a moment, then Jack said, "Billy's having the Big Breakfast and tea, and I'll have a tea, thanks. And a slice of toast on the side." Jack beamed at Roy, and no more was said about anything as he paid for the food and headed back to Billy.

So, Chloe was indeed Mary's mother – that much he'd had confirmed. Now he had to put the pieces together and somehow make sense of it all.

"So, what did you want to ask me?" Billy asked.

Since Jack already had the answer to his question, he had to think of something else fast.

"I wondered how Chloe was, that's all. Behaving herself, I hope," Jack said to Billy with a grin.

Saved.

"Yes, she's fine, and thanks for your help there, Jack. She doesn't need grief on top of everything else."

Everything else? Jack wondered if he should ask, but decided to leave it alone. There was no sense in causing more upset by exposing what was obviously their secret. He hoped Roy wouldn't say anything to the authorities about Chloe abandoning her baby until this was all sorted out, and since he seemed like the caring sort, he felt confident of that. And Jack was the authorities anyhow.

"You're welcome, Billy, though I can't help a second time, so remember that, eh?" He nodded as Roy placed a Big Breakfast down in front of the boy, and a plate of toast for Jack. It was both the distraction they needed and the ideal opportunity to change the subject to something less serious.

"How's the Hansen's disease going, then, Billy? Trade picking up?" he asked, biting into a slice of buttered toast.

Chapter Seventy-Four

It's a beautiful new day.

Jack was finally beginning to see the light at the end of the tunnel – and it was no longer an oncoming train. Since his run-in, quite literally, with Mo and his meeting with Billy, he had almost every piece of the Meadows' puzzle figured out and a good chunk of the other, though Leanne and her family were still blissfully unaware of the crossover they were involved in and the upset and hell that was yet to come. He'd spent a couple of hours talking with Eddie over a pint about how best to move forward, and they had decided on their strategy with Dave Meadows at least. Then, against his normal way of doing things, he had asked for Janine's advice as well, giving her the broad outline, no names. As a woman, she had a different perspective to offer, which he valued; he wanted to make things as easy as possible for Mrs Meadows when the time came to tell her.

It seemed "Sausage man," or Bernard Evans as he was legally known, had indeed buggered off to France and, according to the border patrol, had crossed over on Boxing Day , which, as it happened, was long before they were properly aware of him and what he stood for. It was now a cross-borders affair, which made dragging him in for questioning somewhat more difficult – far from ideal.

Rob Styles, on the other hand, hadn't been as thoughtful in his getaway and was lazing in his mother's flat watching television when Jack's colleagues knocked on the front door. He was now sat uncomfortably in cell number two with a plastic cup of water for company, awaiting his solicitor and his chance to explain. Jack knew by the man's actions that he'd be singing like a budgie to reduce his sentence. He was already pacing his cell like a cat on a hot tin roof. There was no way he'd enjoy life behind bars, where he'd be on offer to his cellmates as a sex object. Paedophiles were not treated well by fellow inmates, even on remand. Meanwhile, there was still work to be done to find their wanted man, who, if he had any brains at all, would now be travelling under a new name with new papers. And in that case, it would be almost impossible to locate him until he offended again.

That left the Meadows debacle. And right now, Jack and Eddie were on their way to arrest Dave Meadows and bring him in for official and in-depth questioning back at the station. The man would find himself booked into cell number three for the night if all went according to plan.

Eddie pulled up outside the house. Cedar Road was becoming a regular destination for Jack. The front door opened as they were getting out. Penny stood in the doorway. Did she know something was up? Unless Jack was imagining it, she looked worried about something.

"Morning, Mrs Meadows. Is Mr Meadows in, please?" Jack took the lead since he was almost a regular on their doorstep.

"Dave? What do you want Dave for, Detective?" She didn't look happy, and Jack wondered if she'd been crying recently, or not sleeping.

"Is he in?" he pushed again.

She opened the door wider and the two men took the invitation to enter.

"I'll get him. Go through to the lounge," she directed, and they obliged. A moment or two later, Dave Meadows walked in wearing a brave face of sorts, closely followed by Penny. Eddie and Jack looked at each other grimly.

"It might be best if we talk to Mr Meadows alone," said Jack as Penny prepared to sit on the edge of the sofa opposite the two detectives. They were both still standing. If Dave was happy for her to stay for the questions, he didn't let on, and Penny promptly left the room. Would she be listening in from the hallway?

"I'll get to the point," Eddie began. "We are here to take you back to the station for questioning in relation to sexual offences against a minor, for starters. I suggest you get your solicitor to meet you there, and tell them it could be a long day."

Eddie stood and Dave backed away slightly.

"What?" he exclaimed. "How dare you, and after all we've been through!"

Jack stood next to Eddie. "Let's talk about this at the station, Mr Meadows."

"Do I have a choice?" he asked, his voice rising in pitch.

"No sir, you don't. And I'd rather not cuff you, so, if you'll agree to calm down and walk to the car . . ."

"Cuff me? Are you mad, man? Am I under arrest?"

"You may well be soon. That depends on your answers," retorted Eddie.

Jack glared across at Meadows, knowing full well that his dental records matched the gum at the scene. Dental records didn't lie. And neither does fathering a child with your own daughter, but that kind of questioning wasn't for the front lounge of his home.

Mrs Meadows chose that moment to walk back in. She must have been eavesdropping.

"Penny, call our solicitor, would you?" Dave Meadows said to her. "Seems I need one."

Penny was about to protest to Jack, but he pre-empted it. "You'd be wise to do so, Mrs Meadows," he said. She turned pale and scurried out of the room.

The three men then made their way out to the waiting car. As

Eddie pulled away from the curb, Jack glanced up at the front bedroom window in time to see the curtain move slightly, as though someone had been peering round it. Penny, he wondered? Or Leanne? It didn't matter, in reality, because whatever either woman thought could be happening, it was going to get a good deal worse when the full extent of the story came out.

Though maybe not for baby Mary. The thought lifted his spirits.

Chapter Seventy-Five

It turned out to be a long day. Dave Meadows was now licking his wounds in cell number three. Dental records had indeed confirmed that he'd left his gum in the house where his daughter Leanne had been imprisoned, and where he'd gone on and indulged himself with a twelve-year-old girl, Kate Byers, who was still recovering in hospital.

Kate was still too traumatized to say much, so Jack thanked his lucky stars Meadows had been dumb enough to leave evidence. His solicitor had argued that the gum could have been left when Meadows had been at the property for a different reason some months back, but Rob Styles had identified Meadows as a customer after he had been shown a photo of him.

Right now, Eddie and Jack were contemplating how far to go with their line of questioning before they tackled the more sensitive blow Dave Meadows was about to receive.

"Let's get it over with tonight," Eddie suggested. "His solicitor is getting fidgety and adding this additional charge in will bring the walls down on Meadows right now. Over and done with, I say. We'll put him on suicide watch and leave him to stew until the morning."

Jack found himself agreeing. After all, they had no reason to tread softly with him. It was the rest of the family they had to think about from now on. Dave Meadows wouldn't be the man to tell them.

"Right, let's tell him now and put it to bed."

"Agreed."

As both men went back into the interview room, the solicitor stood and started to say something but Eddie waved him quiet, speaking over the top of him as he asked his question.

"Mr Meadows, you used to visit an address in Manchester regularly, didn't you? For sex, I mean?"

Jack sat quietly, watching Meadows' body language as Eddie spoke.

"Did I?"

"You did. But then you stopped going"

"Again, did I?"

"Yes, you did. Because the girl fell pregnant. And her parents moved away so she was no longer 'available,'" he said, making quote marks in the air.

Nothing from Meadows for a moment, and then Jack noticed a change in the man's face as realization dawned.

"That girl had a baby," Eddie said. "A little girl, in fact. But here's the thing – due to her circumstances, she couldn't keep the child. Instead, she abandoned it at the local church, where, thankfully, an elderly lady found her and took her to the hospital, where she has been cared for."

"That's all very sad, Detective, but what's that got to do with me?" Meadows said, clearly trying to be brave.

"Well, we took some DNA from the baby, and guess what? It's a match to you as the father. Your DNA was already in the system from that bar fight you got into some time back, and ping! There you were, flashing away at us like a beacon."

"There must be some mistake! That can't be me. I've never visited a woman in Manchester."

"Oh, it wasn't a woman, Mr Meadows. No, it was a girl. Of fourteen. A girl called Chloe. Pretty name, don't you think?"

"You've got it wrong!" Meadows shouted. He leapt up from his chair in anger, tipping it backwards.

"DNA doesn't lie, Mr Meadows. Now, this is where it gets really interesting, so sit back down." The air was thick with tension as everyone waited for him to resume his seat. "You had another child when Leanne was born, didn't you?"

"What's that got to do with anything? She died at birth!" Spittle flew from his mouth.

Meadows' solicitor tried to intervene and speak, but Eddie cut him off.

"You named her Charlotte, I believe. We've yet to get to the bottom of exactly what happened there, but the child you and Mrs Meadows buried was not Charlotte."

Eddie let his bombshell sink in a moment. Both detectives knew there was more to come.

"I don't believe you!" Meadows shouted. "Why are you making this up? How low will you people go!?"

Eddie ploughed on with the rest of the unfortunate tale. "It's a shock, I realise. But Charlotte survived. She was adopted by a couple in Manchester." Eddie leaned across the flimsy table and spoke into Meadows' face. "And you used to visit her. And it was you, Mr Meadows, who got her pregnant. You, sir, are the baby's father."

Silence.

Then Eddie carried on. "So you have another daughter, one you believed to be deceased, as well as a third daughter, and that makes Leanne the baby's half-sister. Are you following me, Mr Meadows?"

All was quiet from the accused's side of the table.

"So, I am charging you with a lot more than sex with a minor. You're going down for some time, Mr Meadows, so you'd better get used to living with four small walls."

Both Dave Meadows and his solicitor sat open-mouthed, not sure what to say to such an abominable mess. It was almost too hard to comprehend. It was the solicitor who finally found his voice.

"I'd like a word with my client, in private please."

"Oh, I bet you would," said Eddie. "And I'd like to see how you'll wriggle out of this one. Meanwhile, my colleague and I will go and refresh our coffees and leave you two to chat."

Jack informed the recording machine that the interview was suspended, and both he and Eddie left the room. Once in the corridor, Jack took a deep, cleansing breath.

"Shit. Holy bloody shit."

"I wonder what he'll do next?" asked Eddie. "And someone has still got to break the news to Mrs Meadows, because it won't be him doing the dirty."

"No. I daresay it'll be me."

Eddie slapped Jack's shoulder and said, "Best that it comes from you, Jack, since you know them better than any of us."

Didn't seem Jack had much choice.

"Let's get a beer after we've done, eh?" said Eddie. "Celebrate."

Jack watched Eddie walk ahead of him towards the squad room and coffee. While he needed a fresh cup of coffee, he didn't feel much like celebrating.

Chapter Seventy-Six

There wasn't much point in telling the rest of the family that night, Jack thought glumly. It wasn't his role to inform them why Mr Meadows had been arrested and what he had been charged with, but he did need to speak to Penny and Leanne about the rest of the situation. No matter how and when he did it, the two women were going to have their worlds blown apart. But Jack knew that if he didn't tell them tonight, he wouldn't be getting much sleep; he'd be lying awake, worrying and thinking about the best way to handle it the following day.

He looked at his watch. It was almost 8 pm.

And then there was Chloe – how and when to tell her? How would she react, and what support would she need? There was too much to think about, and that was why he was still sat in his car in the station yard, having avoided Eddie's celebratory drinking session. He found himself calling Janine. She'd know what to do.

Her bright voice as she picked up the phone sent a tingle through his body. Even after their years of marriage, she still made him hum.

"Hello, my love," he said softly.

"Are you alright, Jack?" He detected the concern in her words.

"I am. But I need your advice again if I can. I suppose I need to know a woman's point of view. It's a delicate matter I'm about to deal with, and I know you'll keep it confidential. Would you mind?"

"Of course I don't mind. But why don't you come home so we can talk properly?"

"I might. That's half of the problem. Shall I do what I need to do tonight, right now or tomorrow, and whom do I speak with first?"

There was a silence between them as Janine waited for him to carry on, and Jack wondered where to start. Then Janine spoke again and gave him the direction he needed.

"Start from the beginning, then I can tell you what I'd do. But the ultimate decision is yours, Jack. You'll know what's best. You always do."

And so, he took a deep breath in and began to tell her about a family that were about to find out about what the father had been involved in and its consequences, finishing off with a little baby and the pink rabbit he'd bought for her and tucked in beside her.

When he'd finished, Janine asked simply, "And what do you think, Jack? What's your gut telling you to do amongst the mayhem?"

"Talk to Mrs Meadows first, and tell her that Charlotte never died and is alive and well, and is now called Chloe. Then tell her that Chloe's had a baby. Then I think I need to tell Chloe straight afterwards. Then let them both come to terms with things. Am I about right?"

"On the button, Jack. That's what I would want. And you can't do that tonight, not really."

"No. I can't."

"So come on home. I'll run you a soapy bath, and tomorrow you can put the world right, at least for one family."

She always knew what to do.

"I'll be home shortly, then. Love you, Mrs Rutherford."

"Love you too."

He sat for a moment longer, fiddling with the car keys in the ignition, wondering how he was going to find Chloe in the morning, and Billy. She was going to need his shoulder for support.

"I'll drive down Pitt Street now, see which garage is theirs. I'll only be a minute or two out of my way. That's what I'll do," he said to himself as he started the engine and prepared to pull away.

Ten minutes later, he was slowly cruising down Pitt Street. There was only the one garage. But how was he going to notify Chloe and Billy that he needed to talk? Knocking on the garage door would raise questions he hadn't the time or energy to answer tonight. He looked around the inside of his car for a piece of paper, found a discarded chocolate bar wrapper and wrote a brief note on the inside of it:

Meet me tomorrow at Roy's. I'm buying lunch. Bring Chloe. I have news. 12 pm. Jack.

That should do the trick and leave him plenty of time. Curiosity and a hot meal should entice them enough to show up, he hoped. He folded the note in half and slipped it under the garage door, saying a prayer the two of them saw it in time. As soon as he'd slipped it inside, he felt better, as though the worst part was over, yet he knew it was still to come, for him anyway. For Chloe? Well, he really didn't know how she was going to react. It could go either way. And Billy? How would he feel? Though he wasn't part of the family, he'd grown to like Chloe; that much was obvious. But this news might mean a change in their own status quo. Would he be resentful, perhaps? Move on without her, even?

"There's no point second-guessing," he told himself. "Que será, será. Whatever will be, will be."

Jack headed home to his waiting soapy bath, feeling better now that the proverbial plate of spaghetti was beginning to untangle itself.

Chapter Seventy-Seven

As he'd feared, Jack slept fitfully and woke with bags under his eyes. When this case was over, he wanted to sleep for a week; perhaps he'd do just that. Janine kissed him on the cheek and wished him luck as he left for Cedar Road. He was sure he could still feel it where she'd left it. It comforted him, like she was with him in the task ahead.

Steeling himself, he knocked on the front door of the Meadows' home and waited. When he heard the chain being taken off, he sucked in a deep breath and let it out slowly. Penny put her head around the door, her red-rimmed eyes meeting his.

"Can I come in, please?"

She pulled the door open wider, though she did not speak. Did she blame him for her husband's arrest? Probably. Without being asked to, he made his way to the lounge and she followed in behind.

When they were both in the room, he said, "I have some news for you. Perhaps we should sit down?" He followed her lead, sitting only when she had. They were in opposite chairs, a low coffee table between them. She still hadn't said anything. She kept her head lowered, looking at the swirly pattern of the carpet.

"Mrs Meadows," he began. "I said I have some news, though it doesn't concern your husband's case directly." Still nothing. "It concerns your daughter, not Leanne, but her twin, the baby you lost many years ago."

Penny finally looked at Jack properly.

"What's that got to do with any of this? And how did you know she was Leanne's twin? I never told you."

"No, you didn't. And I realize how sensitive this is, but during an investigation into another, seemingly unrelated crime, it came to light that Leanne's twin is actually still alive. She never died, Mrs Meadows. She's still with us."

The silence seemed to go on forever, and then a half-strangled sound erupted from her mouth. Her hand flew to cover it as she wailed. Jack leaned forward to place his hand on her arm in comfort, and she let him keep it there until she'd calmed a little. Tears continued to roll freely down her cheeks. This wasn't what Jack had imagined. Denial maybe, before it had sunk in, but not this. Penny Meadows was acting as if she'd known the child hadn't died at all. But how could that be?

"But you buried her," said another voice behind Jack. It was Leanne; her mother's distress had brought her into the room.

"I never believed them, never. I told them they'd made a mistake, that my baby had been mixed up somewhere. A mother knows . . . a mother knows when a child isn't hers. The baby they gave me, the dead one – I never believed it was mine. I never believed them, never..." Penny trailed off. Leanne went to her mother, wrapping her arms around her shoulders awkwardly as she sobbed gently.

"You say she's alive, Detective? How did you find her?"

Oh lord. Here I go ...

"Charlotte, as you christened her, is now called Chloe, and was adopted by a couple in Manchester. For reasons I can't go in to right now, she found herself pregnant and frightened and decided to leave home before her child was born. She came to London." He paused to give them both a little time to digest what he'd said so far. "She had a baby girl and left it on the doorstep of a church, where a stranger found her, and she was taken to hospital. You may have seen something in the paper. It was just before Christmas, so the hospital named her Mary."

"I remember that," said Leanne. "So my sister is alive and well, and I have a niece?"

"Yes, your sister is safe and well," said Jack.

Penny Meadows wiped her eyes and tried to smile. "I can't believe it. I can't. Even though I knew she wasn't dead, I still can't actually believe she *is* alive. It's a miracle! When can we meet her, Detective?"

"There's a little more to it, I'm afraid."

"Oh?"

Jack turned to Leanne as he spoke. "Baby Mary is not your niece, Leanne. She's your half-sister."

There was a long silence.

"I don't understand," said Penny Meadows at last. "How can that be? You're saying ...Oh god, no! You said Manchester ... Oh god, oh no!"

"Mum, what is it? What aren't you telling me?" Leanne looked at Jack for an explanation. He was going to have to tell her after all.

"The girl your father was seeing in Manchester was your sister Chloe. Mary is his child."

Leanne burst into tears now, and she and her mother cradled each other, sobbing. Jack quietly excused himself and went to the kitchen to give them some privacy. He made a pot of tea, found cups and took it all back to the lounge on a tray. They looked up at him, red-eyed, as he stepped into the room.

"I've made you some tea. It might help." It sounded lame, but he hoped they appreciated his trying. He put the tray on the table in front of them, and Leanne set to pouring and handed a cup to her mother.

"When can we meet her – Chloe?" she asked.

"Soon I hope. Soon."

Chapter Seventy-Eight

❦

Chloe stared at the note Jack had written.

"Do you think my caution has been revoked?" she asked Billy, suddenly afraid. What was his news?

"He'd have asked you to the station, not for lunch, silly," he joked, trying to keep things light, but wondering himself. "I don't think they can revoke it anyway," he added. But she looked troubled. "You think it's something else, like your little one?"

"I can't think of anything else, and if it is, I'm really in trouble. I abandoned her, remember?" The strain in her voice was obvious, and again Billy tried to convince her.

"As I said, I'd say that kind of conversation would be at the station, so no, he's not going to arrest you for abandonment." He put his arm around her shoulder and pulled her in close. They were sat on their makeshift bed in the garage, figuring they'd hang out there until it was time to leave for Roy's Café. Through the grimy window, they could see that a pale-yellow sun had risen in the sky, though it hadn't the strength to warm the place at ten in the morning. But at least it was showing itself, that was the main thing; everything felt better when the sun made an appearance.

"Look, I wouldn't worry. And you're assuming the news is about you. It could be about me. Or neither of us, for that matter."

Glancing up at him, she said, "I like you, Billy Peters. You're so reasonable. And sensible. And nice."

"You make me sound like a boring old fart, Chloe Mathews," he said, bending slightly to plant a kiss on her forehead. "Anyway, stop over-thinking it and look forward to a steaming hot meal with a knife and fork. I fancy pie and mash for lunch. What about you?"

"Same."

Jack was emotionally exhausted, and it was only lunchtime.

And there was more to wade through. Between Eddie and forensics, the list that had been found in the young woman's stomach had finally been completed. Dave Meadows was on that list – another nail in his coffin, and more strength for the CPS to agree on charges. Not that they needed any more; the guy was almost buried in crap, it was so far up his neck.

He'd been at Roy's for a few minutes, taking pleasure in a quiet cuppa while mulling over how to proceed. In reality, he knew precious little about Chloe and Billy, and had no idea whether he should even be discussing what he was about to discuss with Billy present, but his gut told him it was the right thing to do. So he'd picked a table in the furthest corner of the café and made camp. He'd also made a call to social services for an update on Mary and was told she was safe with her foster mum and was making good progress. Jack remembered the pink rabbit and smiled. He hoped it was still with her; it was his only way of reaching out to the child.

Maybe he and Janine should apply for adoption again ...

The sound of the door opening interrupted his thoughts, and he looked up to see Billy and Chloe walking towards his table, both looking like they were about to be yelled at. He stood and smiled, hoping to reassure them.

Roy hesitantly made his way over.

"Can I get you all a hot drink before your lunch?" he asked. His apron showing signs of baked beans from earlier in the day.

"Tea, please, Roy," Jack said, and the others followed suit. When he was safely out of earshot, Jack said, "Don't be looking so worried. Nobody is in trouble. Okay?"

Two nods.

"But I'm guessing you're wondering why I asked you for lunch, so let me tell you. But first, let me also tell you this is rather sensitive, and it concerns you, Chloe." Billy and Chloe exchanged a glance. "Chloe, am I able to talk in front of Billy here?"

"Yes. He's my friend. What's going on? You're scaring me."

Roy delivered three mugs of tea and retreated back to the kitchen. Nobody touched their tea.

"Chloe," Jack began, "let me tell you again that you are not in any trouble. Let me also tell you I know you recently gave birth, and that, for your own reasons, you took the little one to the church."

Chloe's face remained neutral.

She must have known it would catch up with her sooner or later, Jack thought sadly.

He carried on. "As you may know from the papers, Chloe, your little baby is safe and well. The hospital named her Mary, as it was Christmas, but it doesn't end there."

Chloe lifted her eyes, which were brimming with tears, and Jack felt pained at telling her the next part. "You see, through another case I've been working on, we had cause to do some DNA matching, particularly a new way of doing it, called familial DNA. Now, I won't bore you with the details, but it means we look for the extended family of the person in question."

He waited for them both to catch up. Finally, he got a faint nod from Billy to go on.

"So it means we now know who baby Mary's father is, and we can prosecute him for what has happened to you."

The tears spilled down Chloe's cheeks now, and Billy reached for a napkin from the nearby dispenser.

"Will I have to see him?" Chloe asked, struggling to keep her voice steady.

"Not necessarily. But it does get a little more complicated from here, and for this part you will need the support of a loved one." Jack was looking directly at Billy, who instinctively reached out and placed his hand on Chloe's. He gave it a gentle squeeze.

"Go on," she said faintly.

"The DNA results led us to a man who had a family of his own. He had twins, in fact. But he and his wife were told that one twin, Charlotte, had died at birth, and so they raised the other twin, Leanne, on her own."

"Right. I'm not sure where I fit in here."

"Charlotte never actually died. There was a mix-up at the hospital, and it turns out Charlotte lived. Chloe, Charlotte is you. You have a sister, a twin sister."

Chloe and Billy sat with open mouths. Finally, Billy spoke.

"Holy hell," he said, and closed his eyes for a moment.

"So, I have a sister, then. Is that what you're saying?"

"Yes, you do. But Chloe..." Jack paused and took a deep breath. "Your natural father is also the father of your child," he said, not wanting it to draw out any further.

Jack and Billy sat silently as Chloe processed what he'd told her. It was a lot to take in. But Chloe was quick on the uptake and decisive in her reasoning.

"It seems both of my fathers have proved to be vile. I think it would be easier if I said I didn't have one from here on in."

Jack was astounded at how strong the young woman sat in front of him was being. She'd grasped the news and was already dealing with it.

"But I have a sister. And a natural mother. Do they know about me? And about Mary?"

"Yes, they do."

"I'd like to meet them both," she said. "Do you think they'll let me?"

"I know they will. I've only told them a short while ago, so they're both coming to terms with the news. I can organize it when you're all ready."

"Billy, will you come too?"

"Of course I will, Chloe."

"Charlotte, eh? Pretty name," she added finally with a weak smile. "What a way to bring the New Year in. I appear to have gained a whole new family."

Billy leaned in, smiling from ear to ear, and kissed her wet cheek. "You'll have to decide what we all call you from here on in," he grinned.

"I'm Chloe. I'll always be Chloe, and I couldn't care less about a surname. Both fathers can go to hell. Perhaps I'll pick a fresh one."

Jack sat quietly, relieved it was all over. If Leanne and Penny wished to tell her the rest of the greater story, that was their business, but Jack suspected Leanne wouldn't be keen to relive and share it, not yet anyway. And there was no need. Chloe had some decisions to make, not only for her own life but for that of her child. Baby Mary was safe where she was for the time being, though Jack would inform social services of Chloe's new situation.

And time was a great healer. He knew that from experience. With a New Year ahead of her and a new family waiting in the wings, the start of the new millennium promised to be a memorable and momentous occasion for Chloe, not to mention a few others.

"Right, you two," he said, getting to his feet. "I said I was buying you lunch, so choose what you want." He motioned to Roy, who approached the table, order pad in hand. "I'm going to leave you to it. I'll be in touch soon." He passed Roy cash to cover their meal and a bit more, knowing he'd give Billy and Chloe the change.

As Jack left Roy's Café, he couldn't help but smile. His step felt lighter than it had done in days. It was a rare pleasure to give victims good news for a change, bittersweet thought it was. He pulled out his phone and called Janine.

"You okay, love?" she asked.

"Couldn't be better," he said perkily. "Can I take you out to lunch, Mrs Rutherford?"

Also by Linda Coles

Jack Rutherford and Amanda Lacey Series:

The Controller

Hot to Kill

The Hunted

Dark Service

One Last Hit

Chrissy Livingstone

Tin Men

A bunch of non-fiction

About the Author

Hi, I'm Linda Coles. Thanks for choosing this book, I really hope you enjoyed it and collect the following ones in the series. Great characters make a great read and I hope I've managed to create that for you.

Originally from the UK, I now live and work in beautiful New Zealand along with my hubby, 2 cats and 7 goats. My office sits by the edge of my vegetable garden, my very favourite authors are Harlan Coben and Michael Robotham and apart from reading and writing, I get to run by the beach for pleasure.

If you find a moment, please do write an honest online review, they really do make such a difference to those choosing what book to buy next.

Enjoy! And tell your friends.

Thanks, Linda

Printed in Great Britain
by Amazon